Regrets

by

Caryn M. McGill

Dedication

To my beta posse: Kaitlyn, MaryLynn, Teri, Lisa T…thanks for your critique and encouragement along my writing journey.

To Darryl Miller, who taught me everything I know about writing.

Chapter One

The putrid smell unsettles my stomach. The air is syrupy sweet, making it difficult to breathe. They shouldn't have flowers in a house of death, especially three-day-old flowers. It seems unnatural. Blossoms are beautiful, cheery, hopeful. But death is ugly, decaying, horrible. I've seen a thousand deaths in my life. It makes you numb after about the hundredth time. Yet, even after all these years, I can never reconcile the finality of it. And then it hits you. Your house, your family…and the numbness isn't there when you need it. Only the pain, the aching in your heart, the loss.

"Grandma, how are you doing?"

She sits next to me on the tufted coach in the front row, her hand on my knee warm, soft, with the perfect skin of a twelve-year-old. I gaze into her bright green eyes to see some distant part of myself. I smile.

I place my hand atop hers and squeeze. "Oh, I'm holding up okay, I guess. Where's your mother?"

"She's with Dad, outside. They're trying to decide if they should bring in Jay. Dad says it's okay, but Mom insists they should have left him home because he's too young for this."

"Oh dear, I don't want to add any more heartache to this terrible day. Maybe I should go out and talk to them." I rub my thumb across the back of her hand.

"Don't bother, they'll figure it out, they always do."

I sit in front of the shiny black coffin. Time seems endless. I glance at my watch—two thirty. I've only been here a half hour. At least it's the last day. Jessie and I sit together, holding hands as a parade of A-list celebrities pass by his body making inane and stupid remarks. I hate this.

"Hi, Mom."

I smile when I see my daughter's face. Her bright blue eyes and cinnamon-hued hair remind me how much she looks like her father. I wish he was here sitting next to me. She takes the seat on the other side of me, lacing her fingers through mine.

"Hi, sweetheart. What did you decide to do with Jay?"

"Steven is staying outside with him for now. We can't seem to agree on whether he should have this experience or not."

I sigh. "It will be over soon, and then we can get back to normal."

The procession of mourners comes to an end. It's four o'clock. I sigh with a small amount of relief. Walking up to the coffin, I study his frozen, perfectly posed face. I caress his hand, then give him a quick kiss on his wrinkly old forehead. Too many lost years, too many tears, our life together should have been better.

We leave the house of sadness to make our way into the limousine. The sickening perfume of fading blossoms lingers in my head. The trip to the cemetery is a short distance. The paparazzi were kept away from the funeral parlor, but there are plenty of them lurking in the background, hiding behind trees or posing as mourners. The crowd of family and friends stand quietly as prayers are read and thoughtful words given. His wishes were for something simple, no eulogies or syrupy speeches, and a quick cremation. People kiss and hug me, offering their condolences. I can't wait for this to be over.

"Did anyone check to see if the caterers arrived?" I whisper to my daughter, keeping my gaze straight ahead.

"Yes, Mark skipped the cemetery to make sure everything was okay at the house because he knew you'd be worried."

I smile at my only daughter. She's a wonderful daughter. A terrific doctor and an even better mother. My life would be so incomplete without her. And my son, Mark, he looks more like me, but he's his father in so many other ways.

The shiny, black, death car pulls up in front of my home, the one I've lived in my whole life. I don't count the years before I was here because I wasn't truly alive then. I dwelt in the shadow of death until seventeen. It was my fault she died. I didn't really kill her, they said, but I knew I had. And *he* knew I had, although he would never admit it to my face.

The day is warm and sunny, which conflicts with my dark and dreary mood. I put my pocketbook on the sofa table and walk into the kitchen and give my son a kiss on his stubbly cheek. Young women think the unshaven look is so hot, but I don't get it. "Thanks for making sure everything at the house went smoothly. It was a huge load off my mind." Mark is a fabulous chef at a well-known upscale restaurant. He took care of the catering for me, and I'm confident this will be the best after-funeral spread in all of Los Angeles.

The wait staff is bustling, plating food and artfully arranging it on the dining room table. Mark is being his usual bossy-chef self, and I smile hearing his voice. If I close my eyes, I can hear his father.

Walking out onto the back deck, I breathe in the salty ocean air. The breeze refreshes me, flushing the sickly-sweet flower smell from my head. An arm surrounds my waist. And then another one surrounds me from the other side. My daughter and granddaughter.

"How are you holding up, Mom?"

"Oh, okay, I guess. I think I'll go for a walk. Do you think it would be okay? No one will notice if I'm gone for a bit, will they?"

"Do whatever you want, Mom. I don't think you have to answer to anybody today." Her smile is warm, comforting.

"I'll walk with you if you want, Grandma." Jessie's offer is sweet.

"Sure, that would be nice."

"Can I come too?"

And so, the three of us kick off our shoes and sink our feet into the warmth of the sun-drenched sand to walk along the beach. Their hands make me feel connected as I hold on to them. There is nothing more wonderful than family. I wish Drew was walking by my side. I miss him. My mood improves as the heat of the sand and sun wipe the chill from my bones.

"Grandma?" Jessie says.

"Hmm?"

"How did you and Granddad meet?"

"Oh dear, it's a crazy story. Sometimes I still can't believe it myself." My mind travels back to the day of that crash. I smile at the memory. The crash that saved my life.

Chapter Two

Pulling into the too long driveway, I hit the remote control that opens the ostentatious wrought-iron entryway. The garage doors part, so I can deposit my car into its resting place for the night. This house is too large for one person and the car too expensive for my taste. The presence of the gates is absurd since the back of the house opens onto the beach. They don't provide any security, so whoever built them must have done it for show, to impress. Both the car and the house ease his guilt, so I shut up and accepted them. The moment of weakness came when I realized it was on the ocean. I've always been in love with the ocean. That was my rationalization, coupled with the fact that he ruined my life.

Walking in the front door, I bolt up the staircase to my bedroom, strip off my blood splattered clothes, and heave them into the hamper. I should have discarded them in the one in the locker room at work, but I was too anxious to leave. It's late, almost midnight, but the horror of the day has me wound tighter than a guitar string. I never have time to run these days, but I feel like if I don't, I might snap.

Dressed in a tank top and shorts, I bound down the stairs, nearly tripping in my haste to get outside. I queue up my MP3 player, shove the earphones in, and slip the device into my shorts back pocket. "The Boy is Mine" is playing. I inhale the warm May air. Maybe I should have considered a career outdoors. Being cooped up all day is sometimes pure torture. But living in Malibu is pure joy. California weather has it all over Paris.

I've been distracted to the point where people are starting to worry about me. It's been like this for months. Jillian, my best and pretty much only friend, offered to spend tomorrow night with me. And it will be the worst night of my life. Well, maybe the second worst. I think I already had the worst night of my life. But then again there's the other worst night of my life, although I was too young to know it at the time. Okay, so tomorrow night will be the third worst night of my life. The deed must be done by midnight. I made this promise to myself, and I mean to deliver.

The night is clear, the full moon bright, and the sultry ocean breeze inflates my lungs with hope, but I know the effect will be fleeting. I stretch, touching my toes, then rotating my torso several times before stepping onto the white line on the macadam of the coastal highway in front of my house. In a flash of headlights, a black Porsche cuts in front of a shiny silver Escalade in a near miss. Geysers of sand spew up from the smoking tires, stinging my face. The car barrels down the beach and comes to a stop on the wet sand where the breakers hit the shore. The ocean is furious tonight, and a wave crashes on the hood, showering foaming seawater over the stalled black sports coupe. I glance over my shoulder, but the Escalade is gone. Jerk. He should have stopped.

I remove the earphones and shove them into my pocket and sprint to the waterline. Waves continue to pummel the car. I peer though the driver's side window. A man is slumped over the wheel. I grab the door handle, but the door won't open. A wave smacks me in the face, and I hold on to the handle to keep from falling. Wiping the stinging salt water from my face, I look through the foggy glass again. He's still unconscious. I try with all my might to release the door, but it won't budge. The vice of panic grips my chest. I must get him out of there. I search for something to smash the window, but there is nothing. In my escalating hysteria I kick the door hard, but my foot slips, and I go down in a heap in the wet sand. "Damn." I try the door again, nothing. I kick at it three more times, releasing my anger with a scream, and the latch releases.

I worry the seatbelt will be frozen as it often is in a crash. But he isn't wearing it. Idiot. How many times have I seen this? People with their faces smashed in, chests crushed, and all because they are too stupid to wear a seat belt. I smell alcohol. Great. He deserves whatever he gets for this lapse in judgment.

I press two digits against his neck. The thump-thump allows me to breathe. I wedge myself between him and the back of the seat, locking my arms around his upper body to disentangle his unconscious form from the lifeless car. It takes three attempts to drag him out. The last heave took all my strength, and the force knocked me to the ground with him on top of me. Waves continue to drench me, and a shiver slides down my spine.

Dragging him across the sand to the edge of my deck could only have happened with the help of massive amounts of adrenaline rushing my bloodstream. I should know by now how hard it is to move an unconscious or dead body. I've done it too many times to count.

He moans. I take his pulse again. It's in the normal range. I give him the once over, checking for broken bones or blood, but everything seems intact, except for small a contusion on his forehead. Lucky. Drunks often escape serious injury while innocent sober people die. Where's the justice in that?

His eyes shiver open. He groans again, reaching for his forehead. The moonlight illuminates his face. Our eyes connect, his the color of an indigo sky.

"Hey buddy, how are you feeling?" The saltwater burns my eyes. I wipe it away with the back of my hand.

It takes a minute for him to focus. "What happened? Where am I?" He attempts to sit, but I force him back.

"Lie still for a minute, so I can see if you're injured. Does anything hurt? I don't see any blood other than this contusion on your forehead. It might need a couple of stitches," I say, knowing what I am talking about.

"My head hurts and my knees, but that's about it."

"That's enough." I slide up his pant legs to examine his knees, moving the kneecaps around. I watch his face for a reaction. "Your kneecaps seem bruised, but they don't appear to be broken." I open the buttons on his white shirt and palpate his midsection, sliding my fingers downward on his abdomen. Everything feels normal.

"You sound like you know what you're doing, what are you, a nurse?"

Always the same reaction. Just because you're a girl, they assume you're a nurse. How many times have I had to endure this comment?

"Lucky for you, I'm an ER resident over at L.A. General. And you should get to the hospital, so they can check you out to make sure there aren't any internal injuries. You probably have a concussion too. I'll call 911."

"No, no way," he says with alarm. "I can't risk it.

I'll be fine."

"Risk what?"

"The publicity."

"Why?"

"I don't want to talk about it. Let's leave it there."

Fine. Wouldn't want to ruin your reputation, I think. He's lucky he didn't kill anybody. Like *me*. Or…maybe that would have been a good thing.

"Well, what are you going to do? You can't drive your car." I look over to see the tide coming in and the car hopelessly wedged in the wet sand, the headlight beams penetrating the breaking waves.

"Let's get you inside, and I'll call for help."

"Please don't call the police."

I study his handsome face for a long minute. His face is vaguely familiar, but I can't seem to place it. "Look, you've been drinking, and you were driving too fast for this road. You're just going to have to be a big boy and take responsibility for your actions." He sits, facing me. A wet strand of cinnamon-hued hair falls over one blue eye.

"Listen, thanks for pulling me out of the car. I'll call someone to pick me up. Could we leave it there?" He attempts to stand but is too wobbly to stay erect.

"Ow," he says, grabbing his knees as he slumps back into the damp sand.

"Come on. This is my backyard. You can use my phone." Am I crazy? Bringing a total stranger, a drunken one, into my house.

He tries to stand again, and I put my arm around him, helping him up. He winces. Now I'm not sure his injuries are so minor. I should get him to a hospital. Why is my judgment impaired?

"Thanks, I appreciate this." We hobble our way up the three steps to the deck, past the pool, toward the back door. "Nice house," he says.

"It's too big for one person." What a stupid thing to say to someone I don't even know. Plus, now I told him I live by myself. How much worse can my judgment get?

A lot, apparently.

Chapter Three

Stumbling through the back door, I walk him into the kitchen and deposit him on a chair. We are both soaking wet. He leans his forehead on his hands, resting his elbows on my table. Don't pass out on me, buddy, I think. I stand there, hands on hips, looking at him. His golden-brown hair hangs over his fingers. He's becoming more recognizable, but I can't quite put my finger on who he could be.

"Let me look at the bump on your forehead." I place my hand under his chin, lifting his head. Pushing the hair off his forehead, I inspect the gash. The bleeding has stopped. "I'll be right back. I'll get something to clean this cut."

Returning with the necessary supplies and my pen light, I tilt his head back and flash the tiny light beam across his pupils. I hold my fingers twelve inches from his face. "Follow my finger," I say. He obeys. "What's today's date?"

"May eighth."

"What year?"

"1998."

"Who's president?"

"Well, in my country, we have a queen and a prime minister."

I detected a trace of a British or Australian accent. "You're British."

"Guilty."

I decide no further interrogation is necessary. He appears coherent.

"You might have a concussion." I dab alcohol at the site of the injury, cleaning the blood away. He flinches at my touch. "Well, this doesn't look too bad, and you're in luck because I happen to have my favorite magic potion on hand." I smile, but he looks back with a frown again.

"Magic potion? What? Now you're a witch too? Or better yet, a witch doctor?"

"Funny. No, but I do have one of the marvels of modern medicine. Liquid stitches. Skin glue. Lucky for you." I flail my fingers through the air, giving my best witch doctor impression. I withdraw the tiny tube from my kit and unscrew the top. "Now stay still. It won't hurt." I squeeze the edges of skin together, making a perfect matching seam. The glue adheres in a few seconds, sealing the site. "There, that wasn't so bad, was it?"

"No. Thanks. Do I get a lollipop?"

"Sorry, all out." Why am I engaging in this ridiculous banter with an inebriated stranger?

"Look," he says, "I know you probably think I'm a jerk, but I only had two beers, and I was in a bad mood, which is my excuse for driving like an idiot. The truth is I'm a terrible driver sober, so I can't even blame it on the two beers. Plus, you guys drive on the wrong side of the road."

He doesn't appear to be drunk. Maybe I overreacted. I don't know what to think as a shiver runs through my soaking wet body.

"I don't care one way or the other. You're lucky you

didn't hurt anybody. You realize you almost mowed me down. Lucky I saw you coming."

"Oh, God, that's a horrible thought. I can't even think about something like that." He holds my gaze as he says this to me. He seems sincere.

I grab the wireless phone from the cradle and hand it to him. "Here, make your phone call."

He stares at it like he's never seen a phone before. "My mobile phone and wallet are in the car. All my numbers are in one of the two."

"You don't know anyone's number?"

"Well, I don't really live here. My friends and family live on another continent, so calling them wouldn't help, and the only people I know here are my agent and publicist, and their numbers are in the phone or on business cards in my wallet."

He stands, holding the table to steady himself. "I'll go look in the car."

"No way, you're in no condition—"

"I'm not letting you do it. I'll be fine."

He opens the door and I rush toward him. "It's too dangerous, the car is probably half under water by now."

"Stop. I'll be fine," he barks. "Do you have a torch?"

"Torch?"

"Flashlight."

I open the cabinet beside the door and hand him the *torch*. I flick on the light switch illuminating the back deck, and he vanishes into the night. I cross my arms over my chest and realize I'm holding my breath. This entire situation is ridiculous. I shake my head and exhale slowly.

A few minutes later, the beam bounces through the darkness, and the handsome stranger limps up the steps.

I open the door and he returns to my kitchen. "I almost drowned a second time. Couldn't find them."

"Seriously? Now what?"

"We could try information, but I think those would be business numbers."

Are you kidding? I will not drive him home. There's a limit to my Good Samaritan repertoire. "Well, where are you staying?"

"Downtown. And I certainly don't want the hotel personnel to rescue me. They pay people to get dirt on you, you know?"

I should come right out and ask him who he is. He'll probably be insulted that I don't recognize him. I rub my temples to soothe the pounding.

"We'll figure something out. Right now, I need to go upstairs and change out of these wet clothes," I say, walking over to the freezer. "I have some clothes you can put on. I'll bring them down. In the meantime, hold this icepack on your forehead until I get back."

Taking the cold compress from me, "Could I trouble you for a glass of water?"

"Sure." I walk to the fridge and extricate the water pitcher, pouring a good eight ounces and place the glass in front of him.

"Thanks," he says to my back.

In my room, I shed my freezing wet clothing and toss everything into the bathtub. I wash my face and hands, brush the tangles from my hair and redress in sweatpants and a tee shirt. What I really want is a shower, but it'll have to wait until he's gone.

I enter the bedroom adjacent to mine and open the closet. I stand there for too long, staring at its contents. The pearly white demon taunts me with its sequined magnificence. All part of the plan, I remind myself. It will be over soon. But, as hard as I try, a wave of despair smacks me in the face. I close my eyes and swallow hard, pushing the sadness down into my gut. Shutting the closet, I approach the dresser and open the bottom drawer. I retrieve a pair of blue sweatpants, running my fingers over the stenciled letters—UCLA. Taking the extra-large T-shirt from the top drawer, I slam it shut. Hesitating a few seconds, I study the well-worn white tee. I press the folded shirt against my face and inhale. Which makes me feel worse.

I find him with his head resting on his arms at my kitchen table. "Hey, I told you to keep the ice pack on your head." I'm hoping he didn't pass out.

He lifts his head from its resting place to look at me. "Sorry, I felt tired all of a sudden."

"Well, here, go change out of those wet clothes." I point towards the open bathroom door. He rises, taking the dry clothing from my outstretched hand.

"Thanks, I appreciate this. All of it, everything you're doing for me."

"Yeah, well, I have no idea why I'm doing it, but you're welcome anyway. When you come back, you can use the phone."

He leaves me standing at my kitchen table as I ask myself again why I have let this strange man into my house and who will come pick him up at this time of night.

Chapter Four

He exits the bathroom dressed in the borrowed attire, his hair finger-combed off his forehead and his wet clothing wadded in a ball. A pang of sadness hits me like a sharp elbow to the chest. I swallow hard. Closing my eyes, I pray for the vision to vanish. I try to regain my emotional equilibrium, what little I have left.

"Thanks again for the dry clothes. Do you have a plastic garbage bag I could put these wet ones in?"

"Sure." I struggle to break eye contact with his mesmerizing cobalt eyes, finding his gaze unsettling, then head for the cabinet under the sink. I wish his car wasn't dead in the water. Then I realize something crucial. His car. We can't leave it there. It must be gone before sunrise, or somebody might see it. Geez, I'm talking like a criminal. What's wrong with me? Getting rid of the evidence before the cops find out. This is insane. And yet I continue aiding and abetting. "We've got to get your car out of here before it gets light out. Otherwise, someone is going to see it and call the police." Oh, my God, I said *we* …when did *I* become *we*?

"It's a rental and it's after midnight. Who could we get to tow the car at this hour?"

I think for a minute, nibbling a fingernail. "Bobby," I say, a lightbulb over my head. I point my finger in the air for punctuation.

"Who's Bobby?"

"He'll probably be pissed, but what the hell. He owes me a few big ones anyway. Time to call in a favor." I am totally ignoring him as I seize control of the situation. Heading for the phone, I hit speed dial.

I get a grumpy, sleepy hello. I tell him what I need, and after he grills me on what happened, I get a reluctant "Okay, I'll be right there." I had to lay the guilt on thick. "Bobby's on his way. He has a tow truck. He'll take the car to his shop, and you can let him know what to do with it when you figure things out."

I study the stranger in my kitchen. He's staring at me. "You're like a human tornado. Is there anything you can't do? Do you have a giant *S* underneath your shirt?"

Now I'm embarrassed. He's got me figured out, and he's only seen me in action for about thirty minutes. Always taking over in a crisis. I've been like that as long as I can remember. Not always to everyone else's liking, however. I can be a little too bossy sometimes.

I smile. "Caught me," I say, "but I'm not taking my shirt off, so you can check." *What the hell? Now I'm flirting with him?*

His eyes widen, but he keeps silent.

I close my eyes and regroup. "I'll make coffee while we wait for Bobby. He lives nearby, so we shouldn't have to wait long." We sit at the table and sip from our mugs, shrouded in silence. The knock on the door comes.

He jumps like someone shot him. "It could be the police. What should we do?"

The fear on his face is disarming. Why do I feel so bad for him? "It's just Bobby." I turn to make my way to the front door. He's on me in a minute. He grabs my arm.

"Wait. We need to think about what we're going to say if it's the cops." Realizing he has me in his grip, he releases me. "Oh, God, I'm sorry, I didn't mean to do that."

I look down at my arm where he touched me. I should be more upset about this than I am. "It can't be the cops. There's an iron gate at my entrance. No one can get in without me knowing."

The knock at the door is more urgent this time. Bobby knows the code to my gate, so he always has access to my front door. "Wait here, I'm sure it's Bobby. Then you can panic if you want. Okay?"

"Okay," he says.

The third knock tells me if I don't answer this second, Bobby is going to break the door down. Bobby's enormous frame fills my doorway, dressed in a black T-shirt and well-worn jeans, his eyes huge. "You scared me when you didn't answer the door right away. I would have called the police in about one second."

"Sorry, this is just a crazy situation. Thanks for coming."

Bobby exhales loudly, his hands on his hips. He struts into my living room looking around for my mysterious stranger. "Where is he?"

"In the kitchen."

"Well, from what you told me, the car is probably totaled by water damage. It will cost him a pretty penny."

"I don't think money is a problem," I say matter-of-factly.

"Oh, so now you know him well enough to know his finances?"

"Actually, I have no idea who he is," I blurt.

"My name is Andrew Foster. Everyone calls me Drew."

I turn to face him. Now I remember. He's the guy in

that blockbuster movie franchise, what was it called again? I work like twenty hours a day, so I don't watch much TV, but I have seen a few of the commercials, and the billboards for the third installment are everywhere. I didn't see the first two, because I rarely go to the movies, but everyone at work was drooling over him, even some of the guys.

It doesn't register on Bobby's radar. He never goes to the movies either.

"I heard you guys talking, and I figured it wasn't the police."

"You're the guy from those movies. I forget the title," I say.

"*New Horizons*, and guilty as charged."

I rub my temples again, working on a doozy of a headache. I sigh. "Bobby will tow the car back to his shop. You can call the rental company in the morning, and they'll tell you what to do."

"Thanks," Drew says. "I'll pay you whatever you want," he says to Bobby.

"How are you getting back to wherever you belong?" Bobby asks, his foot tapping on my hardwood floor.

"Ah…I'm trying to get somebody to pick me up, but it's difficult getting anyone to come out at this time of night. I don't know many people here," Drew offers.

"I can take you in the truck. Where do you have to go?" Bobby really wants him out of here. I realize there are about thirty miles between where Bobby is and where Drew has to go. But that distance takes at least an hour to travel.

So, what do I say? "I'll drive him to his hotel." I can't believe I just broke the promise I made to myself like ten minutes ago.

Chapter Five

"I don't know," Bobby says, suspicious again. "Why don't you try and call him a cab?"

"Because we both know that even if it wasn't the middle of the night, getting someone to come this far from the city is unlikely. And he could be recognized by a driver. He's trying to avoid that." Bobby doesn't say anything because he knows the truth of what I am saying. "Really, Bobby, I'll be fine. I'm a big girl. You don't have to worry about me."

Bobby crosses his arms over his ample chest, flexing his biceps for added emphasis. It's obvious he spends plenty of time in the gym. "Well, I'll load the car onto my truck, but just so you know, I'm sure it's pretty much trashed. You can check with me tomorrow and tell me what you want to do. I can give you a full assessment then."

"Thanks, I appreciate you doing this for me." Drew attempts a smile.

"I'm not doing this for you, I'm doing it for my sister."

Attitude, attitude, Bobby. I didn't even meet my stepbrother until I was seventeen, but he acts like he owns me sometimes. It's sweet, yet annoying.

I walk to Bobby and put my hand on his arm. "I'll get him out. Don't worry. Just get the car out of here."

Bobby is on Drew in a minute. "Just to be clear, it's

not the police you should be worried about. Because I'll tell you right up front that if anything funky goes down with my sister, you won't need the police; you'll need a hospital."

"Bobby," I shout. "That's not necessary, stop it."

"It's all right," Drew says. "I don't blame him. I have two sisters, and I would feel the same way."

Bobby seems to catch his breath, calming his mood. "Well, all right, as long as we're clear."

"I understand perfectly. I'll be out of here soon. I promise."

Bobby's eyes are wary as he shifts his gaze from Drew to me. "All right. You sure you're okay?"

"Yes, Bobby, I'll be fine," and Bobby turns to make his getaway.

"Thanks," Drew says. "I can't believe all the trouble I caused you tonight. I'm sorry." He looks at me with those clear blue eyes, which unnerves me again. Exhausted, I sink onto the couch. I have to be at work in like five hours. It'll take me at least two hours to get him back to his hotel and make the return trip.

Then the medical training kicks in again. With a concussion, somebody should wake him up every hour to make sure he doesn't slip into unconsciousness. Crap, this is getting way too complicated.

"Look, I agree it's unlikely you can get somebody to pick you up at this time of night. And then there's the issue of a possible concussion. Somebody should wake you up every hour to make sure you're okay. Besides, I have to be at work at seven o'clock. So, why don't you crash on the couch, I'll wake you up a few times to make sure you're okay. You can find someone to pick you up in the morning. I would drive you, but it's like two hours round trip."

"No, that's too much to ask. I've already overstepped my boundaries. And with you helping with the car and everything, it's enough."

"I know. This whole night has been ridiculous. Let's just try to get through it, so we both can forget about it."

His gaze fixes me. "Somehow, I don't think I'll ever forget this night."

This catches me off guard. What a strange thing to say.

It doesn't take me long to convince him my plan is our best option. He didn't try to leave very hard either.

I grab some pillows and blankets from the upstairs linen closet. I set the kitchen timer for an hour. He settles onto the couch while I take the chair with the ottoman beside him. Throughout my internship and residency, I learned to sleep anywhere, anytime. I turn off the lights but leave the kitchen one on so as not to be totally in the dark. I try to be quiet, but for some reason my heart is racing. This is the most outrageous thing I have ever done. Allowing this total stranger to sleep on my couch. I must be insane. I am startled by his voice.

"You never told me your name," he whispers.

"Rea."

"I've never heard that before. Is it short for something?"

"Andrea, but nobody calls me that except my father."

"Okay, Rea. Thanks for being my angel of mercy. I'll never forget you for helping me out tonight."

"You're welcome." And neither of us talks again until I rouse him from his slumber an hour later. He seems a bit disoriented at first, but I attribute it to waking

Caryn M. McGill

in an unfamiliar environment rather than anything to do with head trauma. I wake him three more times until I have to get up for work. This house is enormous, so he probably won't hear me rummaging around upstairs.

I tiptoe past him and into the garage, leaving a note on the coffee table.

Drew,

Nice to meet you, even with the unfortunate circumstances. Please lock up on your way out. Go out the back door so you won't have to hassle with the gate. Get yourself to a hospital if you feel dizzy, your vision becomes impaired, or have a persistent headache. You might want to have a plastic surgeon check out that cut, since being a PRETTY BOY is a requirement for someone in your line of work. :)

Best of luck,

Rea

My workday is a nightmare. I let the saga of my night adventure slip to my best friend, Jillian, being stupid enough to tell her his name. Her eyes tell me I made a huge mistake. And he didn't want publicity. It'll take a nanosecond for this to be broadcasted around the entire hospital. I love Jillian, but she has a big mouth, no, a huge mouth.

"You mean Andrew Foster? Hollywood heartthrob, superstar, the guy in every girl's fantasy dreams and probably some guys' too?"

"Geez, Jillian, fangirl much?"

"You're not trying to pretend this isn't a big deal."

"He's just a movie star. No biggie. Like I care about that stuff."

Jillian groans, hanging her head in her hands, elbows on the counter. "You're ridiculous."

Sure enough, people come up to me all day long asking if *he* was really in my house. At least one good thing came out of it. Everyone momentarily forgot what tomorrow is and what I promised to finish tonight. Before midnight, I remind myself. It must be done before the clock strikes twelve.

The respite is short-lived, and later in the day, things start to unravel. Jillian won't let me out of her sight. The rest of my friends are hovering like they're afraid I'm going to jump off the roof or something. Finally, I can't take it anymore.

"I'll be fine. I promise. You don't have to worry about me. I'm going to do it tonight, and I don't need anyone's help. You can stop feeling sorry for me, and leave me alone." I recite this mantra to my boss, my dad, and everyone else in my universe.

Jillian won't let go. We've been best friends since the first day of med school. She, Greg, and I were in biochem together. She dated him first. "I don't think you should do it alone. I'm coming over whether you like it or not."

"Jillian, I know you love me, and you're trying to do the right thing, and I appreciate it, I do. But I have to do this myself. I'll be okay. I promise if I'm not okay, I'll call you."

"I don't know. If it was me, I don't know if I could get through it by myself. Are you sure?"

"I've had to take care of myself since I was five. I'm used to it. Stop worrying about me, okay?"

"Okay. But promise you'll call me if you need moral support."

"I will." I glance at the clock, it's four in the afternoon. Four more hours on my shift. I'm exhausted from lack of sleep, not to mention the stress from last night coupled with the dread that lies ahead. I have totally lied to Jillian. I am not at all sure I can do this on my own. I've put it off for six months. I could have done it any day before this day. But no, I waited until the last second. But then I wonder. Does any of it matter? Is this just the ceremonial beginning of the end?

Chapter Six

My depressed thinking is interrupted by my boss. "Dr. Tasson," he calls out from across the corridor. "Listen, you should go home early today. You know, considering what tomorrow is, I think you will be too distracted to focus on work."

"I already have tomorrow off. I don't need to go home early too."

"Well, I think you do. So go on, get out of here, and take care of yourself. Everybody's thoughts are with you. When Monday comes, it will all be behind you. Now that's an order, so go home." He leaves me standing there but not before giving me an awkward, yet heartfelt, hug, which is totally out of character. I didn't even think he knew I dated Greg.

I am so sick and tired of everyone's pity. Then again, I should include myself in that crowd. I deserved better. How much tragedy can one person endure?

I make my way to my car under the sad, watchful eyes of my friends and colleagues. It's creepy, like they're all shaking their heads behind my back. "Poor Rea," they say. It's sickening but true. Poor Rea.

I stop at the market to buy some groceries. I have absolutely no food in the house since I usually eat at the hospital. But to fortify myself for the task ahead, I decide to make myself a nice dinner. The condemned woman's dinner. I even buy wine. Hmm, maybe that wasn't such a great idea now that I think of it. Alcohol could make this night a lot worse. On the other hand, maybe I need to get drunk, then I could sleep through tomorrow. Well, duh, that is the plan. Eternal sleep.

I hit the button to open the absurd gates, enter the garage and shut the engine. I walk through the door leading to the kitchen and place the groceries on the counter next to the sink. A voice emanates from the living room. Idiot, he left the television on. Then I look to the back door, it's wide open. Thanks for locking up, dude. I guess he's not exactly Mr. Responsibility. His publicist probably wipes his ass. I bet the guy doesn't do one goddamn thing for himself. I let out a frustrated sigh, throwing my keys on the kitchen table and shutting the door too forcefully. I hang my coat on the hook near the side door before heading upstairs for a hot shower and some comfy clothes.

I enter the living room and stop short. Asleep on my couch. At least I pray he's asleep…and not…*dead*. My career flashes in front of my eyes.

I walk over to the couch on silent cat feet. I stand over him to see if his chest is moving up and down with his breaths. Looks like it. I find his wrist, checking for a pulse. He awakens, startled by my touch. I jump backwards as if I witnessed a corpse reanimating. He stands, his six-foot frame towering over me.

"Geez, you scared me half to death. I thought you were dead," I shout.

"Well, you scared the crap out of me too," he says like he has a right to be here.

I perch my hands on my hips. "Why are you still here?"

"Ah…uh…," he stammers, "I called my agent and

my publicist at their offices, but it was too early, so I left messages. I figured I should leave, but without my wallet I have no money, no credit cards…nothing. So, I started walking, but my knees were killing me, and besides there's like no civilization here. No stores, no gas stations and a car didn't even pass by. So, I came back. Luckily, I forgot to lock the back door. I lay down in front of the TV, and I guess I fell asleep."

He's got to be kidding me. This is ridiculous.

Now what? Should I offer to drive him back? That's a couple of hours I need for my dastardly plan. We're both standing in my living room with our hands on our hips. This is outrageous. Why can't I get him out of here?

The phone rings, startling us. I pick up the receiver and glance at the tiny screen. Damn, my father, again. If I don't answer, he'll keep calling until he gets me. "Hi, Dad," I say. "Yeah, I'm fine. I know I've put it off too long, but I'm going to take care of everything tonight, I promise. You can come over tomorrow if you want and see for yourself."

"I don't think you should be alone tonight. Jade and I can come over and help."

"No, Dad, I want to do this myself."

"I don't think…"

"I know, I know. I haven't been able to do it for six whole months, but I promise I will get it done tonight. You'll see."

He sighs, and I imagine him pinching the bridge of his nose, his eyes shut tight. "Fine, but if you change your mind, call, and I'll come right away."

"Okay. Thanks, Dad. I'll talk to you tomorrow."

Too little too late, I think, hitting the button. Where were you when I needed a father? A continent away, that's where you were.

The phone rings again. Jillian, and I give her the same line. Again. But she has other things on her mind too. "Have you heard anything from Andrew Foster?"

I'm not about to tell her he's still here. She'd freak. "I didn't give him my number." Which is true. "Listen, I've gotta go. I've got things to do."

"Okay, I'll call you later."

"I'll be busy, so don't freak out if I don't answer."

The phone rings again. It's everybody in the entire world I know. I tell them all the same thing. I'm fine. I will get it done. I'll still be alive tomorrow. I lie, lie, lie, and lie some more. Drew is frowning at me.

"You have a lot of friends. They all seem to be checking up on you for some reason. Is everything okay?"

"None of your goddamn business." My words hurl at him like a snowball hitting a metal shed. "You need to get out of here. I already told you I have important things to do tonight, and I can't get started until you're gone."

It's like I slapped him.

"All right, sorry." His voice is too small for him.

I march into the kitchen, and he follows. I stare at the grocery bags on the counter. I realize I'm starving, and I promised I would cook myself a nice dinner. I forgot to eat today, like most days. The night is getting away from me. I planned on having total control of my plan for the rest of the day. Things are already going awry, and I haven't even gotten to the hard part yet.

"Look, I need to make dinner. Why don't you try your phone calls again because I don't have time to drive you back to the city?" Pulling the food from the bags, I keep my back to him. I need him to leave, now.

"Okay," he says, sounding a little disappointed. "I'll use the phone in the living room so as not to bother you." And he is gone from the kitchen.

I peel and chop things. Olive oil heats in the frying pan. Lettuce is torn, tomatoes cut. What's taking him so long? What is he doing in there?

He is suddenly standing at my side.

"I left messages. No human voices were exchanged. I'm sure somebody will call me back soon, and then I'll be out of your hair for good."

"Fine," I say, thinking about what lies ahead on this terrible night. I need to get started. It's going to take me several hours to get everything done, and I promised it would be over by midnight. I will make the deadline if it kills me, as it should.

Now I feel bad. "Why don't you take my car? Get somebody to return it tomorrow. I don't have to work tomorrow, and besides I won't be needing it anyway."

I throw the pork chops into the scalding pan. They came two in a package, which now seems prophetic is some weird way. The sizzling oil splatters across my scrub shirt. I jump back and step right on Drew's foot. "Ow," I say in response to the oil spatter.

"Ow," he says in response to me stomping on his bare foot.

I turn to face him. We both crack up laughing. Our laughter becomes uncontrollable for some odd reason. Suddenly, it's quiet as we stand there looking awkwardly at each other.

"I'm sorry," I say. "I shouldn't have yelled at you. It's just…" I shake my head. "Never mind."

Turning back to the stove I flip the meat. Suddenly, I want him to stay for dinner. This is absurd. What am I thinking? But it seems my mouth isn't connected to my brain, and with a mind of its own, it says, "I have too much food. You might as well eat something while you wait for someone to come and rescue you. If you don't hear from someone soon, take my car. There's no rush to return it."

I have to get dinner over with, and I can't waste time waiting for him to leave. Sounds like a good rationalization. It's food, not a dinner date.

Chapter Seven

Drew stares at me as if he can see right through me. It's like I'm standing naked in my own kitchen. It's unsettling.

"Sure, that would be great. I haven't eaten anything all day."

"Yeah, sorry, there isn't much food in the house. I usually eat at the hospital."

"Regardless, I wouldn't have eaten anything, I've already imposed on you way too much."

I put the food in the oven to keep it warm while I run upstairs and change out of my oil-spattered scrubs. My face stares back at me in the vanity mirror. A weary face. Where is my old one? The one with hope painted on it. The bristles of my brush drag through my long brown locks. I let it fall around my face. My hair is always tied up or back these days, I haven't taken any time with it in months. It's barely clean half the time. No makeup either. When did I stop wearing makeup? When did I let myself fall apart? Oh yeah, I remember, the day I found him dead.

I twist my hair into a clip and skip the makeup.

He pours the wine. I serve the food. It's awkward. Neither of us says anything. He helped me set the table, which just added to the uncomfortable situation. Like we are a couple of some familiarity when we aren't. The food tastes wonderful. I haven't cooked in months. I miss cooking. It always gave me the feeling of home. The home I never had.

"This is really good." His comment interrupts my sorrow-fest.

"Thank you."

"I never get to eat home cooking, it's always hotel food or takeout. It gets on your nerves after a while. I miss my mum's cooking. Not to mention I always eat alone unless I am at some event, and well, that's not socializing with friends, you know. It's business. It sucks."

I don't know what to say. It's as if we have the same life, yet, at the same time, they couldn't be more different.

"When were you last home?"

"Six months ago. I had a break from filming last year and went home for a bit, but I've been doing the world press tour these last few months, just me and Lisa, my personal assistant. I've been to seventeen countries. The last leg is the U.S. as it's the biggest market and closest to the premiere."

My knife cuts into the chop. "I think most people would envy your glamorous life. I doubt anyone would think you lived like that."

"I know. It feels terrible to whine about it. Mostly I keep it to myself. My mum can sometimes tell when I talk to her on the phone, but I always tell her it's her imagination, and everything is fine."

"Tell me about your family."

"I grew up outside London, in Chelsea, but my parents opened a vineyard when I was twelve. They met in Paris. My dad was studying to be a sommelier, and my mom was in culinary school. They were at a wine tasting."

"That's funny, I attended boarding school in Paris. It's my second home."

"Cool. Well, my dad says meeting my mother was a *coup de tonnerre.*"

I smile. "Like a thunderbolt, love at first sight."

"Exactly, they both said that." He takes a sip of his chardonnay. "So, like I said, when I was twelve, they bought this land tucked away in the St. Mildred's Road Allotments and built a winery specializing in organic and hand-crafted wines. They grow their own grape varieties including Phoenix, Orion, pinot noir, and Bacchus. They're also part owners of the larger Ravenwood Vineyard in East Sussex."

"Wow, that's amazing. I don't know anything about winemaking."

"Unfortunately, it's made me a bit of a wine snob, but I try not to let it show." He smiles, perfect white teeth and sumptuous lips on full display. He certainly has movie star good looks.

"What about your family?" he asks.

"Just me and my dad. He has a new family, and well, it's complicated, and I don't talk about it."

"What about your job? Do you like it?"

"I love it. It's stressful, long hours, and sometimes there isn't time for anything else in your life. But that's a good thing right now."

Drew stares at me. I said too much. And I was trying so hard to stay focused, stay in control. But now I have let a sliver of my pain escape. Maybe he didn't hear it.

He doesn't say anything as the pleasant conversation has been replaced with an uncomfortable silence again. Now I want him to leave. Why hasn't anyone called him back? Something about this whole thing is wrong. I mean, seriously, this is the twentieth century. How hard is it to get a message to somebody to come and pick you up? Especially, somebody like him. Besides, shouldn't his security people be out looking for him by now? I bet if I turned on *Entertainment Tonight*, they might have a missing person story on him right this minute.

"Are you sure you are all right?" he presses me. "You look a little pale all of a sudden."

His piercing blue eyes fix me, and I can't breathe. This is too weird. This shouldn't be happening, tonight of all nights. The air in my kitchen has become thick with tension. I need to escape. Without answering, I stand. My chair scrapes along the tile floor and tips over. I run out the back door racing across the back deck. I cut the corner around the pool too close and nearly fall into the rippling blue water of the deep end. I sprint down the beach, sand flies off my feet and I struggle to breathe.

He grabs onto my upper arm, dragging me backward. Both of his hands trap my upper arms, and I am halted in my tracks. He turns me around to face him. The water washes over my bare feet. His face mirrors my panic.

"What's the matter? What did I say?" His voice is forceful as he presses me for an answer.

"Let go. You're hurting me," I scream. But I'm not struggling under his restraint.

"No. I'm not letting you go until you tell me what's going on. People have been calling you all night to see if you're okay. You say you won't need your car anymore, there's some guy's stuff upstairs in the spare bedroom, but he doesn't seem to be around." He pauses for a brief minute before he levels the dagger aimed straight at my heart. "And what's with that giant rock on your finger? Where is this guy? If I was engaged to you, I would be here with you. I wouldn't let you out of my sight for long."

Now I'm pissed. "What were you doing snooping around that room? You had no business going upstairs in my house. How dare you." I pull my arm away so I can smack him in the chest.

"I went up to take a shower. I'm sorry but I didn't think it would be a problem since you weren't here. The salt water from the night before made my skin itch. But you still haven't answered my question. What is going on, where is this guy?"

My mouth won't work. My tongue feels swollen. All the saliva has evaporated, the air in my lungs gone. No words come out. Especially not those words. I will not say them, never, ever again. And I'm terrified he saw what was hanging in the closet.

He releases me but he's still close. Too close. "Tell me. I'll listen, no matter what it is. Just tell me."

I stare at his caring face, his kind eyes, and suddenly my body is liquid. My knees buckle, and I collapse in a heap on the sand. The baby waves lap over my feet. The familiar high-pitched whining of a flock of seagulls jolts me back to reality. "Huoh-huoh-huoh," they say. Or is it "No, no, no…you shouldn't be doing this, Rea."

He is sitting next to me on the wet beach.

Didn't we do this yesterday? Why am I here again? With him? In the wet sand?

"Please, Rea, tell me what it is."

I bury my face in my hands. I can't, I can't tell him. I'm sick of talking about it. Thankfully, everyone at work has stopped asking me about it. Until today.

We sit for a long while, and my lungs reinflate. I turn and look at him. "He's dead." I wait for his reaction. I bet he wasn't expecting that answer. That'll teach him to be so nosy.

"Oh, God, I'm so sorry. I had no idea. I thought you were going to tell me he turned out to be a jerk or something, that maybe he cheated on you. God, Rea, I'm sorry."

Tears are pouring out of my face, and the salty drops mix with their mother, the ocean. I put my forehead on my knees, wrapping my arms around my legs. A ball of misery. Somebody throw me in the ocean. A hand is rubbing my back. His touch unnerves me. Why is he still here? This is screwing up my plan. Time is running out, and I have so much to do by midnight. I need him out of here.

I lift my head but can't make eye contact with him. Gazing into the dusky sky over the ocean, I say, "Look, thanks for being so sympathetic, but you need to go. I have things to do tonight and I'm already behind schedule. Go, take my car. I'm sure people must be worried about you by now. They probably have the cops out looking for you."

"I'm not going anywhere until I'm sure you're going to be all right. And from where I'm sitting, you look like you're nowhere close to all right."

I lie back in the sand, my head cradled in my hands. *Why is he still here?* I ask myself for about the hundredth time. This is none of his business. A shooting star streaks across the sky. I wonder who it is.

Drew settles onto his side, his elbow wedged in the sand, his head atop. "What happened to him?"

His voice is soft, like a warm breeze on my face. I

don't want to talk about this with anybody and not with a total stranger. But for some reason, he doesn't feel like a total stranger. I turn and study his sweet face. It welcomes me in, and for some strange reason, I want to tell him.

"He killed himself."

Chapter Eight

"Not intentionally. We worked together, studied together and basically did everything together. We fell in love, and he moved in with me. He asked me to marry him, and my father was thrilled."

Drew doesn't say anything, his eyebrows knit together.

"I should have known something was wrong sooner. We worked long days, late nights, trying to keep up with our studies, classes, and endless shifts. It was awful. No sleep, no food, no personal time. All to finish the year with the best grades and the best shot at a good residency. I started to notice he was off… I didn't know what it was at first but then I began to suspect he was availing himself of pharmaceuticals he shouldn't. I confronted him, but he laughed it off as something everybody did for a little extra help getting through the day. I didn't like it but for some unexplained reason, let it slide. One night we had a huge argument, and he left the house furious. We both had to work that night, and about ten hours into our shift I went to find him. One of the nurses said he was sleeping in one of the on-call rooms, so I thought I would go in and surprise him, apologize for doubting him. By the time I found him, his body was cold. He'd overdosed. I knew he was walking on dangerous turf, but I ignored all the signs. I should have done something, anything…turned him in… Whatever it took, I should have done it."

Sitting up, I run my hand through my hair, but it's trapped in the clip. Removing the restraint from my hair, I heave it into the ocean. The warmth of my hair on my shoulders eases my pain a small fraction. I can't believe I told him all this. I can't decide if I feel better or not.

I turn my head again and study this stranger sitting next to me in the sand. I wish he wasn't here, but then again, for some strange reason, I am glad he is. "Tomorrow was to be our wedding day," I blurt. "That's why everyone has been checking on me."

"Oh, God, no."

I can't believe I told him that.

"So what do you have to do tonight that's so important?"

"None of your business."

"Maybe it should be my business. I think you're in over your head here. You're trying to convince yourself you're fine, but from where I sit, I think you're in trouble."

"You know nothing about me. We're total strangers."

"I disagree."

"Well, I'm reliving my father's life. A life I hate." I laugh. " 'The sins of the father…' "

"What does that mean?"

I didn't realize I said that last part aloud. "Nothing, never mind." He'll never know how my life has become a cruel rerun of my father's. The one he tried so hard to save me from. This painful realization only adds to the misery of this horrid day. I don't want to think about the worst day of my life, the one I don't really remember but still know every sordid detail about. I should tell him.

But I don't even know him, and after today I will never see him again.

And I have important things to do tonight.

"Look, you have to get going. Take my car and go. I'll get Bobby to pick it up. I appreciate your kindness, but you need to leave." I stand. Drew stands next to me.

He takes my hand. His thumb rocks the ring on my finger back and forth.

"Why are you still wearing this?"

Too long. Six months, almost to the day. And this is the day I plan to take it off. But I need to get him out of here, so I can get the job done. All the jobs for tonight. Suddenly I am awash in my pain again. The cold, hard rock is on fire on my finger. I need it off. It's burning my hand. My body is a giant scream.

I ignore his question and pull my hand away, reaching for the ring with the other. It will not move. I can't decide which hand is paralyzed more, the one trying to take it off or the one strangled by it. A scream escapes me. I want it off, *now*. I look up into Drew's clear blue eyes. "Please… Please… Get it off me. I can't do it, you have to help me. Get it off, please, please."

Drew's eyes are enormous, his eyebrows arched. I don't think he knows what to do. Who is this crazy woman he has stumbled upon in his wild ride? The woman he thought was all sane and established. The one with the nice house, nice car, and respectable medical career. I tricked him. He has no idea what he crashed into last night. I fooled him, like I have fooled everybody into thinking I am all right when nothing could be further from the truth.

His fingers grab the ring. He studies me, then pulls hard. The ring scrapes over my knuckle, and I am finally free.

"Throw it in the ocean. Do it, do it now!"

"I don't know," he says too calmly. "It looks expensive. Are you sure about this?"

"Yes! Yes! Throw it in the ocean, get rid of it, hurry!"

Drew turns toward the waves, but he's still looking at me.

"Are you absolutely sure?"

"Yes," I urge. "Do it! Do it now!"

He winds up and hurls the crystalline icon of my agony into the roiling waves. There is a hint of a sparkle as the moonlight strikes it at the highest arc of flight. Silently, it drops into the ocean. My heart skips a beat, maybe ten.

The ring is the catalyst that sets my plan in motion. There can't be much time left as I bolt for the house. I run up the steps to the deck, giving the pool a wide berth. Under the kitchen sink I find the box of black trash bags. Drew is on my heels as I bolt up the stairs.

Entering the horrid room, I throw open the closet doors. The white gown is like a demon in the night as it taunts me with its sequins and baby pearls. I am momentarily frozen with the vision of me wearing it, walking down the aisle alongside Greg.

Shaking myself out of my stupor, I rip it off its hanger, as tears slide down my face, tiny rivulets of pain. I heave it into the middle of the room, then turn to assault the rest of the closet contents. Greg's shirts, his suits, his coats. Hangers break. A huge pile forms in the center of the room. I follow with the clothing from the dresser, tearing out each drawer, adding to the mountain of the remnants of Greg's life. Next comes the bedding as my human tornado strips all reminders of our life together into shreds and deposits them in the center of the room. I look up to see Drew with his hands in his hair, holding on to some semblance of sanity, I guess, as he watches me clear the room of anything left from my prior life.

The bathroom is next as I find myself standing in front of the mirror over the sink. I know my escape is behind the glass door. Suddenly I can't move. My arms are pinned at my side. He peers at me from behind. His arms are around me, his pounding heart against my back. His breath warm on my ear. "Stop," he says. "Stop it. That's enough."

I am frozen in space and time. A statue made from lost dreams.

"Breathe," he orders.

I do as I'm told.

"In and out, slowly."

My shoulders relax, my breathing calms. Does he know what's behind the mirror? He can't. But then again, he was up here taking a shower. Maybe he does know.

His arms release me, and he turns me to face him. His thumbs wipe the tears off my cheeks. "I'll clean out the bathroom stuff. Get the garbage bags and start bagging the clothing. Go. Do it," he says with authority.

I don't move. I started this, and I mean to finish it. I'd been planning this night for weeks. But I don't need his help. I don't want his pity.

"Go," he says more forcefully as he pushes me through the bathroom door.

He follows me out to retrieve a trash bag, then returns to the bathroom. Dutifully, I load the clothing into the dark plastic bags. My mind is numb. I am lost, my plan askew. Drew discards the contents of the medicine cabinet and Greg's toiletries from the shower. He stands in the doorway, bag in hand.

Together we finish packing all the belongings into the hellish trash bags. A mountain of black plastic faces us. We're both out of breath. Sweat covers my body in a glistening dew of pain.

I grab two bags and bolt down the stairs. I need to get this stuff out of here. It has to be done by midnight. Dragging the heavy load out the garage door, I face the alarm pad for the front gate. I frantically punch in the alarm code. It blinks red. Damn it. I do it again, red again. "Damn it!" I scream through my tears.

His warm hand has hold of mine.

"Stop it. Calm down. What's the code?"

"It's his birthday. It's his fucking birthday!" I shriek.

"Okay, tell me the numbers. I'll do it."

"0304."

The gates creak open. We drag our bags down the slope of the driveway to deposit them on the curb. It takes three trips until the room is cleared.

Out of breath, exhausted, I walk out onto the back deck. I take a seat on the steps leading to the ocean. The chimes on the old clock in the kitchen signal midnight. I made it, almost. Laying my hands across my knees, I lean my forehead on my arms. Nearly everything on my list for tonight is done. Drew sits beside me on the step. It is quiet except for the sound of water, the waves from the ocean, and the swirling water in the swimming pool. His hand is on my neck, he gives a little squeeze.

I can't believe he is still here. I turn my head, still resting on my arms. He looks at me, his gaze piercing the deepest recesses of my soul. Who is he? I ask myself. Why did he crash into my life yesterday? It's midnight, and he's still here. This can't be happening.

His hand slides down my back. It moves back and forth in a gentle expression of sympathy. But it doesn't feel like sympathy. It feels like electricity. How long has it been since a man touched me lovingly, even a friend? A long time.

"I could use another glass of wine," I blurt.

"I'll get it."

In a minute, he's back with the bottle and two glasses. We sit together in silence sipping the soothing golden liquid. I'm at a crossroad, my finale derailed for the moment. He should leave, but I don't want him to.

I get up from the suddenly uncomfortable step and deposit myself on one of the chaise lounges adorning the pool deck. It's built for two, and Drew settles in beside me. This it totally screwing up my finale.

Chapter Nine

Drew breaks the silence. "So, what did you mean before by 'the sins of the father'?"

I turn my head and our eyes meet. "Why do you care about any of this?"

"I don't know. Just tell me. I'm not leaving until I get it all out of you."

This need to interrogate me should annoy me, but for some reason I want to tell him. I cannot understand why.

"You probably know who my father is," I say looking up at the brilliant starlit sky. "Being in the business and all. My father is James Tasson." I wait for the impact of my announcement to hit. I sense the expression of awe on his face before he utters a single word.

"You mean, the director, James Tasson?"

"Yes." I almost smile at the shock in his voice.

"He's your father?"

"Yes," I repeat.

"He's rumored to be difficult to work with."

"Yes." I'm starting to sound like an imbecile. "He thinks too many actors are lazy, shallow, and only interested in fame and fortune. Don't show up to his set unprepared. But he still makes great movies, and everybody wants to work with him."

"I've heard."

I decide to cut him a break and tell him why my father is such a jackass. "My father was an up-and-coming director when he met my mother. She was an ingénue breaking into the big time. They became Hollywood's *it* couple. They got married, and it was hailed as Tinsel Town's wedding of the year. Not long after, my mother became pregnant with me. She freaked out about how it would ruin her career. My dad wasn't sympathetic and dismissed it as hormonal craziness. A few weeks after my birth, he came home to me screaming in my crib. My mother had sent the nanny home early and when he went upstairs, he found her dead on the bed, overdosed on pain pills. So, for all his trying to keep me from a situation like his, I wind up repeating his sin. He should have done something. I should have done something. Children suffer for the sins of their fathers, or mothers, which I did, but then I managed to duplicate those sins."

"I don't think it's that simple. You're making it sound like it was fate, or karma."

"Isn't it?"

"I think it was crappy luck. Bad things happen to good people, and good things happen to bad people. There's often no rhyme or reason."

"Well, there's a rhyme in my head even if there isn't a reason."

Drew refills our glasses.

The dam has broken and the flood gates open. I can't stop myself. "After that, I was left in the care of a new nanny and a series of babysitters. When I turned five, he shipped me off to a Catholic boarding school in Paris.

"No one ever said much about my mother's death. The company line was she was sick, and we couldn't take care of her anymore, so God took her. This infuriated me. I kept thinking, I would have taken care of her. This haunted me until I was sixteen when Sister Mary Katherine, my biology teacher, explained people die from pathogens, or random accidents, and the like, and God had nothing to do with it. I found this profound, coming from a nun. In retrospect, I realize all the sisters were well-educated and progressive. I'd call them feminists. They were fierce and preached their belief that women were as intelligent and could be as successful and powerful as men, maybe even more so.

"I didn't know my mother committed suicide until Jane—the dorm's premiere gossip monger—announced it to my face one night when I was ten. I acted like I knew, but the vice squeezing my chest said otherwise."

"I'm so sorry. It must have been awful for you, and at such a young age. Do you and your dad talk much these days?"

"Yeah, we mended most of our fences, although I can't say we ever talked about any of the old stuff. We agreed to forget it and try to be nice to each other from then on. I don't think anything will be any better if we vented our anger and frustration about the past. It's not like we can go back and do it over again."

"I guess not," Drew says in a quiet voice.

"So, what's the deal?" I ask, studying his handsome profile. "Why are you still here? I mean, this is getting a little ridiculous."

"I can't explain it, but something told me I needed to stay."

"Aren't people worried about you?"

"Well, I might have fibbed a little. I left messages saying I was staying with a friend, so I guess they're not overly worried about me."

"What?" I say, not hiding the startle in my voice. "You didn't tell them about the car accident? And really, we're not friends..." As soon as the words leave my mouth, I feel bad. I mean, recent events should earn him the instant merit badge for friendship.

Drew turns his head to look at me, his smile wide. "You honestly can say that?"

I sip my wine and regroup. "Well, I guess not. It does seem after tonight, we might be fast friends."

"Good. Because if you didn't feel that way, I would be upset."

Now what? It's after midnight, and he's still here. He can't sleep over again. I can't rationalize he needs medical attention like last night. But I doubt someone is going to come and retrieve him again at this time of night. Tomorrow is Sunday, and I don't have to work. Oh, my God, I'm making plans for tomorrow. This was not part of the plot.

"So, how are you going to get back to your hotel? You can still take my car if you want."

"I don't know. I'm not anxious to get back to my empty hotel room. Are you desperate to get rid of me?"

Uh-oh...he's calling me out. And I'll admit I'm not in any hurry to let him go.

"Why don't we have another glass of wine before we decide on a plan?" I say. Now, that's a stupid suggestion. He shouldn't be drinking if he's going to take my car back to his hotel. But we both ignore the rational thoughts for the moment as we settle into the chaise lounge built for two.

The conversation is substantive at times and silly and light at others. But all of it is easy and as I look into his playful eyes, I see a man who interests me, a kind man who seems as lost as I am, only for different reasons. The question of him leaving never comes up again as the night air lulls us to sleep, the soothing sounds of the water whispering in my ears.

Chapter Ten

My eyes shiver open. I drink in the serene panorama before me. The sun risen, the surf calm, the sky clear blue, like Drew's eyes, not the drabby gray cloudless sky I'd become accustomed to…in my head. A new day. A day of promise. A day of hope.

Everything is wet. My hair, my face, my clothing. Again. The morning has blanketed us in a mist of glistening dew as we slumbered in the chaise lounge, back to front, Drew's arm slung across my hips. How bizarre is this? What would Jillian say? My mouth turns up in a crinkle as I picture her face. *"He slept over? Are you kidding me?"* I laugh out loud, stirring Drew from sleep.

"Hey, luv," he whispers near my ear, sending a shiver down my spine.

I turn under his arm and lie back against the lounger. "Morning. I guess we passed out last night. Solved the transportation problem."

"I guess so."

I groan. "My back is killing me from sleeping on this lounge chair."

"I'm with you," he says. "All of a sudden my hotel bed doesn't sound so bad."

"You're singing a different tune from the one last night." I flash him a look of disdain.

He smiles. "What's for breakfast?"

"I need a shower, then we can talk food. You can use the other shower if you want." The harsh reality is I have no food because I had no intention of eating breakfast this morning.

****

He's out of the shower wrapped in a towel, standing at my open bedroom door. He looks just…scrumptious. I'm dressed, hair down, makeup on. I can't believe who I am today. When I woke up yesterday, I didn't think I would be here.

"Looks like I don't have any clothes, and we discarded all the stuff from the spare room. I thought maybe we could go get a few things for me to wear. Then, later I could go back to the hotel. I confess I'm putting it off as long as I can. I don't want to go back, alone, with nothing to do."

I feel the same way. It's Sunday, and I have the entire day off. I hadn't made any plans for obvious reasons. Now the entire unscheduled day looms large. The phone rings.

"Hi, Dad."

"Everything okay?"

"Yeah, I'm fine. I took care of everything, just like I planned."

"Maybe we could go out to dinner."

"Thanks, but I'm not really in the mood to celebrate. Just be happy I'm okay and have made peace with the day."

"You sure?"

"I am. Maybe next week."

"Okay. I'll call you later in the week."

"Great. Bye." Jillian is next, and we have the same conversation, while Drew leans against the door frame in his damp towel.

"You have to stop listening in on my conversations," I say, returning the phone to its cradle. "It's not polite." Once again, I feel he knows more than he should.

He crosses his arms over his well-toned chest, one hip pressed against the door frame, feet crossed at the ankles. "So, I thought everyone was calling you last night because of your wedding day, but there's something else."

His smile looks so innocent. I can't believe I'm going to hit him with this. Oh, well, he asked for it.

I look him squarely in the eye. "It's my birthday."

His brow furrows as all the pieces of my horrible life meld into one big terrible scene. The light bulb lights but his face is dim, dark.

"You were getting married on your birthday?"

"Yes. And it took me all this time to dispose of the dress, the ring, and all his stuff. I promised myself I would have him completely out of my life by midnight last night."

His relaxed pose vanishes, and he stands tall, taking a step toward me. "Oh, God, Rea, I didn't realize it. I don't know what to say."

"There's nothing to say, Drew. It's done, it's over, and I'm facing the day with more optimism and enthusiasm than I ever imagined. I won't lie. Having you here was something I never bargained for, never could have imagined. So I guess I should thank you. Thanks for sticking by me during one of the worst nights of my life. I'll never forget it."

We stand there, wearing the awkward moment like a scratchy sweater. He walks toward me and wraps me in a bear hug, my face pressed against his bare shoulder.

A forgotten stirring jolts my body. It's been a long time since I felt...anything.

The phone rings again, and he releases me. I retrieve the phone from its cradle. How many more phone calls must I endure before this all ends? "Hey." I close my eyes and sigh.

"You okay?"

"I am."

"Happy birthday."

"Thanks."

"What should I do with the car?"

"He's right here, you can ask him yourself." I turn toward Drew.

"What the hell is that dude still doing at your place?"

"It's a long, convoluted story. I'll explain later."

"How about you explain now?"

"Bobby, please drop it. I'm okay."

Bobby is silent, and I fear a fight is brewing. I'm fond of Bobby and somewhat comforted he feels the same way about Dad as I do. He too is an only child and was around ten when Dad married his mother. Bobby never spent much time with him either and followed his own pathway, away from the famous James Tasson. Bobby hated school, and he wasn't a great student. He barely graduated. I've often thought he probably has some undiagnosed learning disability. He turned down a free college education and convinced Dad to let him use the money to start a car repair business. Bobby was happy to let dad buy him off, just like I did.

I hand Drew the phone. "It's Bobby. He wants to talk to you." If Bobby knew Drew was standing half-naked in my bedroom, he'd have a fit.

"Hey, Bobby." A pause. "Okay, got it. I'll have the

rental company get in touch. Thanks again for your help."

Drew hands the phone back and I place it near my ear, relieved to hear the dial tone. "What did he say?"

"He called it; the car is totaled. I need his number so I can contact the rental company."

"I'll write it on the small white board on the fridge." My stomach growls. I look up into Drew's deep blue eyes and smile.

"I guess it's time to talk food. And clothing," he says.

"I've got nothing in the house for breakfast because I usually get something at the hospital or grab something out. We can stop at Jenny's Diner. They're famous for their breakfast crepes, but they have everything. Then we'll find you some clothes. You'll have to wear the stuff I gave you for now, then we can add them to the trash pile."

He steps closer, close enough to touch. Our eyes meet. He leans in, his head tilted to the side, his eyes half-lidded. I focus on his parted lips, and everything goes quiet, like the moment of silence between lightning and thunder.

He nudges my chin up with his knuckle and kisses me softly. The taste of him nourishes me. He kisses me again, harder, deeper, a kiss that breaks open the sky and steals my breath, telling me every other kiss in my life has been wrong. A fervent need I've never known commandeers my soul.

I sense a rush of helplessness, a sinking yielding, a surging tidal wave of heat. His solid arms are around me, keeping me upright, my chest pressed against his. A swimming giddiness spins me round and round. His insistent mouth parts my lips again, sending tremors along my nerves, evoking sensations I didn't know I was capable of feeling. And I'm kissing him back, clutching him as the only solid thing in a dizzying world, gripping his rock-hard biceps, our mouths melding in one last kiss.

Oh. My. God.

The kiss ends, but I want to kiss him again, and again, and… What am I doing? When I pictured this day, it didn't include me kissing a guy. Kissing anyone.

"Happy birthday," he whispers near my ear.

He pulls back, and I stare at him, dumbstruck. The spark of him lingers on my tongue.

"Was that okay?" he asks.

Good God, yes, I think. It was fucking great. "I…I…yeah, it was okay. Actually, it was great."

"I didn't overstep?"

"Ah…no."

"Good."

He releases me, but I can't take my eyes off his chest. I want to touch it. Run my hands over his firm body. Oh, God. Stop it.

"I guess I should get dressed."

Good idea, before I make a total ass of myself.

"Any chance you have a spare pair of sunglasses and maybe a baseball hat I can wear?"

I frown.

"Incognito mode, if possible."

I get it. If he's recognized, there's a good chance of getting mobbed or the paparazzi showing up.

"I think I have some shades that aren't too girly and a hat."

He leaves me standing there, my body aflame with

desire. Jesus fucking Christ.

My car is the twin to his rented one, only it's white and a convertible. We put the top down to bathe in the sunshine on this magnificent day. Maybe the most beautiful day I've ever seen. The wind whips my face as I drive down the coastal highway towards my favorite shopping spot. I look over at my passenger's bright smile. God, he really is a handsome dude. I see what Jillian and all the girls were talking about. He looks so happy, almost as good as I feel. And that kiss—I can't stop thinking about it. I haven't recovered. Not sure I ever will.

Chapter Eleven

We enter Jenny's Diner, hoping the disguise is effective. I often came here with Greg, but not since his death. I pray no one asks where he is.

Thankfully, a server I don't recognize seats us in a booth near the back. Drew keeps his shades and hat on, and we order the crepes, stuffed with scrambled eggs, mushrooms, and Swiss cheese, and hash browns on the side. And coffee. I might need more than one cup.

Breakfast is pleasant and uneventful, and the check arrives. I put down my credit card.

"I never let a girl pick up the check," Drew says.

"You can make it up to me." Okay, that sounded bad. How will he interpret that?

"Deal," is all he says.

But it isn't our server who returns with my card and the receipt, it's the owner, Jenny. I'm in the process of signing it when she says, "Rea, I hate to bother you, but I'm worried about that kid over there. Do you see the couple seated by the window?" She points with her chin.

The man and woman have their backs to us, and I see a child of about seven, opposite and between them. He's looking right at me. "I do."

"The boy has a swollen eye and a split lip. The adults ordered pancakes and bacon, but when Molly asked the boy if he wanted pancakes too, adding that we make Mickey Mouse pancakes, the boy said yes, but the man said the boy won't be eating."

"Have you seen them before?" I ask.

"No, never, but my gut tells me something's wrong."

"So, you're not sure if they are his parents, and you think he's in danger?"

"The server said she has five kids, and knows when a kid is scared. I believe her."

"Okay, I get it. Get me a piece of paper and something to write with, like a marker. And do you have a wireless phone?"

"Yes."

"Bring it."

Jenny returns with the phone, a piece of white paper, and a black Sharpie. I write in bold letters: R U OK? and hold it up for the kid to see, his eyes still glued to me. He slowly, barely perceptibly, turns his head from side to side. Twice. I nod my head in acknowledgement.

"Let's see if we can get him alone, so I can get a closer look," I say.

"How are you going to manage that?" Drew says.

The bathrooms are visible from our seats, and I point toward them, hoping the child will understand my request. He says something to his parents, then gets up and walks toward the restrooms. I slip the phone in my pocket. "Follow me," I instruct Drew. "Don't let anyone in."

"What will I say?"

"You're an actor, improvise." I follow the child, take his hand, and usher him into the ladies' room. I kneel in front of him. "Hi, my name is Rea, what's yours?"

"Billy."

"Billy, I'm a doctor. Do you know what that is?"

"They give you shots."

I smile. "Sometimes, but it's only to keep you safe, to keep you from getting sick." I take both his hands. "My job is to keep children safe. Can you tell me how you got hurt?"

"I'm supposed to say I fell down the stairs."

"Who told you to say that?"

"Kenny."

"Who is Kenny?"

"My mommy's boyfriend."

"Is Kenny here with you?" He nods in the affirmative. "How did you really get the swollen eye and the cut lip?" It isn't the only injury. There are distinct finger marks around his neck and bruises on his legs.

"I didn't eat my peas."

"And Kenny was mad?"

He nods again. "He said I can't eat anything else until I eat them. He saved them."

"Is it okay if I lift your shirt and take a look at your tummy?"

Another nod. My stomach knots as I see the contusions on his tiny belly. I palpate his side, and he winces. A chance his spleen is bruised. I turn him around to view more discolorations on his back, older ones. Damn, this kid took quite a beating. And it isn't the first time. I'm surprised he's still standing.

"Sorry," I hear Drew say. "There's somebody sick in there. Give them a minute."

"I'm looking for my kid," an angry male voice says.

I lock the door and dial 911.

"911. What is your emergency?"

"My name is Dr. Andrea Tasson. I am reporting a

child in danger. Please send a patrol car to Jenny's Diner, off Highway One. I have the child secured in a restroom. Please hurry."

"Yes, Doctor." The 911 operator hesitates for a few seconds. "There are two units in the vicinity, I will send them immediately."

"Thank you. I won't release the child until the police arrive."

Drew's voice again. "I doubt your kid is in there. It's just my girlfriend, and she isn't feeling well."

"Bullshit. He said he was going to the bathroom. The stupid little shit can barely read. He probably went into the wrong one."

Sirens blare in the distance, and I hold tight to the boy's small hand. He's obviously undernourished, and my pulse quickens. How could anyone treat a child like this?

"Get out of my way, dude," the man yells, and the door handle jiggles. "Let me in."

"Over here," Drew yells.

I hear a woman's voice outside the door. "Excuse me, sir. Can I see some ID?"

"Why?" the man says. "I haven't done anything wrong."

I unlock the door, Billy clutching my hand. The female officer makes eye contact with me.

"We have a report of a child in danger. Is this boy your son?"

The woman at the table is standing beside her boyfriend. "I'm his mother," the woman offers.

Another female officer approaches while two male officers stand at the door.

"What is your name?" the officer asks the boy.

"Billy."

"Is this your mother, Billy?"

The boy nods.

"How'd you get the swollen eye?"

The boy looks up at me. "It's okay, you can tell the police lady. We all want to help you."

"He fell down the stairs," the woman offers. "He's very clumsy."

The officer extends her hand. "Come, Billy, let's talk outside." The boy grasps her hand without hesitation, and she leads him away.

"Wait," the man says. "You have no right to talk to him without our permission."

"Actually, I do, sir." And she turns toward the exit with the boy in tow. One of the male officers holds the door open.

The man attempts to pursue. "Get your hands off my kid."

"Sir," the remaining officer says, "let's not make this more difficult than it has to be."

He pushes the officer out of his way, but she grabs his arm, kicks the back of his knees, and he falls chest first onto the floor. She has him handcuffed in under five seconds. The officers escort the couple outside and secure them in a cruiser.

One of the male officers reenters the restaurant and approaches me. He sticks his thumbs in his apparatus-laden belt. "Good call," he says. "The kid informed us he'd been beaten by the boyfriend, and this isn't the first time. The mother confirmed his story but claimed the kid misbehaves and they're trying to correct his bad behavior. The kid's six."

"Make sure he gets to a hospital," I say.

"Definitely. We're enroute to L.A. General."

"Good, use my name and ask for Dr. Jillian Ortiz."

"Will do."

"Do you need a statement from me?"

"We'll include you in the report. Give me your name and number in case the DA needs more information."

I comply, and they drive away.

Jenny shakes her head. "Jesus. How can anyone do that to a child?

"Nice work," Drew says. He looks at Jenny. "Both of you." We exit the diner and climb into the car. "That was awful. Do you see stuff like that a lot?"

"Enough."

"It hurts my soul to see something like that."

"It should."

Chapter Twelve

We drive the mile to Celeb Wear Boutique. We enter, and Bethany beelines toward me.

"Hey, Doc, how are you, where have you been? I haven't seen you in months." As soon as the words leave her mouth, she remembers. She bites her bottom lip, then, "Oh God, Rea, I can't believe I said that. I'm sorry."

"It's okay. I'm doing all right. Better than expected."

"Today was the day, wasn't it?"

"Yeah, but I'm fine."

She glances at my companion and her lips quirk up. "Well, I guess sooo… Are you going to introduce me?"

I turn to Drew, hoping to reassure him the paparazzi won't be showing up in the next few seconds. "Bethany is discreet. There are a lot of celebs who come in here, but she never gets involved in the publicity stuff, although she's been offered some serious cash to reveal any dirt she can get on people." Drew removes his glasses and hat. "Bethany, this is Andrew Foster, Drew, this is my friend, Bethany." Andrew reaches out to shake her hand. Beth swoons.

After the nice-to-meet-yous, I shake Beth out of her movie star stupor. "Drew needs some clothing. Can you help us out?"

"Sure," Beth says. I imagine what she must be

thinking. What's a movie star like him doing with me and without any clothing? She gives me a wink and a smile. I let her think her sordid thoughts without offering any explanation.

"There's just one problem," Drew says. "It seems I've lost my wallet. Can I come back and pay you tomorrow?"

"Sure," Beth says. "We'll put it on account. I'm sure you're good for it."

"Great," Drew says. "Thanks."

"Come on. I'll help you pick out whatever you need." This is going to be the highlight of Beth's day, I decide, maybe even her year.

"Great," he says again. "Let's start with pants and maybe some shorts. Oh, and a bathing suit." And the two of them are off to the dressing room.

They spend about a half hour picking out assorted items, including a pair of navy-blue topsiders and Teva sandals. I poke around perusing stuff I never wear. It seems like I have forgotten what it's like to be a girl. Standing in front of a sapphire blue cocktail dress, I admire the beautiful fabric and skinny rhinestone belt. I imagine wearing it to some place fun when my fantasy is interrupted by his voice.

"You would look great in this dress."

I meet his smile with one of my own. I say nothing.

"Why don't you let me buy it for you?"

"That's ridiculous. I never go anywhere that would require something so glamorous. My life is pretty much scrubs, pajamas, and jeans. Not terribly exciting."

"Hmm…" He is thoughtful for a few seconds. "The premiere for my new movie is Wednesday. Come with me as my date. So you see you'll need the dress."

"That's absurd. I don't belong anywhere near a movie premiere. It's out of my realm of reality."

"Come on, I hate these things. Having you with me would make it so much better."

"No way. Not for me, but thanks for asking."

"I hate to do this, but I was there in your hour of need last night. I think the least you can do is return the favor and come with me on my awful night."

My lips part, anger rising in my chest, but before I can utter a syllable, he stops me.

"Oh, God, I'm sorry, I didn't mean my premiere night is anything even close to what you went through. It was totally insensitive. I'm so sorry. It was a stupid attempt at a joke or to coerce you to come with me or... Oh, geez." He pinches the bridge of his nose, like my dad does. "I'm sorry Rea. I'm just an ass sometimes."

I press my lips together. My anger simmers lower than a second ago. Of course, he didn't mean it. Think a minute. Don't overreact. His hand is on my arm. The second he touches me, the anger melts away.

"Forgive me, please, Rea. I couldn't bear the thought of upsetting you."

"I know. I know you didn't mean it. It's okay. I'm not mad."

"Oh, God, thanks...but, please? Come with me. I really want you there."

"I don't know. I probably have to work anyway." I can't believe I'm even considering something so outrageous, even for one second. Besides, my father would have a cow if he found out I was at a movie premiere with this guy. A smile crosses my face. Yeah, he would have a friggin' heart attack. And wouldn't that be just perfect?

Drew interrupts my evil thoughts of revenge on my unsuspecting, controlling father. "I'm buying you the dress anyway. You have a few days to decide if you want to come with me. I'll wear you down by then." His impish smile has returned.

"I'll think about it. You can buy me the dress. It's tempting, at least for now."

Off to the dressing room, Beth has me inside the dress in a few minutes. I prance around in front of the mirror when Beth grabs my hand, pulling me outside. Drew stands there admiring my girlish look. I haven't felt like this in, gosh, maybe ever. I twirl around like a five-year-old in her first party dress. Drew's delight enhances my enchanted mood.

"Wow, you're a knockout. You'll kill at the premiere."

I'm not so sure. I have no business being at a movie premiere, on any level. But I put my insecurities aside for the moment, not wishing to ruin the fairy-tale moment.

We exit the boutique with our bags and deposit them in the trunk of the car. Drew turns to me and says, "Is that a bookstore?" He sounds like a kid who spied a candy shop.

"Yeah."

"Can we go in? I haven't been in a bookstore in ages."

"I guess so." Neither have I, I realize. Who reads for leisure these days? Certainly not me. I can't remember the last book I read for sheer pleasure.

"Cool," he says walking toward the entrance. I'm right behind him, and soon we are combing through the tomes of fiction. The smell alone is exhilarating. We spend about forty-five minutes selecting a half dozen hardcovers for the pure fun of it. Making our way from the pay-for library, we once again head to the car. This time it's my turn to take a detour.

"Let's go into the grocery store. I'll get something to make for dinner."

"Great," he says, "I haven't been in a food market in months. Could we buy some fresh fruit and maybe some biscuits…I mean cookies?"

I smile. He sounds like a ten-year-old again. "Sure, why not?"

Groceries in the cart, we approach the checkout. How did I get here? At the supermarket with a man. This man. A gorgeous man. A famous man. This seems so normal, shopping together, planning dinner together, having breakfast together—stuff Greg and I rarely did. I suddenly wonder if I'm setting myself up for a fall. Am I so desperate to replace my life with Greg that I will throw myself at the first guy who gives me even the slightest bit of attention? And he's an actor. I must admit my dad is probably right about many of them being shallow, narcissistic druggies. But, then again, there seem to be a lot of celebrities who are doing it right. They do good things with their money, they have a high level of social conscience, and they get married and have kids. Like normal people…whatever the hell that means.

Drew lags, probably distracted by some childish treat he hasn't had in ages. I turn to see him standing at the bakery counter. Exactly as I thought, as a grin captures my lips.

But then I see what he is asking the clerk behind the counter. The tube of red gel spells out my name. A herd of butterflies attacks my gut. Now who's acting like a ten-year-old?

"What are you doing?" I whisper.

"It's your birthday. You should have a birthday cake. Did I spell it right?"

My eyes well. A giant lump lodges in my throat. I try to swallow it, but it's stuck.

Drew looks down at me. "Oh, Rea, I didn't mean to upset you. Why are you sad?"

I didn't plan to be alive on this birthday. Now, there is a cake with my name on it. The impact of this day is smacking me in the face, hard. The red welts from the harshness of the reality sting me. I can't allow myself to fall apart. Not now, not here, not at all. I'm going to be all right. I'm over the misery. I can have a good life. I can leave the past behind. Get a grip, Rea. He's being so nice to you, embrace the kindness, the caring. You deserve it. It's okay to let someone be nice to you.

The log jam in my throat opens, my pulse rate slows. I quell the tears.

"You spelled it right." I inhale slowly and let it out. "I'm sorry. I'm not sad. It's just…well, nobody ever bought me a birthday cake before."

Chapter Thirteen

His arm is around me. I feel safe and secure under his protective touch. "I don't understand. Never a birthday cake? How can that be?"

"It's complicated," I say. "Story for another day."

"Then let's get out of here," he says. "We can read our books on the beach for a while. We'll have a decadent day before we face the realities of a new week." He grabs the pink box tied with red and white string, and we once again make our way to the checkout.

"Your card is declined," the clerk says. The woman ahead of me at the counter is tiny, short dark hair, clad in a shabby jean jacket over a short black dress. I scan her order—baby formula, diapers, wet wipes, some apples, bread, pasta, rice, and beans.

"Do you have cash? Or another card?" the clerk asks.

"No. How short am I? I can put some things back."

"I've got it," I say. I hand the clerk my card. The woman looks at me, and I see a weary face, suntanned, but lined, creases around her eyes and on her forehead.

"I can't accept…"

I stop her. "Please, I'm happy to help."

"I can pay you back."

"Not necessary. You can pay me back by doing something nice for someone else."

"Thank you, miss. I will say a prayer for you."

"That would be nice."

The clerk scans my card, helps her pack her goods, and she departs. Before she does, she turns and says, "God bless you."

I smile.

I pay for our groceries, and we are soon driving back to the house.

"You are an amazing woman," Drew says. "That was a classy move. And now I'm convinced you have a giant *S* on your chest."

I ignore the super-hero reference for the second time. "She looked like she's had a hard life. People need to suffer less. Get more help."

"I agree that I need to do something charitable. I've thought about it. I could never spend all my money. And I think people with this much money should do something altruistic, charitable, with it. It's too much money for any one person to have. I still marvel that we pay our actors and professional athletes more than we pay our teachers, social workers, and nurses, who do the lion's share of good in this world."

"Wow," I say, "Not your typical celebrity from where I'm sitting."

"Did you know your father has several foundations to support struggling actors?"

My eyes widen. What? My father helping the downtrodden? Doesn't sound like him. "He does?"

"Yeah, he renovated a bunch of old apartment buildings in New York, Chicago, and right here in L.A. The rent and food are cheap, sort of like in homeless shelters. Casting directors often tap them for quick roles for extras. It's pretty cool. When I first hit New York, I stayed at one for two weeks."

I find this incredulous. My father never had the time or inclination to take care of his daughter, yet he's taking care of thousands of actors. Someone who supposedly doesn't even like actors.

Drew is staring at me. "You didn't know…"

"No, and I'm shocked. I thought he wasn't fond of actors."

"I think he got a bad rap. He had a bad time with Frank Biggers on his first movie. The guy was a bit of a prima donna, and they didn't get along. There were some quotes from your father that didn't present him in the greatest light. But it was a long time ago, and yet it still follows him around."

The craziness of this whole situation taunts me. How could my life have changed so drastically in two days? I try not to overanalyze it and tell myself to enjoy it and not think about tomorrow.

We return to the house and unload our purchases. The day is still bright and beautiful, and we settle into the lounges on the back deck. It feels great and decadent, like Drew said, to have nothing to do but relax by the pool with the ocean twenty feet away. Suddenly my home is a vacation villa. Greg and I rarely took time to enjoy the amenities of the house as we were so obsessed with studying and work. Racing to get the best grades and the best residencies. I begin to wonder if our life was that great. And if our life would have been any better in the future.

The sun is sinking low on the horizon as we clean up the dishes from dinner. We wash the pots and load the dishwasher like a normal couple. It's odd how comfortable it has become in such a short time. He tracked down the number for the agency representing him and awaits a call from his publicist. Suddenly, I'm afraid of being alone. Maybe I set myself up with false hope, and as soon as he is gone, I will fall into the bottomless abyss of despair again.

"What's the matter?" he says, interrupting my miserable musings. "You look like you saw a ghost or something."

"No, nothing, I'm fine. Let's go for a swim in the ocean. Come on." I run out the back door before tears can find their way out. No more tears, I scold myself.

I strip off the baggy sweatshirt covering my bathing suit, letting it fall onto the sand, and splash my way into the breakers. I dive headfirst into a wave at least as tall as I am. Surfacing, I look behind to see him following me into the roiling ocean. The cold water shocks my body, banishing the momentary icy shadow of gloom.

He secures my hands in his as we bob up and down in the never-ending waves. We laugh and try not to swallow salt water as we dodge the giant mounds of menacing water. Playing a game of chicken with Mother Nature with my new friend is exhilarating. We tire and struggle to make our escape from the pounding surf. Standing on the sand, saltwater drips off our chilled forms. Our breathing is rapid as we recover from the intensity of staying afloat in the powerful force of nature.

I pick up the discarded sweatshirt and run back towards the deck where I deposit it on a chair. I dive into the pool. Pure decadence. Swimming in the salty ocean, then being able to shed the saltiness from your body in the sweet warm water of the freshwater pool. I can't remember the last time I did this. Drew is beside me in an instant. Our eyes meet; smiles turn to something more serious. His arms are around me as we stand chest deep in the heated water. I return his embrace. Faces close, his lips brush against mine. His skin is warm against my cool body. He pulls me in close, our bodies crushed against each other as the kisses become pure ecstasy. I close my eyes and let myself drift in the warmth of his touch. I can't hold him close enough. I'm so hungry for his body, his love.

Our lips part and he smiles. "Time for cake," he says, jolting me from an amatory trance. He pulls me up the pool steps by my hand. "I'll be right back."

Is he kidding? I had something sweet in mind, but it wasn't cake. Maybe he's a tease. But it didn't feel like it. I wrap myself in a towel and settle on the lounger, confused, bewildered. He's probably made love to hundreds of women. Okay, that might be a few too many. But definitely more than me. I might be out of my league here.

Back from the kitchen, cake, plates, and forks in hand, he sets everything on the side table. I swing my legs over and stare at the cake with my name on it.

"I couldn't find candles, but I'm guessing you don't have any."

"No birthday cake or candles have crossed into Tassonland. This is a first."

"Well, I'm singing anyway, and you can pretend to blow. Use your imagination."

I laugh at the absurdity of this entire situation. What a nut. And off he goes…

"Happy birthday to you, happy birthday to you…"

He sings the entire song and for some strange reason I'm laughing so hard, tears stream down my face.

"I hope you're happy crying," he says.

I catch my breath. "You know, I never cried as a kid.

Not when I broke my ankle or got five stitches in my foot or when I was scared, or anything. Not even when Greg died. I know that sounds messed up, but it's true."

Drew shakes his head. "Well, as a kid, I was a total crybaby. I still am. I cry at the drop of a hat. I'm considered one of the best criers in the business. I'm proud of it."

"And now I can't even count how many tears I've shed since I met you."

"That sounds terrible. Who wants to be with a guy who makes her cry."

"That's not what I meant. It's a good thing. I'm feeling things I never felt before. Or things I've never acknowledged before. It's very…freeing."

"Glad to hear that. Now blow."

I inhale deeply and exhale forcefully at the imaginary candles. Drew claps, hugs me, and whispers near my ear, "Happy Birthday, luv."

He feeds me cake like I'm a three-year-old. And it's the most delicious cake I've ever eaten.

We drink more wine as the sky grows dark and the stars appear on the nighttime stage. After another luxurious swim in the pool, he leads me up the steps and pulls me down on top of him, in the same place we slept last night. His arms secure me to his chest. My arms surround his neck as I lean in to kiss his sumptuous lips again. The heat of his hands spreads across me as he slides them up and down my wet skin, and I lose myself in the essence of him. I never want this moment to end. The perfect ending to the perfect day. The complete antithesis to what it was supposed to be. I thought I would be in hell today, but instead…I'm in heaven.

Our smiles merge in a warm kiss. His fingers trace

small circles on my back. It tickles, and I moan, maybe more of a chuckle. His hands slide down the curve of my back. "Can we take this upstairs?" he whispers.

Oh, God. Yes.

Chapter Fourteen

We stand facing each other at the foot of the bed. "I don't have protection," he says.

"I'm on the pill."

He grins. "Excellent."

His fingers tug at the tie on my bathing suit top, and he slides the straps off my shoulders, letting it fall to the ground. His perfect eyes are on me, making me swoon. He takes my head in his hands and pulls me toward him. The taste of him intoxicates me. His kisses drift down my throat, hot and sweet on my neck. Pleasure spools up my body in long, thick ribbons as the familiar heat of passion spreads across me like a tender memory.

The bottom is next, and I am rendered free to love him.

He sheds his bathing suit and scoops me up in his arms and carries me over to rest on the cool sheets. I lie naked against his chest, our bodies bonded together by desire. Warmth floods through me. The feel of his flesh against my flesh is agonizing in its intensity as we lie together, eyes reaching into each other's soul.

Strong hands circle my back, and I'm lying on top of him. My long tumble of damp hair cascades over his chest. I can't take my eyes off his beautiful face. Long fingers tuck the loose strands behind my ears in an affectionate caress. He drags his thumb down the side of my face, across the line of my chin, settling on my bottom lip. He tugs on my chin, parting my lips to meet the curve of his. My hands travel across his firm biceps, traveling over his shoulders and around his neck. I clutch him against me as my body melts into him.

Another wicked kiss sends delight throbbing through me as his fingers tease at my back, down my thighs. His lips find the curve of my neck, the arch of my shoulder, then the place where my ribcage meets my waist. I yield to his desire and sink into that familiar space I so desperately need to fill. And now the moment is upon me, he is upon me as a soft moan of pleasure escapes my throat.

We are pure movement, pure desire. The first wave washes over me like liquid fire, my back arches, my toes curl, and I fall off the cliff into a pile of tingling ecstasy. The aftershocks pulse through me as the roller coaster slows to a stop.

His voice grows low, almost a growl, as his passion erupts in an uncontrollable shudder. My heart flames as my breath slows, our hearts beating in tandem.

****

The morning arrives, but this time we are in my bed. Warm and cozy in contrast to the two nights we spent previously. The bedside clock announces 7:10. My boss said to come in whatever time I wanted, knowing I'd have a difficult weekend. Of course, I didn't think I'd be at work at all today.

His arms are wrapped around me as we lie like two silver spoons in a velvet-lined drawer, his leg slung over my hips. The sun is emerging through the slats in the window blinds, his warm breath tickles my neck, and I try not to laugh out loud. I don't want to disturb him in his perfect embrace of me. We lie there for a while, him asleep, me basking in the glow of the perfect morning.

Now I have to pee. It's unbearable, and I slide myself out of his body hug. Of course, he wakes. I run to the bathroom, wincing at the soreness between my legs. It's been a long time, and I think we might have overdone it last night. Yeah, overdid it…but totally worth it.

I return to the warmth of the bed and slip my arms around his neck, both of us resting on our sides. Our gazes meet.

"Morning, luv," he says.

"Morning." I smile, reveling in this perfect moment, a moment my wildest dreams could never have imagined. But back to reality. "So, I thought your publicist would have called by now."

His eyes widen. "Well, my bad, but I told them not to have her call until this morning."

I frown. "Are you ever planning on leaving, or did you intend on staying all along?"

"Are you trying to get rid of me?"

"No," I say through a smile.

"Well, you're on to me. As soon as you plucked me off the beach the other night, I decided I was staying forever."

His look is more serious than it should be in response to my sarcasm. I wonder if there is some truthfulness in what he said. I dismiss it as folly. Sounds like a line from a movie, I chide myself. Don't be such a jerk.

I roll onto my back, focusing on the ceiling fan. My hands are over my head, nestled in the softness of the pillow underneath. He props himself up on one elbow. I study his adorable face.

"I mean it, Rea. I don't want to go back to my hotel.

I want to stay here with you. Don't make me go back there. Please."

The intensity of his look unnerves me. Is he serious? I mean, we met three days ago. Yet I cannot deny the intensity of the feelings I have for him in such a short time. Could he feel the same? *Come on, get a grip, girl.* He probably does this kind of thing all the time in every city he visits. My father's words come back to haunt me. *This is what they do. They take advantage of you, and then they're gone.*

I don't know what to say, what to think. "You can't be serious, Drew. We barely know each other, and you want to move in with me? How long will you even be in town? After the movie premiere, won't you be off to some new location?" Although I never lived with my father, I knew the drill. He always promised but only managed to visit me at school once a year if that, constantly involved in some project or on location in some remote part of the world.

"Even if I have to be out of town for any length of time, I want to come home to you. I want to be with you. I know it sounds ridiculous, and you're right, we just met. But I know in my heart I want to be near you. You're like fresh air I haven't breathed in a long time. I don't want to leave you. I don't want to be without you."

This torrent of emotion overwhelms me. This can't be right. Things like this don't happen. It's the stuff of moviemaking, not reality. But again, I can't deny how right it feels to be near him. How comfortable it is being with him. I've never jumped into bed with someone this fast, ever. I haven't even slept with that many guys. Why would I let him in, physically and metaphorically? It doesn't make any sense, yet I cannot deny the truth of it.

He just feels right. Like we've always known each other, like we're meant to be together.

He laces his fingers through mine and kisses my fingers. "Tell me you feel the same way. I know you do. You just have to admit it to yourself."

I don't say anything as I try to digest his words. I look deep into his eyes, and all I can see is love, like he has stardust running through his veins. And I believe him for some strange reason.

"I don't know," I finally utter. "It seems crazy. How could we feel like this after only a few days? I don't know how to answer you. It's Monday morning, I have to go to work, and you said you have TV talk show appearances all week. Our lives are totally different. I don't think our life together could work. The odds against us being together seem monumental."

I can't believe we're talking about a life together, like forever. What's wrong with me, with us? To think we could ever have a life together.

He keeps at me. "Look, I know it seems outrageous, but I know how I feel, and I've never felt like this about anyone before. I knew it the minute I opened my eyes on the beach and saw the most beautiful woman I'd ever seen."

His look is so sincere, and it unnerves me. This can't be happening. I must be dreaming. Maybe I am dead. I'm lost in some surreal death dream. Wishful thinking, the love I wish I had but would never find because it doesn't exist. I don't exist.

"But, Drew, it seems…" His fingers press my lips closed.

"What have we got to lose? Why can't we try, and see what happens? Take it one day at a time. Let's not think past that for now."

The idea of him moving in with me terrifies me. I just cleared out Greg's stuff. Moving out one guy's belongings and immediately replacing them with another's? It seems wrong. But I remind myself Greg has been gone six months. Not gone, dead. Just because I refused to accept he's dead and let his stuff languish, shouldn't confuse me with the fact that he's been gone a long time.

"I don't know, Drew. This has been fun. It's been great and I can never forget how you being here the other night is something I...I...will never forget. I can never repay you for what you did for me. But I'm not interested in getting into another relationship. Not now, maybe not ever. When the time comes for you to leave me, I'll fall apart again. I can't risk it. I don't think I could recover again. I'm done with letting myself love someone. I have my work. That's all I want. That's what will be important to me, what will keep me alive."

I bury my face under my arm. I can't look at him. The morning has brought clarity. My resolve must be strong. I can't let myself love anyone, ever again. It's too hard. It's too painful. I'm done with it.

His warm hand grabs my wrist and pulls it off my face. I keep my eyes closed tightly. I know if I gaze into his beautiful blue eyes, I will melt.

"Rea, look at me." His voice almost sounds angry.

I ignore him, turning my head away. I won't do it. I won't look at him.

He grabs my chin between his fingers forcing my face forward again.

"I mean it, Rea, look at me."

I open my eyes.

"I'm not your mother. I'm not your father. I'm not Greg. I will never leave you. I promise. I'm not going anywhere. You can count on me. I mean it. Just because they have all left you doesn't mean I am going to leave you. You have to trust me."

Tears well again. I promised myself I was done crying. I pinch my eyes, staunching the flow of tears.

"You can't guarantee you won't leave. What if you get hit by a car? Or you're in a plane crash? Or someone mugs you or…oh, God, I can think of a thousand things. Like you'll meet some Hollywood hottie on one of your movies, and you'll be sick of me. It happens all the time."

He actually smiles.

"This isn't funny," I say, faking a pout.

"Yes, it is. You sound like a teenager. We're not in high school. I'm an adult, and I know what I want, and I don't make stupid decisions often. Well, maybe the other night a little, but that was out of character for me. Look, Rea, there are no guarantees in life. What are you going to do, drop out because you've had crappy luck? Give up on being happy because your parents screwed up, and so did your boyfriend? You have a whole life ahead of you. Even if it isn't with me, you have to think about what you want in life. I am telling you right now, I have every intention of spending the rest of my life with you."

I'm speechless. I've got nothing here. It's as if he's gazing into my soul, wrapping me in the blanket of his own soul. Warmth banishes the cold dead feeling I have embraced for so long. Could he mean what he is saying? I can't think of a retort to his declaration of unconditional love. This is insane.

"Look," he says, "let's go back to what I said before. We'll take it one day at a time. Let me stay with you this week, and come to the premiere with me. You can make that much of a commitment, can't you?"

"I don't know, I guess so. But…"

His fingers are against my lips again. "I'll take that as a yes."

His mouth is on me. The kiss unleashes a dervish of butterflies in my stomach. I sink into him. But suddenly he is pulling me off the bed and toward the ensuite bathroom.

We shower together and make love again…I'd never had shower sex and no idea that sprayer attachment could be so…*hot.*

"What time do you have to be at work?" he says as we towel off.

"I have a light schedule today, so I can make my own hours," I say, having had no intention of going to work at all.

"And what time do you get off?

"I'm not sure. I'll let you know."

"I'll take care of dinner. I'll be here when you get home. Now, scoot. Go get ready."

He walks out of my bathroom, leaving me standing in a naked stupor.

Chapter Fifteen

I tread toward my closet and exit with a pink tee-shirt dress and my well-worn, white slip-on sneakers. I dress, combing my wet hair into a slick-backed pony. I dot my cheeks with blush and slide on some lip gloss.

We deposited Drew's purchases into the bedroom at the end of the hall yesterday…too creepy settling him in Greg's old room. I assume he has gone there to don his new duds.

He stands in my doorway wearing navy-blue shorts and a white, short-sleeved button-down. His hair is wet and finger-combed into submission. "Got scissors?" he asks, holding a dangling price tag in his fingers. My bedside landline rings. "Hope that's Lisa," he says. It is, and I hand him the phone. "Yeah, I'm good. I had a fender bender and got rescued by a good Samaritan. I've been…ah…recuperating at a friend's house. I'll give you the address." He covers the receiver with his hand, and I recite my address. He repeats it and ends with, "Thanks, Lisa, see you around ten."

****

I arrive at work fresh-faced, rosy-cheeked, and humming, garnering stares from the nurses. Entering the locker room, I run right into Jillian changing clothes.

"Thank God," she says, rushing me and hugging me so tightly I can't breathe. "I was so worried about you. I called a bunch of times but kept getting voicemail.

Didn't you get my messages?"

"I'm fine," I whisper near her ear. "You didn't have to worry. And I was busy all day and didn't check my voicemail."

She holds me at arm's length, dressed in her bra and scrub bottoms, her brown eyes scanning my face. "You got rid of everything?" My left hand is in hers, her eyes laser focused on my ring finger. "Even the ring? What did you do with it?"

"Some fish probably swallowed it."

"What?"

"Or maybe some guy with a metal detector will find it on the beach and hit a big pay day."

"You threw it in the ocean?"

I don't respond, extricating my hand from hers. I throw my backpack into my locker and secure fresh scrubs from the cabinet.

Her gaze stays fixed on me, and she frowns. "What's with you? You look different."

"Nothing. It's just me." I drag my dress over my head and hang it on the hook inside my locker. "Nothing's changed," I say, donning my scrubs.

"I'm not buying it. Your gray pallor is gone. You look...I don't know...alive again."

I laugh. Yeah, I was almost dead, but I won't give her the satisfaction of acknowledging her accurate assessment. "You've lost your mind. I'm fine." I drape my stethoscope around my neck, shoving the chest piece into the breast pocket of my white coat, slam my locker shut, and twirl the lock. She does the same.

"By the way, did you see that kid on Sunday? I told the cops to ask for you."

"The starving kid who'd had the crap beaten out of

him?"

"Yeah, Billy."

"You called the cops?"

"Yeah."

"Good call. We got him placed with social services. I feel bad for the kid."

"Tell me."

I dig into pre-rounds, conferring with the overnight staff on patient status, to prepare for nine a.m. rounds with my attending for the day.

I return my last chart to the desk and turn to face the eminent and arrogant Dr. Luke Frick. We call him Dr. Prick behind his back. "Tasson, you're with me. We have a blunt trauma arriving. I paged Cardio. Get a chest tray on standby and let the OR know we may need to jump the line." Trauma always overrides rounds.

"Yes, sir." I do as told, then rush to the ER entrance doors to stand beside Dr. Frick.

"Incoming," the charge nurse shouts. Two EMTs are pushing a gurney through the entranceway.

"Talk to me," Dr. Frick says, removing his stethoscope from around his neck.

"Brian Pitt, twenty-four, MVC, blunt trauma to the chest and abdomen, multiple rib fractures, patient's splinting, oxygen saturation in the low 90s."

"Bay three," the charge nurse orders.

I join the parade of medical personnel marching into the curtained cubicle, standing at the patient's bedside opposite Dr. Frick. He listens to his chest while I hook him up to the Holter monitor.

Dr. Frick says, "It's a bad lung contusion. Not sure how long he'll remain stable. He's likely hemorrhaging. Let's get a chest tube in and rush him up to CT. Then into the OR, depending on his chest tube output and what the scans show."

"O2 is seventy," I say.

"Where's that intubation tray?" Dr. Frick barks.

I tug the wheeled metal table toward me.

"Have you done one of these before, Dr. Tasson?"

"Yes, sir."

"Good, let's go." I swab the skin with iodine and grab the scalpel, making a one-inch incision into the pleural space between two ribs, then attach the tube to the canister. Blood enters the clear plastic tube.

"Good," Dr. Frick says, "let's get him up to CT."

We wheel him into the elevator and cut the CT line, the technician having already been alerted. A few seconds later the images post. "I'm seeing multiple displaced rib fractures and a massive pneumothorax on the right side," Dr. Frick announces. "We're going straight to the OR. Is Dr. Mullaney there?"

"He's waiting for you," I say.

"You want in on this?" Dr. Frick says.

"Yes, sir."

"Good, let's go."

I stand alongside Dr. Frick as we scrub each finger, between the fingers, and the back and front of our hands for the requisite two minutes. Then we attack our arms, always keeping the hand higher than the arm. Meanwhile, a nurse is tying a mask around my mouth and nose, and another slips me into a gown and ties it behind my back.

We enter the frigid operating room where Dr. Mullaney, the cardio-thoracic attending, is assessing the patient's injuries. I stand opposite him, alongside Dr. Frick. "Dr. Tasson, welcome to my OR," he says.

"Thank you, sir. It's a privilege."

"Lungs are shredded," he says. "We need to figure out where this blood is coming from."

"You going to do a lobe resection?" Dr Frick asks.

"He's bleeding out. We'll use a hilar clamp to temporarily stop the bleeding and do a wedge resection. Retraction, suction," he orders.

A nurse hands me the retractors. My mind goes to a terrible place. *Henry.* Several months ago, fellow first-year resident, Henry Sattler, was assisting during a hysterectomy with Dr. Gleason. He'd been awake for thirty-seven hours and fell asleep on his feet with the woman's ureter clamped in a retractor. He hit the floor taking it with him. Of course, the attending is responsible for all the residents under his care, and Dr. Gleason ran Henry ragged, but Dr. Gleason found a way to get Henry thrown out of the program through nefarious means. But Henry didn't simply exit the program, he took the express elevator off the roof and killed himself.

"Dr. Tasson," Dr. Frick says, "you in the game?"

"Yes, sir," I say, securing the necessary tissue.

The anesthesiologist announces, "Vitals dropping. BP is in the eighties."

"Keep suctioning," Dr. Mullaney tells Dr. Frick.

"Systolic is in the seventies. Got to move faster," the anesthesiologist says.

"Saying it won't make it happen," Dr. Mullaney says.

"Pressure is dropping," the OR nurse says.

"Load him with fluids," Dr Mullaney orders.

"Systolic in the 60s. He's about to code," the anesthesiologist says.

Dr. Mullaney removes the clamp, and we hold our collective breaths. All eyes on the patient's lung.

Chapter Sixteen

"Pressure is coming back up," the nurse says.

"Okay, Dr. Tasson, what's the next step after the clamp is removed?" Dr. Mullaney asks.

"Ventilate the lung and wait to see if it reinflates."

"And if it doesn't?"

"Means there's still a leak, which we'll have to repair."

"Good." We watch as the lung inflates and deflates, appearing normal. Sighs of relief abound.

"Looking good," Dr. Frick says. "We'll monitor the chest tube for air in post-op."

We tell the family we stopped the bleeding, and there was minimal tissue removal. He should recover.

I re-enter the ER and find Jillian.

"How'd it go?" she asks as she reads through a patient's chart.

"Awesome. I was lucky to catch a case like that."

"Yeah, I think Dr. Frick has his eyes on you."

"For what?"

"Not sure, but he's definitely giving you more attention lately."

"Incoming." Two EMTs are pushing a gurney, shouting vitals to the charge nurse.

"Bay two," she orders.

The morning had already been intense and there are ten more hours on my shift. Off we go…

I follow the gurney into the bay. The male EMT announces, "Ashley Jordan, twenty-two-year-old female. Opioid overdose. We gave her Narcan fifteen minutes ago." The EMTs and nurses lift her from the gurney and deposit her on the bed.

I approach, stethoscope in hand. But I'm momentarily frozen. Her face is gray, her lips and fingernails blue. She's staring over my shoulder, her green eyes two discs floating in tiny red puddles, her pupils the size of periods on a page. I come out of my stupor and listen to her heart. "I'm Dr. Tasson." I check her pulse. It barely registers, her skin cold and clammy.

"Boyfriend found her and called 911. She's pregnant." The EMT hands me the empty prescription bottle.

The profundity of the moment hits me hard. This could have been me. Although no one would have found me in time to reverse the overdose. My eyes well, and I swallow hard.

"Blood pressure eighty-five over fifty," the nurse says.

"Ashley," I say, "Are you a user, or is this a one-time deal?"

Her gaze drifts in my direction. "I can't have this baby."

"I understand, but there are other ways to deal with this."

"I know. I panicked. I spent my entire life in the foster care system, and I just couldn't deal."

"Well, we've got you, and we're going to help." I squeeze her hand, and she squeezes back, her fingernails digging into my palm. I smile. "Don't worry. We'll sort this out, and you're going to be okay."

"Get Dr. Kelly down here for a psych consult," I instruct the nurse.

"Yes, Doctor, right away."

****

"That damn full moon," Dr. Kelly utters, his pen scratching his signature on the chart.

"Agreed," I say. There's always increased activity in the ER during the full moon. Not a real believer in astrology, however, I can't deny the statistics.

There are two more suicide attempts today. One successful. All patients in their twenties. I can't shake the coincidence of it all, my emotional equilibrium teetering on a razor's edge.

I escape into a storage closet, and my knees give out. I huddle in the corner and wrap my arms around my knees, my forehead pressed into the metal shelving. I came close…so close…too damn close.

****

It's a little after eight when I enter my garage, noting the blue sportscar in my circular driveway. I enter the kitchen and a savory waft overwhelms my senses. Drew is standing at the stove stirring something. He turns. I laugh, seeing him in my pink apron. "Well, aren't you a sight?" I sidle up to him and wrap my arms around his waist.

He leans over his shoulder and pecks my lips. "Not much of an apron guy, but I have a limited wardrobe and didn't want to risk getting tomato sauce on my shirt."

"So you're back."

"I said I'd make you dinner, and I'm a man of my word."

"What did your *people* say? Were they worried about you?"

"A bit. They called everyone they could think of, but I'd slipped out rather effectively, and no one even knew where to look. I have a new rental. I told them what happened, then I called Bobby and let him know they'll pick it up."

I peer into the pot and inhale. "What are you making?"

"Lasagna stew. It's my mother's recipe. She's a professional chef."

"Smells great."

He turns in my arms and his hands land on my hips. "How was your day?"

"Challenging," I say. "I got in on a thoracotomy. MVC. Pretty exciting."

"What's an MVC?"

"Motor vehicle crash."

"Is that EMT talk?

"Yup."

"And what's a thoracotomy? Cracking open someone's chest?"

"Pretty much. But he's doing well. Will make a complete recovery. But the ER was a madhouse. I'm blaming the full moon. It happens fairly regularly."

"Is that a scientific observation, or are we talking witch doctor again?"

I smack his chest. "You're an idiot."

"I know, but I'm your idiot."

His words hit me hard. Does he belong to me now? Do I belong to him? There's an old Native American adage that if you save someone's life, they belong to you. Does he think I saved his life? Does he know he actually saved *my life?* Hmm. Does anyone ever really belong to another person? Okay, overthinking here. Stop it. One day at a time, like Drew said.

"I'm going to take a quick shower before dinner," I say, and sashay myself out of the kitchen.

When I return, Drew is pouring cabernet into two stemless wine glasses. The shower didn't wash away the angst from the day's events. I saved three lives today, but the one lost weighs heavily on my heart. And then it hits me. I'm going to change my specialty from trauma surgery to psychiatry.

Chapter Seventeen

Tuesday, I arrive home after midnight. Drew is asleep in my bed. He wakes as I shrug out of my fourth set of scrubs and throw them in the hamper. I crawl into bed and snuggle up to his back, my arm slung across his hip.

"Hey, luv," he says, "long day."

"The longest. The ER was a zoo."

"So sorry, luv. I tried to wait up."

"Yeah, don't ever do that. There's no way I'll ever know what time I'm coming home."

"Got it."

He faces me on his side and grabs my hand, pressing it against his chest, his fingers laced through mine.

"Remember, we have the premiere tomorrow."

"Yup. I got someone to cover the end of my shift so I should be home by five."

"And I'm doing *The Tonight Show* Thursday night. But it's taped at five, so I should still be home for dinner."

"Gotcha. I won't be home till at least seven. I'll get takeout."

"And I leave for New York Sunday afternoon to do the morning shows, *Letterman*, and *SNL*. I'll be back the following Sunday."

Here we go, just like Greg and me, schedules that keep you from spending any time together. Doomed again before we ever start. And I'm sad.

"It won't always be like this," Drew says as if reading my mind. "It's because I have a movie coming out."

I want to believe him, but…

****

Premiere day arrives, and I'm nervous as I slip into the silver patent-leather peep toes. I never dress up, ever. Drew is fumbling with his tie as I put the finishing touches on my makeup. My heart is pounding. I'd give anything to be in the ER saving somebody's life—even digging a tick out of some old guy's ass like I did today—than doing this. In about one minute, *I'll* need CPR.

"The car should be here in ten minutes. Will you be ready?" Drew says, viewing his reflection in the mirror. His cinnamon-colored hair is gelled to perfection, as he gives it a final tousle. He is so incredibly handsome.

"I'm ready. I just have to put a few things into my purse."

Drew turns toward me and breaks into a wide grin. "You look great. You should dress up more often."

"You're just being nice because you know I'm like one second away from totally freaking out."

"Yeah, that's it. You really look like crap. I'm just making stuff up, so I can drag you to the premiere where everyone will say terrible things about you." He comes over and stands in front of me.

"Sorry," I say, chagrined. "I'm not good at taking compliments. Thanks."

"Really, luv, you look ravishing. Maybe we should skip the premiere and stay home."

"Don't fool around. One word and I'm outta this

dress."

"Don't tempt me. We better go." He gives me a tiny peck on the cheek.

The limousine arrives right on time to whisk us off to Hollywood Central. I lean against Drew's shoulder in the back of the shiny black town car.

The car gets in the queue for arrivals. The red carpet, ugh. I hope I don't have to talk to anyone. Maybe I can go in and get my seat early and wait while Drew does his interviews. Yeah, that's it. Be inconspicuous. That'll work.

As we pull up to the curb, he says, "So, look, this is going to be the moment when we let the cat out of the bag. You realize bringing you to the premiere is going to alert the paparazzi we're together. We talked about this, right? You're prepared for the onslaught? If we handle it properly, I'm hoping it will die down in a few weeks. Once they find out who you are, they'll be relentless until they find everything out. Hopefully, it won't take forever, and then we'll be done with it, providing we don't do anything stupid."

"I know, we talked about it already. I hope I can handle it. I mean, you don't think they'll find their way into the hospital? That would be wrong, right?"

"I'm not sure what to expect. We'll have to wait and see how it plays out."

We're greeted by the mob of frenzied fans. Photographers are everywhere. Lights flash, and girls scream. Someone opens the door, and Drew steps out to wave to his adoring fans. The lights are momentarily blinding. He turns to offer me his hand, helping me exit the shiny black limo. This feels so wrong. A world I never imagined entering. Why did I agree to come with him? I should let him handle his career, and I should handle mine. We should stay out of each other's work life. Yeah, too late now, I remind myself. Way too late.

Gosh, how can anybody see anything with all the flashing lights in your face? It's a wonder people don't fall flat on their faces, especially in these effing shoes. Girls are yelling Drew's name, screaming so loud it hurts your ears.

We walk up to the front of the theater, hand in hand. If he lets go of me, I might run. And he knows it too, his vice-like grip pinning me to his thigh. He drags me through his interviews as reporters ask him who I am. Some even try to engage me in conversation. I give the same response to each one, the answer I rehearsed in the shower.

"This is Drew's night. He's doing all the talking." I smile my best movie-star smile as we plod our way down the line of entertainment reporters. I don't think I've had my picture taken this many times in my entire life.

Then I see him. Oh, my God. I can't believe it never occurred to me. I had a whole week to think about this, but with work and spending time with Drew, somehow it never crossed my mind. What an idiot. He's going to be furious. I grip Drew's hand so hard he looks right at me. We've moved away from the last interview booth.

He frowns. "What's the matter?"

"I…I totally forgot…" I stutter, nodding my head toward his angry face. "I never even thought about him being here." He's walking right for us. I hold my breath.

"Andrea," he says. "What in hell are you doing here? And with this guy?"

"Hi, Dad."

"Hello, Mr. Tasson. It's nice to finally meet you. I'm

a huge fan of your work." Drew offers his hand in a friendly gesture. My father ignores him.

"I said, what are you doing here?"

"Dad, you're being rude. Please don't embarrass me in front of my friend."

The two men make eye contact while I squirm. But now I'm angry. How dare he act this way in front of Drew, in front of me? He has a lot of nerve telling me what to do, and I'm not about to put up with it again. Not this time and not anymore. I'm not a child.

My father thrusts his hand forward and they shake, but he doesn't say a word to him.

"That's better. Now, Dad, this is my friend Andrew Foster, and he invited me to his premiere, and I accepted. So here I am, and you're just going to have to get over it. I mean, you don't want to make a scene now, do you?"

My dad isn't often silent, but he is now. I can see the anger simmering behind his dark eyes, but my anger is also floating behind mine, and he better damn well see it. I haven't exposed him to my wrath in a long time, but I am prepared to level him if I must.

"How did you meet him?"

Well, that's the question of the century, and I have no intention of giving him the slightest detail. Drew has my hand in a death grip. "Let's just call it serendipity."

"Fine," he says, "We'll talk about this later," and he walks away.

Both of us stand there awash in his rudeness. "I'm sorry. I should have prepared us both better for this."

"It's okay. Forget it. Once he gets to know me, he's going to love me."

I laugh out loud. "You're ridiculous. I don't think I've ever met anyone so eternally optimistic. It's quite unbearable to us pessimists." I have the unique ability to catastrophize any and all things.

"Come on, let's get our seats. I should warn you I hate seeing myself on screen, so expect me to be skulking in my seat with my eyes closed most of the time."

Before we can make it to our seats, Drew says, "Hey, there's my agent."

A tall, Hollywood-thin woman, her blonde hair coiffed in a tight bun, approaches. She's wearing a tiny black dress, a little too short for someone her age. But then…Oh, God. Of all the luck. Things are spiraling downward fast. How could I have forgotten all this stuff?

"Drew, you look wonderful." She grabs his bicep. "Where did you disappear to? I was starting to worry. I was so relieved when Lisa said she finally found you. And you moved out of your hotel? Where are you staying? What about security? I need to know where you are going to be…"

Then she sees me. Our eyes lock.

"Who's this?" she asks. But I know damn well she knows who it is.

Before Drew can introduce us, I jump in. "Hi, Ava."

Chapter Eighteen

Ava looks at me for a studied minute before she says anything. Come on, Ava, you know who I am, spit it out. Don't play stupid because you know I'll call you out.

"Oh my God, Andrea? Is it really you?"

"It is."

"Well, look at you, all grown up." Her gaze reverts to Drew, then me, then back to Drew. I'm enjoying watching her squirm. I had no idea she was Drew's agent. We never discussed it, not that I know any agents. But I know this woman, even though I haven't seen her in probably twenty years.

Drew breaks the tension, his look incredulous. "You two know each other?"

"Oh, yes, Ava was my nanny when I was little. What was I, maybe three or four years old?"

"Ah…ah…yes, that sounds right."

"Unfortunately, Ava was much fonder of my father than me," I say to Drew. "Isn't that right, Ava?"

"Well, Andrea, I wouldn't say that. I…"

"I walked in on them one morning. She was in bed with my father."

Drew is slack-jawed, and I'm enjoying this way too much. I blame Ava for getting me shipped off to boarding school in France. She had the hots for my father, and I heard they were together for a while after I got banished to another continent. But my father dumped her. I guess she recovered.

Nobody says anything, and so I decide to act like a grown up and take the high road.

"Well, Ava, it was a long time ago. Let bygones be bygones. Don't you think?"

"Ah…yes. It was a long time ago. I was young and stupid. I never meant to hurt you, Andrea. I was quite fond of you, but I got a little starstruck for a minute. I'm sorry if I caused you any hurt."

Ava was charged with getting me to France and depositing me at school. I was terrified, but my way of dealing in those days was shutting it all away. My fear, my feelings of abandonment, my belief that I was unworthy of love. I couldn't have put that mindset into words then, but I can now. And truthfully, she was wonderful. She bought me new clothes and gave me a pink teddy bear I still have stowed away in the back of a closet somewhere.

"All is forgiven. Let's start over." I extend my hand and she takes it. "Any friend of Drew's is a friend of mine."

"Does your father know you're here?" Ava scans the crowd, holding my hand a little longer than she should.

"He does," I say. "He isn't thrilled."

"I imagine not."

"Well," Drew says, obviously relieved the awkward moment has passed, "let's get our seats."

"I've instructed the usher to show you to your place," she says. And she turns on her three-inch black heels and marches in the opposite direction.

"Any more surprises up your sleeve this evening, little Miss Hollywood?" Drew says as we walk into the dimly lit theater.

"I don't think so. At least I hope not." I slip my arm through his. "This is entirely too much drama. I'll take a life and death situation at the hospital over this stuff any day."

We are escorted to our seats, and the director and producers ascend the stage. They give a small speech thanking their supporters and the studio and introducing the cast. Drew waves and takes a bow to thundering applause accompanied by hoots and hollers. They tell us to enjoy the show. The lights go out, and I can pretend it's the two of us snuggled together in a darkened movie theater. Except there's Drew, twenty feet tall, kissing some unbearably beautiful actress. I don't like it one bit, and I whisper my sentiments into his ear. But he just smiles at me, not taking the bait.

****

The paparazzi nickname us "Andy squared." Andrea and Andrew, Andy and Andy…totally ignoring our preferred nicknames—Drew and Rea. It's positively revolting, and if I thought the attention at the premier and on TV was awful, I was totally unprepared for what would happen when I returned to work the next morning.

I'm changing into scrubs in the locker room when Jillian crashes through the door. She barrels toward me. This can't be good.

"I am so mad at you I could scream."

Well, you are screaming, I think.

"I had to see it on *Access Hollywood* last night. Andy Squared? Seriously? You guys are a thing? I mean, I am your best friend. Or have you dumped me for some Hollywood A-lister?"

Jillian has lost it. I should have told her I was going to Drew's premiere. I should have told her he's still at my house. And I can't decide what's bothering her more, that I never got around to telling her or I'm suddenly leading what she thinks is the glamorous lifestyle of the rich and famous. Something I rejected a long time ago.

I let her rant until she vents all her frustration, standing with my arms crossed over my chest. Luckily, we're alone in the locker room and not near the nurse's station. Even though it won't take long to saturate the hospital gossip sponge, it would be worse if everyone witnessed my best friend's meltdown.

"Are you done?"

"Yes," she says.

"I'm sorry, Jillian. I didn't think it through. It happened so fast. I still can't believe I was there. You knew he was at my house Friday night; I told you that much, right?"

"Well, yeah, but I thought he made an appearance, and that was it. Was he there the second night? I mean, no wonder you didn't need anybody else, you had *him*. If that didn't serve as a distraction, I don't know what would."

"That's not fair, and it wasn't like that."

"Oh? Then what was it like? I mean you show up Monday looking all dewy and refreshed. Glowing. Perhaps the afterglow of…amazing sex?"

I huff. I can't do this now.

"Is he still there?"

"Look Jillian, I don't have time to give you all the gory details. I promise I'll tell you everything, just not right now."

"Fine," she says. "But I want deets. Every single one. *And,* I want to meet him."

Now I smile. "Okay, I promise, soon. Now we're

going to be late for rounds, and I don't want to get chewed out by Dr. Prick. Come on, let's go."

We march out of the locker room as others are entering to deposit stuff in their lockers before starting the workday. Their stares are unsettling. I close my eyes and remind myself it will get better. Drew warned me about this, and I am beginning to understand how awful it has been for him. It will pass. Just hang in there. I repeat this mantra as eyes peer at me all morning long. Apparently everyone watched *Access Hollywood* last night.

The ER is besieged by a rash of incoming. A sightseeing bus collided with a semi on Highway One. Pretty sure the semi wasn't supposed to be on Highway One. An onslaught of broken bones, torn flesh, and head trauma swamp us for the next five hours. Four fatalities. One a ten-year-old girl. X-rays, stitches, casting limbs, CT scans, emergency surgeries. Everyone is feverishly working to save lives, everyone on-call is here. It's terrifying and exhausting.

My shift is about to end when the EMTs crash through the entry doors.

"GSW, a police officer," the EMT barks. "Gunshot to the left shoulder, hypotensive, blood pressure eighty over fifty-four. He's lost a lot of blood. We put in two large-bore IVs."

The patient is a young Black man, a rookie.

"Trauma one," the nurse orders.

I follow the gurney into the bay, "On three," I say. Two nurses and I on one side, the EMTs on the other, we grab hold of his clothing. "One, two, three…," and we simultaneously lift him onto the bed.

"What we got?" Dr. Frick says, arriving at the

bedside.

I give him the vital statistics.

"Lynn, draw labs," he orders the nurse. "I want one 7.52, 23, and a T. Hang a unit of blood, O neg. Prepare to intubate." The remaining nurse and I cut off his bloody clothing as Dr. Frick continues his examination. "Positive breath sounds on both sides. Pulse is thready. I need to see what we're dealing with."

I spread jelly on his midsection and hand him the transducer. "What do you see, Dr. Tasson?"

I study the display. "Right upper quadrant clear." He moves the probe downward. "Pelvic area clear." The wand travels upward. "Right upper quadrant, cardio sac clear." He moves left. "Left upper quadrant, I see free fluid, most probably his spleen."

"Excellent, Dr. Tasson." He frowns. "Blood pressure is plummeting. No time. Let's get him to the OR. You with me, Dr. Tasson?"

"Yes, sir."

Chapter Nineteen

We enter the OR prep area and scrub and gown. "Busy day," Dr. Frick says, "how you holding up?"

"I'm good," I say. But I'm going to sleep like the dead tonight. That's if I can sufficiently destress. This day reinforces my decision to transfer to psychiatry. I've already changed my scrubs three times.

"Then let's save this police officer's life," Dr. Frick says. He winks. Cool as a cucumber. How does he do that? I guess years of experience and a stellar success rate.

I follow him into the operating room and stand opposite him, a nurse beside both of us.

The officer's torso is draped, a rectangle cut out. I swab the area with betadine, and Dr. Frick makes the first incision. He announces, "We're here for an exploratory laparotomy and probable splenectomy. Stay on top of the blood. Estimated blood loss at least five hundred."

"BPM and pressure are falling," the anesthesiologist says.

Dr. Frick says, "Lungs are filling with fluid. We got a bleeder somewhere. Prepare a chest tube."

He makes another incision, and I insert the plastic tubing. Blood immediately fills the tube.

"Good," Dr. Frick says.

"Stats are improving," I say, reading the monitor. "BPM 34, BP 86/50, PLETH 89, RESP 16."

"Okay, on to the next problem." Dr. Frick makes a third incision and I hold the retractors.

Settled in the ICU, I stand by Officer Selleck's bedside. He's probably about my age, and I lament his near loss of life. Intubated and in a coma, his outcome is uncertain. "Come on, Aaron, fight," I say, holding his hand and hoping his subconscious hears me.

Dr. Frick is beside me. "The waiting room is overrun with police personnel. You up to giving them an update?"

"Sure." I let go of the patient's hand.

The room is a sea of blue uniforms and shiny silver badges. Those sitting, stand. A tall Black man comes forward. "I'm Captain Seaver, his CO."

"Captain Seaver," I say, "have you been in touch with his parents?"

"They're on a plane. Should be here in a few hours."

"Okay, well, he's out of surgery. We removed his spleen and the bullet. He's intubated and in a coma. He's not out of the woods yet. The next twenty-four hours are critical. We're hopeful. And we can use blood donations."

"Not a problem. I'll see to it. Can I see him?"

"Yes, follow me."

"I'm posting an officer at his bedside and two outside his room."

"Of course."

Captain Seaver turns and addresses his officers. "All leave is canceled, and overtime approved until we find these suspects. Anyone who can donate blood, please do so. Johnson, Elsis, Brighton, you're with me."

Three officers, one a woman, approach, and we walk the hallway together.

Captain Seaver takes the young rookie's hand and squeezes. "Come on, Officer Selleck, you need to fight," he says, echoing my words. "That's an order."

And the day's hits keep on coming—two women in labor, one delivering in the ER, a young man of seventeen experiencing an acute psychotic episode who'll be here for days waiting for a treatment facility, and another suffering from drug withdrawal, also awaiting placement. We can only hold these patients for seventy-two-hours, and if they are unwilling to agree to treatment, we set them loose, even though they are a danger to themselves and the public. We can get a court order, but it's extremely difficult to commit someone without their consent. And even if they agree to treatment, often their insurance doesn't cover sufficient time for a program to work. A sad and untenable situation.

Before rounds Friday morning, I summon the nerve to approach Dr. Kelly. I ask his secretary if I can see him, and she allows me entry. "Sorry to interrupt, but I need to speak with you."

He sits at his desk, his wire-rimmed glasses low on his nose. He drops his pen and leans back in his chair, hands clasped on his desk. "Of course, Dr. Tasson. Have a seat. How can I help?"

I sit in the armchair facing the desk and make my pitch. "I'd like to change my area of specialty."

He frowns, but his expression isn't threatening. He's never threatening, and one of the only attendings on staff who isn't. His white beard and bushy eyebrows remind me of Santa Claus, a skinny one.

"To…?"

"Psychiatry."

"This is a serious decision, Rea. You've nearly completed a year as a surgical resident. It could set you back an entire year."

"I know, but recent events have made me rethink my decision. I believe mental health is an undervalued specialty, and I would like to become an advocate for those who often cannot advocate for themselves."

"Would you care to elaborate on these recent events?"

"Not really, but I know as part of a psychiatry residency, I will be required to go through therapy myself. And I think that would be a good thing."

The corner of Dr. Santa's mouth turns up. "You can enter therapy without pursuing a psychiatric degree."

"I know, but I think my experiences could help me help others."

"I see. And you've extensively researched this decision?"

"I have. I need someone to sponsor me, and I admire you very much. It would be a privilege to have you as a mentor."

"I appreciate your kind words. I believe the trauma you've experienced in your life could make you an excellent candidate for our program. If you're sure, I will speak with the appropriate personnel to initiate the transfer."

"I'm sure."

"Fine. I'll let you know as soon as I hear something."

Dr. Frick orders me to round on his post-op patients. "Check if Mr. Salazar's biopsy results are in. Review tomorrow's patient's PTIs. Bed seven, Sarah Hawkins, when her blood sugar stabilizes, shut off her insulin drip.

The patient in bed three can go home, and have her check in at the clinic in two weeks."

"Yes, sir," I say as I finish scribbling notes on the pad always in my pocket. You never want to forget instructions from your attending. Never, ever.

I recognize a repeat patient standing at the nurse's station. "Mrs. Spencer. How can I help?"

"I woke up feeling a bit dizzy, dear, it's probably nothing, but at my age, better safe than sorry."

Mrs. Spencer is eighty-two years old, a widow with an active sex life. Last time we treated her for gonorrhea. Seems to be a problem in the senior living apartments nearby. We treated four other members in the same community. Sheesh. They get laid more than most of my colleagues. And she's a relative of Dr. Branson, chief of Cardiology, who was a tad embarrassed at her last visit, but also impressed, like the rest of us. "Come on," I say. "Let's get you checked out."

"Don't I need to check in?"

"Nope, you're a VIP. Come on, let me take a look." I settle her on a bed and wrap the blood pressure cuff around her frail arm. Chief Resident Cecily Lily makes an entrance. I won't be missing her either. Some wonder if she's bipolar because her mood swings are legendary, angry one minute and sweet the next. It's not a verified diagnosis, however. But she is way too impressed with herself and thinks she has Dr. Frick in her back pocket. Not so evident to the rest of us.

"Mrs. Spencer, it's good and not good, to see you again," Dr. Lily says. "Why are you here?" Per usual, Dr. Lily is on autopilot. She's like a machine and not known for her bedside manner. As a cardio resident, her motivation is to impress Dr. Branson. Her stethoscope presses against Mrs. Spencer's chest.

"Feeling a little woozy, and I didn't want to take any chances," Mrs. Spencer says.

Dr. Lily glances at the monitor. "She's a bit tacky and her BP is slightly low. Open your mouth for me." She shines her pen light in. "You're a bit dehydrated. As long as you're here let's run a few tests. Make sure nothing else is going on."

To me she says. "Let's run a CBC, CMP, urinalysis, and give a bolus of IV fluids."

"Yes, doctor," I say. I could have done this all myself, but Cecily can't keep from butting in on even the smallest cases. It's like she owns the ER.

Chapter Twenty

I hang the IV bag for Mrs. Spencer as she slogs me down memory lane. She was a professional dancer and madly in love with one of the men in her troupe. "My lost love," she says. "I kept waiting for him to sweep me off my feet. Too many romance novels. I never told him how I felt. You know," she says, her voice dropping to a whisper, "marrying a Black man in those days was frowned upon."

I smile. "I imagine so."

"But I did marry Mason, a lovely man, a solid man, a safe man, but not exactly the man of my dreams. You know I still dream about Maxim?"

"Well, marrying the man of your dreams doesn't happen for most of us." I think of Drew. In my wildest imagination, I would never have imagined a man like him would literally crash into my life.

I make sure Mrs. Spencer is comfortable before I attend to my assigned tasks. I remove the insulin pump from Sarah Hawkins and check on Mr. Salazar's biopsy results, which diagnose pancreatic cancer.

Later that afternoon, I check on Mrs. Spencer, but her bed is empty. I walk the halls asking if anyone has seen her but no luck. Crap. Dr. Lily will have my head. Thirty minutes later, I find her in the North Wing chatting up an orderly, towing her IV stand behind her.

"Mrs. Spencer, why are you out of bed?"

"Oh, hello, Janie. I got up for a few minutes and got turned around. And now there is someone in my bed."

"Mrs. Spencer, I'm Dr. Tasson. Who is Janie?"

"Aren't you my granddaughter?"

"You're confused, Mrs. Spencer. And this isn't your room. It's the right number but you're in the North Wing, your room is in the South Wing." I take her arm and steer her down the hallway.

"Oh dear, I'm a little confused."

My guess is the UTI test will be positive because she's suffering a bout of dementia.

I settle her back in bed and attach the monitor leads when Dr. Lily arrives. "What happened?"

"She wandered off and seems to be suffering from delirium. Probably a UTI."

"Let's put her on telemetry and get blood cultures and put her on a broad-spectrum antibiotic," Dr Lily orders. "And let's get her to the ICU." She looks at the monitor. "She's more hypertensive than tacky, and septic."

****

I have the weekend off, and so does Drew. We spend it like we're in some G-rated sitcom, except for the amazing sex—cooking, sunning, swimming, reading, watching TV, or listening to tunes. It's pure delight.

It can't last.

Late Sunday afternoon, the car to the airport arrives, and Drew kisses me goodbye.

"Don't get in any trouble in the Big Apple," I warn.

"Never. I'm a good boy." He winks.

"The jury is still out," I say.

He gasps, feigning shock. "I only have eyes for you, luv."

He kisses me again, and off he goes.

Monday morning, I arrive on shift, and as soon as I near the nurse's station, I hear, "Dr. Tasson."

Dr. Frick. "We have a transfer from PIH Health. An ortho consult. The patient was cliff diving. PIH did what they could, but they aren't equipped for this level of injury."

"What did he break? Tibia, femur, humerus, pelvis?" I ask.

"Yes," Dr Frick says.

"Yes, which?"

"All of them."

Gulp. "Any major head injuries?"

"Seems his head was spared. Although I seriously question his sanity."

The EMTs burst through the entrance doors, shouting their obligatory assessment and handing me the chart. "Patient with all four limbs in traction."

"Don't worry," says the patient. "It's worse than it looks." He smiles.

Well, it looks pretty bad, I think. And how can he be in such a good mood? I read the anecdotal record as the patient is wheeled into trauma room four, and the parade of medical professionals follows.

"Dr. Tasson, give us a report."

"Matthew Smith, forty-four, patient versus boulder twenty-four hours ago, GCS fifteen, no evidence of TBI. Has left sided pneumothorax with a chest tube placed at the other hospital. Sustained multiple fractures to all four extremities, ribs, as well as stable spinal fractures."

Dr. Wellington, chief of orthopedics arrives next. "I got the call," he says.

"Matthew, this is Dr. Wellington, chief of

orthopedic surgery. Do you mind if he takes a look?" Dr. Frick says.

Dr. Wellington moves closer to the patient. "Have we ordered CT angio on all four extremities, checked the blood flow?"

"I was about to," Dr. Frick says. "Tasson will see to it."

"How does it look? Do you think I'll be back to base jumping in a few months?" Matthew says. We stare at him. "Kidding," he says. "I know I'm lucky to be alive. But I did promise my nephew I'd teach him how to ride a bike this summer. I'd like to make good on that."

Dr. Frick ignores his comments. "We need to look at your scans and x-rays, but I'm not going to lie. The damage is extensive. If anyone can help, it's Dr. Wellington. He's the best. We'll do everything we can."

"Dr. Tasson, page me when those scans are up," Dr. Wellington says.

We have him in CT, and the images post. "How many bones did he break?" I ask.

"I've counted seventy-five so far," Dr. Frick says. "He's got commutated fractures in all the long bones."

"Jesus," I say. "I've never seen anything like this."

"That makes two of us, probably all of us," Dr. Frick says. "Plus, the ribs and spine have process fractures."

"Yeah, we don't have to worry about those, they'll heal themselves. It's incredible his spine is still intact." I turn to see Dr. Wellington surveying the CT images. "Nothing is where it's supposed to be. It's like a jigsaw puzzle. We can put him back together, one surgery at a time. The question is, do we do them all at once, or spread them over a few days. We need to reconstruct the right femur using cadaver bones to fill in this defect here." He points to the scan on the left. "Then we'll wash out and fix the left extremity since it's already open."

Dr. Frick says, "If we fix everything at once, he'll be under anesthesia for an extremely long time, up to twenty hours. That's a long time to be under. It could result in clots, bleeding. If the tissue loss is too severe, we might have to amputate. We have to weigh it against the risk of waiting because sepsis could set in."

"Let's get him back to his room, then we'll update the patient and talk this out with him," Dr. Wellington says.

I return the patient to his room and wait for the attendings.

"What's the prognosis?" Mr. Smith says. Before I can answer, Drs. Frick and Wellington arrive and explain the pros and cons for his surgeries.

"All or nothing," the patient says. "Let's do this."

"Is there anyone you want to discuss this with? A family member?" Dr. Wellington says.

"Nope, it's just me, and I've decided."

"All right, we'll be back when everything is in place," Dr. Wellington says.

I follow the two surgeons from the room. Dr. Wellington sighs. Pinching the bridge of his nose, he speaks with his eyes closed. "So we'll repair the four extremities all at once. Probably about nineteen hours in the OR, and a shitload of complications along the way. It's going to take two teams, one to help me repair one extremity and then prep the next. We'll need like six surgeons."

"I'll take care of it," Dr. Frick says. "Tasson, you want in?"

"Yes, sir." I scrubbed in last month on an

amputation, and I'm hoping we don't have to do that again.

"We should be ready to go in two hours," Dr. Frick says. "I'll keep everyone updated in the event of complications."

I've only been on shift for an hour, but somehow it feels like I've been here a whole day already.

Dr. Lily approaches. "Mrs. Spencer's results are in. She's positive for a UTI. Let's continue her antibiotics and more IV fluids."

"Yes, ma'am," I say.

"You in on the big ortho case?" she asks.

"Yes, ma'am."

"Me too. Crazy case."

"Me too," Jillian adds as she stands beside me.

"Nothing like it, for any of us," Dr. Lily says.

We enter the OR. I've never seen this many personnel working on a case.

Chapter Twenty-One

"CT angio shows diminished blood flow all over the place," Dr. Wellington says. "I'm still trying to wrap my head around it. He's up to ninety-two broken bones."

Jillian and I stare at each other, matching raised eyebrows. "That has to be some kind of record," she says.

"Are the cadaver grafts ready?" Dr. Wellington asks.

"Thawed and prepped, and Matthew is ready too," I say.

It's a full house. We should have sold tickets. Even the gallery is packed with observers. Dr. Wellington announces, "This is Matthew, and he's a veteran and a hero, and we thank him for his service, and we're keeping him alive today. Let's do this, all or nothing," he says, repeating the patient's earlier words.

He gives us a pep talk. "This is a long surgery. You will get tired, hungry, your feet will hurt, and when that happens, think about Matthew because there's no margin for error. We will get through this together."

****

Nineteen hours and seventeen minutes later, Jillian and I sit on the floor of the locker room, our backs against the metal cubicles. I rest the back of my head on the locker. "Motherfucker," I exclaim. "That was something else. What do you think the guy's chances of recovery are?"

"Never mind recovery. How about survival? That amount of stress and anesthesia takes its toll." Jillian sighs. "God, I haven't been home in two days. It's like I live here."

"That's why we're called residents because we live in the hospital," I remind her.

"I haven't seen Brian in three days. We're like ships passing in the night."

I think of my life with Greg. Same thing. And I'm not sure my life with Drew will be any better. He's gone this entire week, and I've been working ridiculous hours. But then I remind myself working in psychiatry will be an improvement. Maybe there is hope.

I arrive home at six a.m. and fall into bed, but only for about five hours. Dr. Frick said we could come in at noon.

Back on shift, I make my pre-rounds. Matthew Smith survived the night and, considering his condition, is alert and in ridiculously good spirits. And he's refusing pain meds. Most patients would be begging for them. How does he do it?

All four limbs are casted and cradled in slings. Tubes and leads are everywhere. The monitor beeps steadily, indicating all his stats are in the normal range. "How are you feeling today?"

"Good. And I've been meaning to ask you, are you single?"

A good question. Am I? Or do I have a transient visitor with benefits? "I'm not sure."

His eyebrows knit together. "I don't understand."

"It's new, and I have a track record of relationships crashing and burning."

"In case you hadn't noticed, I'm an expert at crashing…in the event you need saving. Besides, I need something to live for."

I smile. "I'm sure you have plenty to live for."

"In the meantime, I have a mother of an itch. Can you scratch it?"

"Where?"

"Right ankle, on the inside."

I grab a wooden tongue depressor from the jar on the counter and slide it under the edge of the cast. "Here?"

"A little to the left."

I comply and move it side to side, then up and down.

"Ah…" he says, dragging it out for a few seconds. "You're a lifesaver. Thanks."

"Happy to be of service."

Dr. Wellington enters, followed by Dr. Frick, Dr. Lily, and a few interns, and asks for a status report. I read from the chart. "Patient Matthew Smith, post op day one, upper and lower limb fractures repaired, right and left lower extremity gastroc flaps in place. All doppler signals are strong and no sign of infection."

"I hear I'm going to be famous," Matthew says. "Writing me up in a journal so I can help the next guy."

I shake my head. Drs. Wellington and Frick don't respond.

"We were able to save all four limbs," Dr Wellington says. "We're hoping you'll walk again and be able to use your fingers and hands, with extensive PT and time."

"Thanks," he says, "to all of you. I mean it."

"I'll come back to check on you later," Dr. Wellington says. "Dr. Tasson will be taking your data for the rest of the day, so if you have a question, you can ask her."

Dr. Frick pulls me aside after everyone else leaves.

"Excellent work yesterday, Tasson."

"Thank you, sir."

"You have so much talent. Are you sure about this switch?"

Apparently, the word is out. "I am, sir."

"My loss."

Next, I check on Mrs. Spencer. "How are you feeling today?"

"Better. Lost my marbles for a few hours. I still don't understand how this happened. I always pee after sex."

I smile and wonder if I'll still be having this much sex at eighty.

Dr. Lily arrives. "What's the patient's status?"

"We're monitoring her fluids and urine output. All good. Her delirium has resolved, and she's been off pressers for twenty-four hours."

"Good, let's move her out of ICU and into a room."

I seek out Jillian and find her at the bedside of an elderly patient, the victim of a stroke. "Her son found her in her apartment. Unfortunately, she'd been there too long, not enough time for us to intervene. Her symptoms won't improve significantly."

"That's a shame. There needs to be more awareness about how early intervention can make a huge improvement in the long-term prognosis for stroke. Like a PSA or something. If people don't know, they can't get help fast enough."

"Yeah, the 'golden hour' should be something everyone knows about."

We exit the patient's room, and I place my hand on

Jillian's arm. "I have some things to tell you."

Jillian looks at me, her eyebrows knit together. "When is that ever a good sentence? And things? Now, I'm really worried."

"It's not bad, actually. It's good stuff."

Jillian drags me into one of the on-call rooms. Luckily, no one is sleeping there, or *having sex*.

"Spill, sister." But she puts up one hand. "Wait, let me guess. Andrew Foster called you."

"Not exactly. He's at my house. In fact, he never left."

"What? What does that mean?"

"It means he was there the night I got rid of all of Greg's stuff. When I threw the ring into the ocean. Actually, he did it for me."

"That's how you got through that night. With an exceptionally handsome accomplice. No wonder you didn't need me." She sinks onto the bottom bunk.

I sit beside her. "I can't explain what happened. The night after he crashed his car on my beach, I came home and found him asleep on my couch. He made some lame excuse about not being able to get anyone to pick him up. He lost his wallet and cell phone in the accident and didn't know anyone's number by heart. He told me all his friends and family live on another continent, and those were the only numbers he knew. But then he said his gut told him I was in some kind of trouble, and he didn't feel good about leaving me. After we got rid of all of Greg's stuff and the ring, we opened a bottle of wine, and well, I don't know what came over me. A flood gate opened, and I told him everything. About my father, my mother, being sent to boarding school…and it was not only supposed to be my wedding day, but also my birthday."

"Jesus, you never tell anybody about that stuff."

"I know. I still don't understand it."

"So, what you're saying is, he's been with you all this time, and you didn't tell me?"

"Yeah, I'm sorry. I guess I can't believe it myself. I keep thinking it's some weird dream, and I'll wake up."

She shakes her head. "You're freaking me out. Does your father know?"

"Unfortunately, he does. He was at the premiere, and you can imagine his reaction."

"He was probably foaming at the mouth."

"Anyway, Drew says he's incredibly lonely. He has no real friends in the U.S. and spends all his time alone in hotel rooms. He can't even go out and get a cup of coffee without being mobbed by the paparazzi."

"I bet it's a nightmare. We all envy the lives of famous people, but it probably sucks."

"At first I thought he was hiding out, but I don't know… There's something about him I can't walk away from."

"So, he's your boyfriend?"

"I don't know. It seems wrong, after Greg and everything."

"How's the sex?"

"Jillian!"

Chapter Twenty-Two

She slumps back on the bed and sighs. "You know I was never crazy about you and Greg. So I say, give it a shot. What have you got to lose?" She sits up again. "Wait, you said there were two things?"

I stare at her for an extended minute. "I'm changing my area of specialty to psychiatry. I'm waiting to hear from Dr. Kelly."

"You're leaving trauma surgery?"

"I am."

"Why?"

"Lots of reasons. We can talk about it later. Why don't you come over for dinner one day next week? Drew is back from New York on Sunday. You can meet him. He's a great cook."

"Gorgeous, rich, *and* he can cook? Girl, you've hit the jackpot. I'm there."

"Your boyfriend can cook."

"Yeah, but he does it for a living." She hangs her head in her hands. "You've blown my mind, girlfriend."

Jillian hugs me, and we slip out of the on-call room and return to work.

Halfway through my shift, Dr. Kelly finds me in the cafeteria getting coffee. He stands beside me, paper cup in hand. "Can we sit for a minute?"

"Of course," I say. My stomach does a little flip. Is the verdict in?

I pay for my coffee and follow him to an empty table near the window.

"I've heard from the powers that be," he says.

"Oh?" I'm not sure how I will react if the answer is no and brace myself for bad news.

He smiles his Santa-smile. "Welcome to psychiatry, Dr. Tasson. A term coined in 1828, probably from the French word *psychiatrie*—where you will learn the science, practice, and treatment of mental, emotional, and behavioral disorders, especially as originating in endogenous causes, or resulting from faulty interpersonal relationships."

I already feel like an expert. Who's had more faulty interpersonal relationships than this girl?

Drew gone until Sunday, I'm back in my old world. Working non-stop, coming home and crashing, desperate for sleep. Drew has called every day, but with the time difference, it's hit or miss, and when we do connect, there isn't much time to talk because one of us is swamped with work.

Thursday morning, I round on Matthew Smith, checking his vitals, helping him scratch numerous itches, and rebuffing his flirtations.

"I'll wear you down," he says. "Just you wait and see."

"Enough, and this conversation is inappropriate." I smile. He's a seriously handsome dude and I'd be tempted if… "You need to rest."

"You can be terrible to me if you want. I'll lie here immobilized and starved for entertainment. I can't even give you the finger."

"You're incorrigible." I check his output in the drainage collection chamber. Oh no…

"I'm not feeling so hot…" Matthew says. He closes his eyes, his head drifting sideways.

The Holter monitor beeps. Lines turn red. "Matthew," I yell. "Matthew, can you hear me?" He flatlines. I lift his gown to check his chest tube and blood is flowing copiously. I press the intercom button. "Code blue! I need help in here." Jillian runs in along with the charge nurse. "Page Dr. Wellington and Cardio, page everybody."

The charge nurse says, "I got it. Dr. Wellington is right outside."

"What's happening?" Jillian says.

"He's leaking blood from his chest tube."

"Damn," Dr. Wellington says. "What the hell happened?"

"I was checking on him, and his chest tube started pouring blood. He's lost over two liters."

"His aorta must have transected. He's bleeding out into his chest," Dr. Wellington says, reading the monitor. "We need to get him up to the OR right now."

"I already alerted them, and Cardio," I say.

"Meet me up there," Dr. Wellington says. "And prep him as fast as you can."

We race the patient into the OR where Drs. Wellington, Frick, and Branson await.

As chief of Cardiology, Dr. Branson is running the show. "We'll do an emergent thoracotomy and cross clamp the aorta as quickly as we can to give anesthesia enough time to catch up," he says. "Then we'll do the repair. Tasson, you're on retraction. Ortiz, you're on suction."

"He's coding," the anesthesiologist says.

"Damn," Dr. Branson says, "he's bleeding out from

a transected aorta."

Oh, God, I think, that's almost always fatal.

"He's critical," the anesthesiologist says.

"I'm doing everything I can," Dr. Branson says. "Do not die on me, Matthew."

There's blood everywhere, dripping off the table, puddling on the floor, soaking my sneakers. Jillian and I make eye contact, signaling Matthew's imminent death.

"Time of death, 9:42 a.m.," Dr. Branson says.

The silence in the OR after a patient dies is the worst silence in the world. The finality of it, the valiant fight over. The loss, the sadness. It's always the same, and it's always heartbreaking.

I follow Jillian into the locker room, paper booties on my feet, my bloody socks and sneakers tossed in the medical waste container. We sit on the bench in silence, heads hung low.

"You were right about his prognosis for survival," I say.

"I wish I wasn't. Poor guy. So young, he had his whole life in front of him."

I change into fresh scrubs, don my spare sneakers, and wrap my stethoscope around my neck, slipping the chest piece into the pocket of my white coat.

Mrs. Spencer is ready to be discharged, and I help her dress while we wait for her granddaughter to pick her up. She regals me with more stories about her lost love and sexual escapades, and I revel in her zest and her positive outlook on life. I'll miss her.

I have Saturday off and spend half of it catching up on some well-needed sleep. I can't purge Matthew's death from my dreams and thoughts. Such a nice guy. What a waste.

I drag my weary body into the kitchen for something to eat. I actually have food in my house these days since Drew has become a regular at the market. I make a frittata for lunch accompanied by a surfeit of fresh fruit. Recently, thanks again to Drew, I've become a fan of the kiwi and also the avocado, although not usually at the same sitting.

I relax by the pool, ignoring my own medical advice about sun exposure, and generally goof off. It's delightful and would only be better if Drew was here. He'll be home tomorrow, but tonight he's doing *SNL*, and I'm stoked to watch it, a little nervous too. My phone rings.

"Hey, luv," he says. "Sorry I haven't had a chance to talk much. I'm overscheduled to the max. I keep asking Lisa for some down time, but she's a woman possessed. So much friggin' press."

"I can't even imagine."

"But this week at 30 Rock has been…not sure how to describe it…fun, but intense. I don't know how they pull *SNL* off. It's a monumental production."

"Well, my week has been insane too. I have so much to tell you. And I invited Jillian over to meet you next week."

"Super, can't wait to see you again. I miss you, luv."

"Miss you too. See you tomorrow."

"Are you going to watch tonight?"

"Definitely, I wouldn't miss it. Are you nervous?"

"There's no time to be nervous. And they're total pros. I'm in good hands."

"Okay, well break a leg…or whatever."

He laughs. "At least if I do break a leg, I know a doctor who will take good care of me."

Chapter Twenty-Three

Snuggled into bed Sunday night, I open a large tome. I've availed myself of my new textbooks and leaf through the pages. My eyes settle on a chapter heading in bold print: Abandonment. It notes three types: A parent who leaves for someone else, a parent with an unreliable and erratic presence, and a parent who dies. Ding. Ding. Ding. We have a three-way winner.

The guidance of a trained professional would help me navigate these dangerous waters, but as usual, I fearlessly jump in. You'd think I would be afraid of…well, *everything.* Then, on the other hand, no one held *mine, and* I fended for myself my entire life. Relying on strangers for my survival—a parade of babysitters, my nanny, and eventually the charitable Sisters of Mercy at Our Lady of Lourdes.

Of course, I'm particularly interested in how development is skewed by abandonment, in my case, left by my mother via suicide, and then by my father, who shipped me off to another continent. As a child of five, I felt like he didn't want me. But as I grew older, and as explained to me by the good sisters, much of it due to the erratic nature of his work—projects being rescheduled, relocated, extended, thus the dependability of him showing up at all, nearly nil. And when he did, it would only be for a few hours and it was strained. He'd often take me to some fancy restaurant where the waitstaff looked down their noses at a six-year-old, waiting for her to break their fancy crystal. No physical contact other than a peck on the cheek at hello and goodbye. He never asked about my life, but instead filled the air with stories of his travails and accomplishments. Things a child could not understand, nor cared to. He always praised my excellent grades and relayed the lauds of the good sisters. And there was always a check. Seriously, I was a child, I didn't even know what a check was. Sister Dolores would find it in my room and tell me she'd hold onto it for me, which I later learned meant she deposited it in my personal account. I could care less. Of course, I saved a tidy sum which enabled me to live a comfortable life. I was the only med student with a two-bedroom apartment in a nice neighborhood. Then came my beachside mansion and a spiffy car when I graduated medical school. I say I've forgiven him, but I still think he could have made more of an effort. I accept he was suffering too, but I was a kid, and he was the adult, and he should have done better.

The alarm pad beeps five times. Someone put in the entry code.

"Honey, I'm home," Drew yells from downstairs. I close the DSM-5—The Diagnostic and Statistical Manual of Mental Disorders, *the* reference book on mental health and brain-related conditions and disorders—and clutch it to my chest.

He flings open the bedroom door like a swashbuckler boarding a pirate ship. "I've always wanted to say that," he announces. He laughs. "Actually, I often did…to an empty hotel room. It was kind of sad."

He drops his suitcase at the foot of the bed and flops on the mattress like a one-year-old Labrador retriever.

His playfulness should be catching, but instead, what do I say? "Did you know homosexuality was classified as a mental disorder until 1973?"

His smile evaporates. "Seriously, I come home excited to see you, and that's your response?"

Sometimes I think I have no social skills at all.

He takes the book from my hands and studies the cover. "Some light reading?"

"Not really."

He tosses it on the floor.

I regroup. "How was your trip? I didn't catch the morning shows or late-night talk shows."

"Well, you were right, it was more terrifying than I thought. But everyone was great. Really supportive. Not like some sets, where people don't mind seeing you fall on your ass. I know one actress who had a toxic experience on set. She said it was so volatile, hostile, it made her physically ill. People were crying daily, so upset by this one person. Apparently, the guy would fire people on a whim, which kept everyone quiet. It was very effective. Then one day, she was like, 'It stops today.' She kept saying to him, it stops, it stops. And she said she'll never keep quiet again."

I immediately think of my father. Could it be him?

"That's terrible. Has it ever happened to you?"

"Not to that extent. It's hard when you're the new kid, and you don't have much clout and you need the job. And it happens more to women, which is a sad commentary in general."

"We have a similar problem. It's sort of like hazing. Several of our attendings think being tough on you is how they prepare you for a grueling profession, but often it's just abusive."

"That's a shame. It seems many people in power abuse their status, no matter where they are. Anyway, *SNL* was great. And they can execute a complete costume change in like thirty seconds. I think more people saw me in my underwear than in my entire life." He rolls onto his back and kicks off his topsiders, his hands cradling his neck on the pillow. He sighs loudly. "Glad to be home."

Home. He might be right. It never felt like this with Greg. Our shifts rarely synced, and the house was merely a place to crash, catch up on sleep. The last month or so we barely had sex. One of us was always too tired. But in a few short weeks, my house has become a home. A safe haven, a comfort zone. A place where two people can build memories, a future, where they can truly be themselves. Where the heart can live without shyness and tears can dry at their own pace. Where you find light when all grows dark.

Egad. Who am I? I've never been one to wax poetic. About anything.

"I'll unpack tomorrow," Drew mumbles through a mouthful of toothpaste. He shuts the bathroom light and slips into bed beside me, kissing my bare shoulder, then his lips capture mine. He forces me down onto the mattress and slides his hand under my blue silk camisole, his head propped up with his other hand. "I love you," he says.

Oh, God. The breath catches in my throat. I stare into his cerulean eyes. First *home* and now the *L-word*. "Thanks," I mumble.

"Don't look so terrified. I wanted to say it before I left, but I didn't think you were ready. And I'm not sure now."

"It's a big word. We hardly know each other."

"I know. But I've been in love before, or at least I thought so, but this is different. It's so much bigger. Thinking of you keeps me awake. Dreaming of you keeps me asleep. Being with you keeps me alive."

I have no words. Not a single monosyllabic utterance can find its way past my lips.

"I know you've gotten crap in the love department. Your mom, your dad, Greg. But you deserve love and affection. You can still share your heart with me even if it's been broken. Have enough courage to trust love one more time."

"Drew…"

"Wait," he says, "let me finish." He inhales deeply and lets it out slowly and deliberately. "I believe in love. I think it hits you and pulls the rug out from underneath you, and then it demands your attention every minute of the day. Love isn't something you find. Love finds you. And when you find the one who's right for you, it's like they were put there just for you. You never want to be apart. I knew it that night on the beach. When you were probably at the lowest point of your life. I always want to be there when you need me. I love you not only for who you are, but for who I am when I am with you."

"Drew," I say again, laying my hand atop his, still resting on my belly, "I'm not sure I know how to love someone. When I think about my relationships with my dad and Greg, I wonder if I was just going through the motions, and…"

"I understand. It's all about being vulnerable. To let someone in, to share your deepest fears and insecurities. To be fearless, an intrepid warrior in matters of the heart."

His words cover me like a warm, weighted blanket. I feel safe when he's beside me and even when he's not. Like I'm tethered to him, our hearts bound together even when he's thousands of miles away. But instead of sharing these feelings, I say, "Who's the psychiatrist here, you or me?"

He laughs. "Deflecting again. You need to quit that."

"I know. I'm not good at expressing my feelings. I'm not even good at feeling my feelings."

"How could you? I'm not sure I could have survived what you've been through."

I almost didn't, I think. "Well, your words mean a lot. They're beautiful."

"Good, because I practiced them on the plane for like an hour."

"Well, you did a superb job. Your director would be proud of you."

"And now, I'm going to make mad passionate love to you. I thought about this for like an hour on the plane also."

He rolls on top of me, his weight pressing me into the downy mattress. He secures both my wrists in his hand and pins them to the pillow above my head and plunders my mouth. He pulls back and nips my bottom lip. "Be prepared to be ravished."

I drink in his male perfection. My heart hammers, and I slip off the precipice into his waiting arms. But I still haven't said the word, the *L-word*. Soon, I promise myself. Soon.

Chapter Twenty-Four

I return home around seven on Monday, and Drew is at the stove again, sans apron, some scrumptious aroma in the air. "I had coffee with your father."

"What?"

"I said, I had coffee with your father."

"I know what you said. I meant, why?"

He turns, leaning his adorable jean-clad ass against the stove, his arms folded over his black T-shirt. "Well, then you should have said why."

"Don't be a smartass. You know what I mean."

"Well, I decided the best defense was a good offense. So, I tracked him down and told him I wanted to meet with him before things were said that shouldn't be. He agreed, and we met for coffee downtown today."

My eyes are bugging out of my head. My father is a scary guy on a good day, and that's if he likes you. His rumored distaste for young actors couldn't have made it easy for Drew to call him, not to mention, he's dating his daughter.

"How did it go?" I'm afraid to hear the details, but I know it's coming anyway.

Drew opens the refrigerator and takes out a bottle of chardonnay. He's quiet. I rummage around for the corkscrew. The waiting is torturous. He's doing this on purpose, making me sweat as I envision the ugly conversation between him and my narrow-minded father.

The wine flows into the glasses in what seems like slow motion. He hands me a glass of wine, then takes my hand and leads me out to the back deck and into our favorite chaise lounge built for two. We're usually naked when we're on it, and my mind drifts to how many times we've made love on this spot. I am momentarily distracted from what lies ahead. I don't say a word as I let him have this moment to torment me. I'm not sure I want to know how it went anyway.

He takes a sip of his wine, swallowing slowly. I'm going to throttle him any second if he doesn't spit it out. But I stay silent.

"I laid my cards on the table. I explained how much I enjoyed my craft, and I was a hard worker and didn't give too much attention to the whole fame and fortune part of the career because I was aware all of it could be gone tomorrow. I told him I don't do drugs, and I was mostly a social drinker and knew my limits. I confessed I was in love with you, I was a good, decent man and would always treat you with the respect and honesty you deserve. I said I hoped he would accept me for who I am and not based on some stereotype he'd likely witnessed in the past, and I wasn't looking for his permission or even his approval but hoped he would see I was the right man for you."

"Wow, good speech. Did you practice it?"

He laughs. "You bet your ass I did. I didn't rehearse this much for any of my movies."

This makes me laugh, and we both share a chuckle at the absurdity of it all.

"And...what did he say?"

"I should have been pissed, but I wasn't. He said

he'd done his homework, fully prepared to find out the worst, and was surprised by what people told him. He said he'd wait and see before he came to any conclusions. I told him that was all I asked, and we parted on decent terms. So I'm hopeful he'll come around."

Okay, so this didn't turn out half bad. I'm proud of Drew. I give him credit for having the balls to call my father in the first place and then to stand up to him once he got in front of him. Impressive.

****

"I'm excited to meet Jillian," Drew says as we sip coffee on the back deck the next morning. "Can I cook?"

"You better, I told her you were quite competent in the kitchen, and her boyfriend is a chef at Bon Appétit Paris, downtown."

"Okay, no pressure."

"He's not coming. He has to work, but still, she's used to great cuisine."

"Are there any rules? She's not a vegan…"

"No, and until she met Brian, she lived on popcorn, soda, and boxed mac n' cheese."

Drew smiles.

We spend most of the day lounging, enjoying the beach and the pool. Drew made a quick trip to the market; he's getting to be a regular local these days.

Jillian arrives promptly at five, two bottles of pinot grigio in hand. "They're chilled," she says. She gives me a peck on the cheek, hands me the bottles, and pushes past me. "Where is he?"

"In the kitchen."

"Right where a man belongs."

I shake my head and laugh.

She drops her purse on the table and lands her hands on her hips. Drew is at the stove and turns, no apron.

"Wow," she says, "it's really you. In the flesh."

"And you must be Jillian," Drew says.

"Or you can call me flabbergasted." She smiles. "Holy shit."

"I'll just call you Jillian."

"God, you're even better looking in person."

Drew doesn't respond and turns back to the stove, placing the cover on the simmering pot.

"Smells great, what are you making?" Jillian steps closer, their arms nearly touching.

"A seafood stew, with brandy and cream, a Caesar salad, and French bread. I don't do much in the dessert department, so I bought a lemon tart."

Jillian swoons. "Yum. Where's the corkscrew?"

I open the drawer and hand it to her.

Dinner is spectacular, and we eat the tart on the back deck, and the conversation turns to the night Drew helped me through one of the worst nights of my life.

"Thanks for being there for Rea. I don't think even she knew how much trouble she was in. You being there was huge. I'm not sure if you realize how huge."

"I have a pretty good idea," Drew says.

"Hey, guys, I'm right here."

They both smile.

Jillian leaves around nine, and Drew and I snuggle on the lounger, finishing our wine.

"So, I have something to tell you.".

A pang lands in the pit of my stomach, but I keep my mouth shut.

Chapter Twenty-Five

"I signed on to a new project today. It's a remake. Sandy Marshall is directing."

"She's great. I love her movies."

"You know her stuff?"

"Of course. What's the remake?"

"I'm under an NDA. It's all hush-hush for the moment."

"Can I guess?"

"You can try…"

"Hmm…" I tap my lips with my forefinger.

Drew crosses his arms over his chest, his eyebrows hike up. "I'll give you a hint, but don't say the name out loud."

I glance over my shoulder. "You think someone is snooping on us?"

"Of course not. Just don't manifest it to the universe."

"Okay, shoot."

"It's set in Paris."

The lightbulb lights. "I got it!" I clap my hands and jump up and down like a three-year-old finding an Easter egg.

"Okay, keep it to yourself."

I drag two fingers across my lips and shut the imaginary lock. Drew grins. "I love old movies. So did the nuns at school. We watched them all the time." I laugh.

"What's so funny?"

"You should have seen the living room on Saturday nights. I was only there during the summers and vacations, when all my classmates were gone, and the sisters let me stay at the convent. Saturday night was movie night, and sixteen nuns were crammed in the tiny parlor, fighting for space, but there wasn't enough seating so there were pillows and blankets, no nunnery attire, just nightgowns and pjs. Honestly, it was like what I imagined a college dorm would be like."

Drew gives me the side-eye. "Sounds weird."

"And there was an endless supply of snacks—popcorn, homemade brownies, and every beverage imaginable." I purse my lips. "Except for alcohol of course."

"Of course."

"It was an old wooden console TV, like maybe twenty inches. It had color, but the movies we were watching were black and white, so it didn't matter. No remote control. And some of the older nuns were hard of hearing so one of us would have to keep getting up to adjust the volume.

"We'd watch the classic movie channel, so we didn't get to choose the feature. It was whatever was scheduled that night. And when it was one of their favorites? They clapped so loudly—not the applause that would come after a performance, but in anticipation of what they knew would be a great performance. I saw all the classics, knew the names of all the stars. In hindsight, I was lucky to have been exposed to so many amazing movies in history and those early years in movie production. So many people have no idea what it must have been like to rely solely on acting. No lighting, no green screens, no special effects."

Drew narrows his eyes. "You accuse me of playing doctor…not in a creepy way…" He laughs. "But now you sound like an expert in my field. I think you're more a part of the Hollywood world than you'd like to admit."

I purse my lips. Maybe he's right. "I doubt it."

"Anyway, sounds like a great memory."

"It is. I learned a lot about love from those flicks. But then again, I considered it the stuff of fairy tales. Nothing even close to reality." I study Drew's face. He's such a good listener, as if he really cares. Well, duh, he *does* care. "But now that I've met you, maybe I was wrong." I take his hand with both of mine. He smiles. "I just might have met the man of my dreams. A real-life movie star of my very own."

"At your service, ma'am. I'm here to fulfill all your fantasies."

"Okay, now *this* is getting weird." I laugh.

"What's so funny?"

"Like all girls, I did have some fantasies of becoming a famous actress but Sister Genevieve, the music teacher, nixed that idea. In seventh grade, she told me I was no longer needed in the choral department, and I should stick to math and science."

I realize I've only seen *one* of his movies, at the premiere, and have no idea of his theatrical range. "So, you can sing and dance?"

"Well, I can carry a tune, and I don't have two left feet. Besides, it's not a musical. I don't think anyone has the nerve to remake that finale. It's iconic. The original garnered eight Academy Award nominations and won six, including best picture. This remake follows the basic story line, but it's been updated. Instead of a World War Two Vet, he's a Vietnam Vet living in Paris trying to succeed as a painter. The rest follows the original plot line."

"So, it's set in the seventies?"

"Yeah, very retro. I'm playing Jerry Mulligan of course, Richie Spade plays Adam Cook, the struggling concert pianist, and they cast Michael Munson as his best friend, French singer Henri Baurel. Megan Street is Milo Roberts, and Gwen Davis is Lise Bouvier."

And here we go. He's leaving.

"Wow, some cast. When do you start shooting?"

"In a few weeks. And of course, we're filming in Paris. I'll be there for the summer."

"Paris? For three whole months?" My pulse accelerates, and I'm afraid. Afraid if he leaves, the insanity will return. I sip my wine and try not to overreact.

Drew laces his fingers through mine and kisses the back of my hand. "You okay?"

"Ah, yeah," I lie.

"So, I thought since you finish at the hospital next week, and your next year of residency doesn't start until the fall, maybe you'd come with me. We could do some exploring and be decadent when I'm not on set, sunbathing, eating the local food. I found a secluded resort and each bungalow has its own pool. We can sunbathe naked if we want. And the housekeeping staff is on call and brings whatever you need. What do you think?"

Okay, so not abandoning me. Yet. I sip more mine. "I don't know…I…"

He puts his fingers on my lips. "Take some time to

consider my offer before you say no."

The truth is, I don't have any plans for the summer. I haven't thought about the future because…I can't even say it in my mind anymore.

"Didn't you say you went to school in France? You must have some friends there."

"Now you've opened Pandora's box. Are you sure you want to see what's inside?"

"Of course. I want to know all of it. I want to see all your scars." He squeezes my hand.

"I'm not sure I want to remember. I've tried to forget. To move on."

"Stop punishing yourself for your feelings. You can't protect yourself from suffering. None of us can. To live is to grieve. You are not protecting yourself by shutting yourself off from the world. A scar is a sign of strength, the sign of a survivor. The pain reminds you you're alive. The scars mean you've survived."

"Okay, Dr. Freud. You asked for it…" I take a deep breath and the dam opens. "When I turned five, I boarded a private plane in the company of my current nanny, who you now know was Ava."

"Yeah, that was a bit of a shocker."

"For all of us. She was like twenty at the time. I had never been around my dad much, so at first, I didn't miss him. I didn't know any other life. She got me settled and took me shopping for clothes and tchotchkes to decorate my room. After she departed, I realized I missed her way more than my dad.

"My dad visited once a year, but truthfully, he was a total stranger. And he never made it for Christmas, so I spent it in the convent with the nuns as everyone else had gone home with family. I was a good little girl. I got good grades and never complained. I hardly ever saw him. He always claimed he was too busy."

Suddenly, I'm in my dorm room. Alone for the holidays. Again.

I peer out the open casement window of my second-floor bedroom. My roommate, Angelique, just departed with her mother.

The biggest snowflakes I'd ever seen are falling softly, silently, blanketing the cobbled pathway I trod to class every day. The complete quiet surprises me. The outdoor commons area is usually bustling with my classmates as we hurry to class. The only sound is Mr. Jackson's boots crunching the snow covering the stone walk as he sprinkles salt on the footpath no one will travel. The aroma of damp pine trees makes the air feel fresh and clean, and I inhale, filling my lungs with the frosty air.

Puffs of snow float on the tree branches, but it's already melting, drip by drip, off the tips of pine needles. Snow distorts the light, casting shadows, adding contrast, and tiny prisms make rainbows dance…a magical fairy world where I imagine the fabled creatures live. The emptiness in my chest is a giant chasm, I wish for a mother, or someone, *anyone* who would love me. Someone who would hug me, kiss my cheek, pick me up when I fell. If kisses were snowflakes, I wanted a blizzard.

In the distance, the sun is setting. The azure sky morphs into shades of orange and red, as the golden globe sinks into the horizon as if the sky is on fire.

" 'Tis the season to be freezing." I turn to see Sister Dolores Thérèse standing in my doorway. Odd thing for her to say, yet she often surprises me with her playfulness. Something I was unaccustomed to and seemed uncharacteristic for a nun. A woman who dedicates her life to religious service, living with vows of poverty, chastity, and obedience in the enclosure of the cloistered convent.

I glance at the thick black belt circling her trim waist. When I first arrived, I was eye-level with that belt, and worried it might be used for discipline in some sordid way. Not sure where I got that idea—the terrifying musings of an abandoned child. The white headdress, covered by the black veil, squeezes her rosy cheeks, making them appear chubbier than they are. Her hands are clasped below the belt, a pose she often took.

"Perhaps you should shut the window," she says. Her smile grows wide, and her blue eyes twinkle.

"My dad isn't coming for Christmas," I say, not a question, a statement, and I return my gaze to the flaming vista.

"He is not."

I sigh. "He said he might make it this year."

"I know, but he did send presents. And sweets."

Of course he did. Purchased by some personal assistant. I secretly thought the nuns delighted when he stood me up because they benefited from the ostentatious cache of foodstuffs bestowed upon the convent. The good sisters took pity on me as I was always the sole resident forsaken in the dorm at Christmas.

"Pack what you need, *ma chère*, and I'll wait for you downstairs," said Sister Dolores Thérèse.

Drew sighs. "I'm sorry. It must have been difficult." He takes both wine glasses and sets them on the side table, then pulls me forward and settles me on his lap. The back of my head rests against his chest; his arms encircle my waist.

"I was pretty much a loner. My self-esteem was in the toilet, and I avoided relationships." I gaze at the ripples in the pool. "When I was twelve, I found an article in a movie magazine my roommate had. I learned my father remarried, and I had a half-brother. Bobby called me one day when I was about fifteen, and we had the same thoughts about Dad. He never saw him much either. I felt a little better knowing that. It didn't take me long to realize how famous he was, especially when *Afterthought* debuted at our local movie theater. I heard he made about a hundred million dollars on it, not to mention winning the Oscar for best director. He sent me money…a lot of money. I'm not sure why. I think to assuage his guilt.

"Sister Dolores Thérèse helped me open a bank account, and I religiously deposited every cent. All my needs were provided for, and we wore a uniform most of the time, plus my father put more money in my house account in the event I needed to pay for something extra. By the time I graduated, I decided I wanted to come back to the States to go to college. I could pay my way through college without his help.

"Anyway, I returned to California and enrolled in college. My dad was nearby, but I still didn't see him often. When I first got involved with Greg, my father was ecstatic. I'm sure he felt like I found a great guy. Someone who was smart with a solid career who'd treat me well. You know, the reason he sent me to France in the first place was because he didn't want me anywhere near Hollywood. No way was he going to let me hang around the entertainment scene with the possibility of meeting some actor.

"And so, the joke is on him. I met what seemed like a great guy, and he overdosed and killed himself just like my mother did. Now, I ask you, how ironic is that? Sometimes I think he got exactly what he deserved for ruining my life. Although once again, I'm the one who got hurt.

"You know what is so ridiculously absurd about this whole thing?" I ask without expecting a response. "My father spent his entire life trying to keep me from this exact experience, and in the end it happened anyway. Just like it happened to him. Life is a cruel joke. My father firmly believes fame corrupts. But it happens everywhere. No matter what you try to do, life smacks you in the face. And it does so with a giant laugh at your expense." My cynical tone settles deep in my gut. Yeah, life is a sick joke, and the punch line always makes you gag.

Drew is still quiet as I ruminate on my pathetic life.

I sigh. "Aren't you glad you asked?" I look up at him and he smiles.

"I am." He slides me off his lap, and I lie beside him. He grabs my shoulder and pulls me onto my side to face him. "Like I said before, you're a survivor. Be proud of that."

I ponder this but don't respond.

"So will you come with me to Paris?"

"The trouble with boarding school is no one is local, and it's been eight years, so they could be anywhere by now. I would like to see some of my teachers again. I spent every summer there. The sisters tutored me, and it allowed me to graduate a year early. And Sister Dolores and I spent lots of time in the city. We regularly visited the theater, museums, and the local cafes." I laugh. "She let me drink coffee."

Drew chuckles. "Very decadent."

"I even stayed the summer after I graduated before I started college, because I had nowhere to go. It turned out to be the best summer of my life." Drew kisses me, his warm breath sending a shiver through me, but I continue. "I was admitted to UCLA as a bio major and went right from dorm to dorm. My father sent a large check, so I could buy whatever I needed for school. And he paid for tuition and room and board, even though I didn't need it since I'd saved all the money he'd sent me."

The urge to see the good sisters suddenly overwhelms me. The closest thing I had to a home, a family. "You know, I think I will come with you." I drape my arms around his neck and kiss him.

"Well, that went better than expected." His fingers run through my hair, and he kisses me. "Way better." Our tongues dance an erotic jig, and our clothes wind up strewn on the deck. His kisses are everywhere. My hair is wound tight around his fist, and he pulls me on top of him, and I fall off the precipice, such sweet torment.

Chapter Twenty-Six

The last day of my stint in the ER confirms my decision to exit trauma medicine. It's a war zone. But my year ends uneventfully, my reviews are stellar, and word spreads about my change in specialty. Dr. Frick, in an unexpected moment of sentiment, expressed his dismay at me leaving his service. I almost think he was more sad than disappointed.

So I will return to year one of a four-year residency in psychiatry under the mentorship of Dr. Kelly. The program focuses on psychotherapy as well as medical care, which I found particularly attractive. At completion, they offer fellowships in addiction plus geriatric, pediatric, and neuropsychiatric medicine.

I arrive home that evening, musing about being on vacation. Three whole months with nothing to do...*in Paris*. Thumbing through the mail, I'm startled by someone sitting at my kitchen table, sipping a Perrier from my fridge. I didn't notice a car out front. "Ava, what are you doing here?"

"Hi...um...I...ah...I was just checking on Drew."

Checking on Drew? What the hell? I throw the unopened envelopes on the table. "I wasn't aware he needed checking on."

"I don't mean to intrude..."

"Then don't," I say with too much attitude.

Drew is suddenly beside me, buttoning his pale blue

button-down. "Hey, luv." He kisses my cheek. "You're home early." His hair is wet, as if he just showered. My stomach knots. What's going on here? Ava is probably old enough to be his mother, however there is such a thing as a MILF.

Ava stands. "Look, Andrea…"

"It's Rea," I remind her.

"Rea. I only have Drew's best interest at heart. I just needed to see where he was living and make sure he's okay."

Heat travels up my neck, flushing my cheeks. Who the hell does she think she is? "Ava…"

"Let's take this down a notch," Drew says. "We're finalizing the contracts for the new project, and Ava volunteered to bring them here rather than having me go into the city. At least that's what you said, Ava." Drew frowns. "I don't need you checking up on me, Ava. Ever. You're my agent not my mother. I'm a grown man, and even my mother doesn't check on me that often. I'm capable of managing my own life."

Ava sinks into her chair, elbows on the table, her head in her hands. "Of course. I'm sorry. I don't know what came over me."

I look down on her, struggling for control.

She makes eye contact with me, hers filled with tears. "Rea, I honestly never thought I'd ever see you again, and…well…there are things I need to say."

I steady myself, holding onto the back of a chair. "Water under the bridge, Ava, it's not necessary."

"It is for me."

I sigh, gripping the chair tighter, but remain mute.

"Taking you to that school when you were five was one of the hardest days of my life."

Your life? I think…

"I know I was only your nanny, but I was very attached to you. I loved you, and I told your father he was making a mistake. You needed him, and sending you away was not in anyone's best interest."

I frown. "You wanted me to stay?"

"I did. Your father and I had a terrible fight over it, but he wouldn't budge. I did my best to convince you school would be fun and you would get so smart and your dad would come and visit often, but I felt terrible, like I was lying to you, and maybe I was. Or maybe I was trying to convince myself." She pauses, wiping her eyes. "You were scary smart, Rea. You beat me at checkers every time, and you were only four. You could knock off fifty of those memory cards in under a minute. So I tried to convince myself this school would be good for you."

"I had no idea."

"After I returned from Paris, I never saw your father again. I attended school at night and interned at a talent agency during the day, and after I graduated, they offered me a full-time position. Over the years we've bumped into each other a few times professionally, but we mostly ignore each other."

I'm off balance. I don't know what to say. Or what to *feel.* I look at Drew, who's standing beside me, his expression too serious. His arms are crossed over his chest. I think back to the morning I found Ava in bed with my dad, and my confession hemorrhages out. "The morning I saw you in bed with my dad was the happiest day of my life. I hoped you were going to become my new mom. I loved you too. You were the closest thing I had to a mother. But then you took me to school and left me there. I was so confused, disappointed, hurt."

"Oh, God, Rea, I'm so sorry. That day completely traumatized me. I've never married, never had children. If I couldn't advocate for or take care of you, how could I take care of my own child?"

Drew interjects. "You had no legal rights, Ava. There was nothing you could have done."

"I talked to anyone who would listen, looking for some way to intervene. But you're right, there were no legal alternatives. Your mother and father were both only children whose parents were dead, and there was no one to help in my struggle to keep you. And your father was a very powerful man, even then."

"Ava, I had no idea. I thought you wanted me gone so you could have my father to yourself."

A crack opens in my chest, and my heart rate plummets from the red zone. An eerie calmness floods through me.

Ava takes my hand. "I'm so sorry, Rea. I never meant to hurt you."

I fixate on her tear-drenched face. She stands. My arms surround her, and I hug her tight, tighter. She returns my embrace, and we hold each other for a long moment. "Let it go," I whisper. "There's nothing to forgive."

She holds me at arm's length and smiles. "Thank you. It means a lot to know you don't hate me."

"I'm okay. We'll be okay. I'm glad we were able to sort all this out. Now let's put it behind us and just be friends."

"Deal." She wipes her face again with both hands. "Where's your bathroom? I think I did the ugly cry."

Drew takes her elbow and ushers her toward the powder room. I walk to the backdoor and gaze at the roiling ocean. For once, I'm calmer than the sea.

His hands are on my shoulders, his lips near my ear. "I think a very large wound healed, for both of you."

I place one hand on his. "I think you're right, *Dr. Foster*." He surrounds my neck with his arms and snorts a laugh. "Perhaps you should be the one in med school pursuing your degree in psychiatry."

"Nah, I'd never make it through med school. Blood, guts, cadavers? I'd either puke or faint, probably both."

"My car is here," Ava says. "I'll take care of the contracts and be in touch regarding travel plans. I'm sending Lisa with you."

Ava departed, Drew says. "I have a surprise for you. Wait five minutes then come upstairs."

I narrow one eye. "What are you up to?"

"What part of *surprise* do you not understand?" He slips away and leaves me wondering. Was he up to something when I arrived, when I imagined something untoward might be going on with Ava? My bad...

Chapter Twenty-Seven

I trod the stairs, imagining what he's been plotting. He's standing at the door to my bedroom, *our* bedroom. He opens the door and I search for signs of his surprise. Nothing.

"Take off your clothes," he says.

One eyebrow arches. "Excuse me, mister?"

He walks toward the bathroom and opens the door. The floor is littered with red and pink rose petals.

"Who's going to clean those up?" I ask.

Drew frowns. "You're going with that?"

I slap my mouth. Will I ever learn? "Sorry, I don't know why I said that."

I step closer. Candles rim the tub, casting a hallowed glow, the flickering yellow shadows mesmerizing.

"I thought you might enjoy some me-time to celebrate your last day of work."

"You set this up before Ava arrived?"

"I did."

"Where did you get the bubble bath? I never bought bubble bath."

"Under the sink."

Then I remember. "Oh yeah, the bubble bath was in the basket my cleaning lady gave me last Christmas." I hug my waist. "I've never taken a bubble bath."

Drew's eyes are wide. "You're kidding. Never?"

"No."

Drew runs his fingers through his cinnamon-hued hair. "First no birthday cake and now this? You've had a seriously deprived existence."

I don't respond to his accurate rendering of my life and slowly shed my clothing. My eyes well as I imagine an archway to somewhere beautiful. "Thank you. It's a lovely gesture."

He comes close and surrounds me with his arms, his lips close to my ear. "I didn't mean to upset you."

"I'm not upset. I'm…overwhelmed."

He pulls away and takes my hand, leading me toward the surfactant foam. I step in and submerge myself in the cool bubbles and calming heat. "Are you coming in?" I ask.

"Tempting, but no, this is just for you. I'm going to order food, and then we'll relax and watch a movie. It's one I know you'll like."

"Sounds delicious."

"I'll be back in twenty." He hits a button on a portable CD player that wasn't there before, and Sade sings "Smooth Operator." One of my favorites. How did he know that? "I made a playlist."

Of course he did. He walks back into the bedroom, and I whisper, "I love you."

But he's already gone.

Drew returns for me, and I sink into the plush white towel he holds out. He hugs it around me. "So, how did you like your first bubble bath?"

"Pretty decadent. It calms the nervous system, reducing stress and anxiety, and improves your mood. I'm sure my serotonin levels are elevated."

He groans. "So, interpreting your science-speak, you're relaxed and in a good mood? Maybe even happy?"

I laugh, and suddenly I'm giddy, laughing uncontrollably. "Sorry. Yes, that's exactly how I'm feeling." I wipe away the tears…the good kind.

"Wow, you said the f-word. I think progress has been made."

"The f-word?"

"*Feeling.*"

Huh, he might be right. In the last twenty-four hours I feel like somebody new. The pressure of my first-year residency is over. I can eat, sleep, and play to my heart's content. And *in Paris.*

"I ordered Thai food. It should be here any minute. I'll wait for you downstairs. I have the movie queued up."

I arrive in the living room in an oversized T-shirt and my favorite sweatpants where Drew is unpacking the food on the coffee table. "Beer or wine?"

"Beer."

He returns from the kitchen with two bottles and hands one to me. We settle onto the couch, and Drew hits play on the DVD remote, and the screen lit up. "Oh, my God. I thought you said you didn't want to see it. That it might screw with your performance."

"I decided to risk it. I think our script is radically different."

The movie is even better than I remember, and Drew sings along with a few of the tunes. No dancing.

We snuggle into bed, and I fall asleep in his arms, my serotonin levels still elevated.

****

"The car is here. Ready?" Drew says as I shut my suitcase and yank up the handle.

"I am."

"I don't think I've ever been this happy. A great project in Paris and my girl by my side. Being on location can be difficult. When you arrive, you usually don't know anyone. It's like the first day of school. Hopefully, you make some friends, but not all sets are friendly. I often get homesick. But this time I'm bringing home with me."

His arms circle my hips, and his chest presses into me. He kisses me, a long, luxurious melding of our mouths. I melt into him, just like always. I can't deny the effect he has on me. And he's right, being together feels like home. Or what I *think* home should be like.

"Let's jet," he says, leading me by the hand, tugging my suitcase behind him.

We arrive at the airport at ten for our ten-thirty a.m. flight. We're flying private, which streamlines everything—no check-in line, you drive onto the tarmac, and the plane is ten feet away, with foodstuffs and beverages to your heart's delight on board. We are in the company of Lisa, Drew's personal assistant for this project. She's as bossy as a schoolmarm, but doesn't garner any complaints from me.

Belted into our seats, I study Lisa. She's very attractive. And Drew has spent a lot of time with her, alone. The green-eyed monster peeks out. "So you and Lisa spend a lot of time together. Didn't you say it was just the two of you during the overseas press tour?"

"What are you getting at?"

"Well, you know, all that time together, did you guys ever…?"

"She's not my type."

"You have a type?"

"She dates women."

"Oh." Exactly how far can one's foot fit into one's mouth? They never covered it in med school.

Drew smiles, taking my hand. "A little jealous, luv?" I don't say anything and lean my head on his shoulder. "I like it."

We eat, drink mimosas, play cards, listen to music, and recline in the soft leather seats, arriving before ten p.m. to a waiting black SUV. Drew introduces me to the driver. "I have hired a car for you. This is John, and he's at your service 24/7. He's French but speaks fluent English. Although I know you speak French, so communication shouldn't be a problem either way."

"*Enchanté de vous rencontrer,*" John says.

"Nice to meet you, too," I say.

John whisks us away to Hotel Chambiges Elysées, complete with balcony view of the Eiffel Tower. Drew doesn't need to be on location for two days, and we check into his promised "secluded little cottage resort" tomorrow.

I open the double doors to the balcony and step onto the tiled floor. I glance at the street below. It's quiet. Only a few cars pass by. A smile captures my lips. It's good to be home. There's that word again. I had no meaning, no memories I could call *home*, but now? Seems I have more than I could have ever hoped for.

His arms around my waist, he nibbles my neck. "Happy?"

"Very."

"I'm glad. You seem happy. Happier than I've ever seen you."

Drew pops the cork on the complimentary bottle of French champagne, and we snuggle into bed naked. The bubbles tickle my nose and I sneeze, but thankfully, I don't spill the precious golden liquid.

"Bless you," Drew says.

"Thank you. By the way, I've been wanting to ask if you'll get a chance to see your family while you're here."

"Definitely. I wasn't going to bring it up right away, but I can't wait for you to meet them."

Meet his parents? Oh God, that sounds serious.

Chapter Twenty-Eight

"Don't look so terrified, I've met your dad and your brother. Now, they're scary. Both of them."

I laugh. True that. Drew's already earned his stripes. "I'd love to meet them," I say. "Just makes this sound so serious."

"I already declared my intentions. I am serious. Very serious. I don't know if I loved you the first moment I saw you, or if it was the second or third or fourth. But when I opened my eyes on the beach that night, and you were staring down at me—the vision of you against the background of a starlit sky, your face wet, a strand of dark hair covering one eye—the thunderbolt struck, and somehow the rest of the world vanished. Maybe being weak in the knees wasn't because I smashed them on the dashboard." He winks.

"Drew…"

"I think when love strikes, it's like lightning, so powerful and intense you can't deny it. It's beautiful and messy, cracking your chest open and spilling your soul out for the world to see. There's no turning back. Once the thunderbolt hits, your life is irrevocably changed."

I don't know what to say to this outpouring of emotion. Emotions are not my forte. Which makes me a good doctor, but terrible in relationships. At least Greg and I were similarly suited. With the death of my mother at such a young age, I never had any real affection. I grew up in a house where no one ever mentioned her, and I quickly learned not to ask. I kept all my sadness and fear locked inside my tiny soul.

"I said too much…" he says. "I'm overwhelming you."

"No, your words are beautiful, poetic, as always. I could never compete."

"This isn't a competition."

"I know, but doctors are stubborn and competitive by nature. And we don't like to lose."

"There's nothing to lose here. Do my words make you feel inadequate? Less than? Because I would never want to make you feel that way. I'm just expressing my feelings."

"I know. But we're complete opposites. You're an artist and I'm a scientist. I attribute love at first sight as pheromonal compatibility. Chemistry—the real kind. There have been many studies done on the chemistry of love. The effects of oxytocin. It's fascinating."

"Okay, I had a hard-on, but I think you nixed it."

"Oh, God. I'm sorry. I'm such an ass."

"Like the night we were awakened by a thunderstorm. I find thunderstorms romantic. But what did you say? 'A cold front must be coming through.' And there went my hard-on."

"Oh, Jesus, I'm sorry. But words and emotion are your craft, and I can't…."

"Look, if this is going to work, you've got to let me inside, even when it hurts. Don't hide the broken parts. You have to love yourself before you can love me. And I think you're starting to understand."

"It's true. I've been more open and honest with you than anyone else in my life. Even Jillian, and she's my best friend."

"Good, then let's keep working on that. Now drink up." We empty our glasses, and he takes them and turns them upside down in the bucket. "I've recovered, so let's christen this bed."

He pushes me down on the plush mattress and parts my legs with his knee. "No more talking." He plunders my mouth, and I sink into the depth of his love. "I know you love me, and I will get you there. In fact, one day soon, I'll bring it screaming out of you."

Well, I did say it, but not loud enough for him to hear, so it doesn't count.

I kiss him. Hard. Challenge accepted. But right now, I intend to scream for a different reason.

****

Breakfast in bed is a requirement on vacation, or holiday, as Drew calls it. I sip my cappuccino and munch a still-warm croissant. Drew dangles a ripe red strawberry in front of my mouth, and I nip it from his fingers.

"Our checkout is at eleven, and the car will take us to the resort. It's only a twenty-minute drive."

Drew is perusing his shooting schedule while I pick up the brochure from the bedside table. "So we can be tourists for a few days. Is there anything special you want to do before you report to set?"

"I hope to mostly relax these next two days. We have all summer to catch the sights."

"How often will you be able to get away?"

"Catch as catch can. I'll leave you a copy of the shooting schedule, so you can see what's planned. But it can be unpredictable. Which is why you'll need this." He rises from the bed and roots around in his suitcase, returning with a small box. Inside is a cell phone. He flips it open. "I've already programmed it with my number and John's. Do you know how to use it?"

I only have a pager, which I use for work, and left at home. "I'm sure I can figure it out." Drew gives me a quick tutorial, and I'm good to go.

"Keep it with you at all times, so I can reach you."

I feel a stirring of…what exactly? Possessiveness? Keeping tabs on me? I've never answered to anyone. Perhaps the result of being abandoned at an early age and nobody cared where I was and what I was doing. I let the feeling pass.

"Have you spent much time in Paris?" I ask.

"I've never been."

"You're kidding."

"Nope, this is a first for me and I'm counting on you to be my tour guide as needed. But I must warn you, I'm not exactly the tourist type."

"Well, there are some places you've got to see while you're here." I read from the pamphlet. "The Louvre and Palais Garnier, and the Arc de Triomphe and Notre Dame. Maybe an event or a game at Parc des Princes, and we should make time for the Luxembourg Gardens."

"I'm at your mercy. Just be gentle. I'm more inclined to spend the days naked in bed with you."

My cheeks flush, the heat of desire always bubbling near the surface with this incredibly handsome and sexy man. I never knew it could be like this. "You'll get no complaints from me."

****

We arrive at the resort and the bellhop takes our luggage from the trunk. John departs. We follow the loaded trolley into the lobby where the concierge greets us. "*Bon jour,* Mr. Applegate." She extends her hand. "My name is Celine. Be assured we have made your anonymity our highest priority."

Mr. Applegate?

"I appreciate that," Drew says, accepting her hand.

"Let me escort you to your accommodations." She turns, and the bellhop extends his hand, indicating we should follow.

"Mr. Applegate?" I say.

Drew smiles. "It's my mother's maiden name. I use it at hotels mostly, or sometimes for reservations."

"And who am I?"

His lips purse. "You're Mrs. Applegate."

"What? We're married?"

"Or you could be my sister." He winks.

I grab his hand and pull him into me. "You're impossible."

"But you love me anyway. Even if you don't know it yet."

Oh, God.

Our suite at Escapade à la Plage takes my breath away. No one would call this a cottage. The large living area has a pitched roof made of golden oak planks. The back wall is composed entirely of glass, and gauzy white curtains attempt to hide the ocean view as they billow in the gentle breeze. Gleaming hardwood floors welcome us in, and the open French doors reveal a small deck with matching rattan lounges and a round marble table between them. A gigantic cream-colored couch lines one wall. Opposite are two chaise lounges in brown Haitian cotton.

My fingers are still laced with Drew's. "Wow, this place is incredible."

"You like?"

"I love."

The bellhop has escaped with his trolley through an archway to the right. "Come, let me show you the sleeping quarters," Celine says.

We follow her into the luxurious bedroom where the bellhop is unloading our luggage. The square room is adorned with similar curtains and a giant circular bed. Everything is decorated in shades of seashell—off-white with pale pinkish hues. I drop my purse on one of the two plush chairs beside the window and step forward. Another deck with more lounges. I guess we'll be doing a lot of lounging…

"What's that?" I say, pointing to the large white basket with a pink and white polka-dot bow sitting in the middle of the bed.

Chapter Twenty-Nine

"Is that my package?" he asks Celine.

"It is, sir. I took the liberty of arranging everything in a decorative basket."

"Excellent, thank you."

"If everything is to your liking, I'll take my leave," Celine says.

"Okay?" Drews asks me.

"Perfect."

"I think we're good. Thank you, Celine."

The bellhop has vanished silently, and I wonder if we should have tipped him. However, I'm sure Drew has taken care of all the amenities.

"Please call the desk if anything is lacking or we can be of further assistance." And she makes her exit.

"What's in the basket?" I ask.

"It's for you, luv. Open it." Drew sits on the edge of the bed and waits.

"A present? For me?" I untie the ribbon and open the lid of the lovely wicker basket, already repurposing it. Inside is an array of lingerie. Everything is pink. I hold up a tiny lacy teddy by its straps. "Wow. I've never had anything like this. I'm not exactly a lace and satin type of girl." I pick up another piece, a matching short robe in pale pink satin.

"I'm going for as many firsts as I can." He smirks. "And you're a beautiful woman, and I want you to have nice things. Plus, I'm already hot to see you in that."

I unpack the remaining items, a lace baby-doll set, camis with matching panties, and French heeled fuzzy slippers... Jesus. "Thanks," I finally sputter. "Everything is beautiful. Did you pick these out yourself?" I worry Drew may be too much like my father. Having his assistant do everything for him. The idea of Lisa picking out all this stuff suddenly turns me off.

"I did. But Bethany helped me with the sizes and delivered them here."

Phew. Not Lisa. A minor assist from Bethany? Okay.

Drew leans back onto the bed, his hands behind his head, and lets out a gigantic sigh. "I think I've died and gone to heaven. In a beach paradise with my girl. Nothing could be better than this."

I kick off my white sandals and snuggle up to him, my hand across his chest. "I thought this would be a working vacation," I say.

"Ugh, don't remind me. I'll be off to the set in two days."

"But you love your work, right?"

"I do, and I don't take it for granted. I'm extremely lucky to be working. For an actor, roles can disappear at any time, so you've got to make the most of it while you have it."

"Based on what I've seen, you'll have a long successful career as an actor if it's what you want."

"The truth is, I'd like to direct. I've done six films but I'm itching to have more creative license to make my own."

"Really? That's cool." But then I choke on my words. A director...like my father.

****

We sleep until ten. After years of sleep deprivation, I could get used to this. Drew rolls on top of me and kisses my neck, his lips nibble my ear, and shivers run down my spine.

"Morning, luv. Did you sleep well?"

"I did." I slip a leg between his and flip him on his back, pinning his hands over his head, my chest smooshed against his. "And now I'm going to make sweet passionate love to you."

He chuckles. "Lucky me."

"Stay perfectly still, mister. I'm doing all the work."

"Yes, ma'am. I'm at your mercy."

"No mercy for you. I intend to torture you into oblivion."

"At least I know if my heart stops you can resuscitate me."

****

Breakfast arrives, and the waiter arranges it on the back deck overlooking the water. The pool water glistens in the morning sun and seagulls glide by, singing their welcome song.

"What do you want to do today?" I ask.

"How about more of what we're doing?"

"Come on, we have to see a few sights."

"You're my guide. Since we've already played dominant and submissive—" He clears his throat. "—not my usual MO, I might add, I'll allow you a little more leeway and let you drag me around town on a pretend leash."

I laugh. "I'm trying to consider that sexy, but not so much."

After breakfast, we swim in the pool, then shower

and dress. I let Bethany pick me out a new wardrobe for the trip, since the feminine side of mine is severely lacking. I don a white sundress with spaghetti straps, a bright red imprint of a peony splashed across the skirt, and slip into strappy red sandals. I tie my hair up in a French twist, feeling very 1950s Hollywood.

"Wow," Drew says. "I like you all dolled up."

"Well, don't get used to it." But then I wish I hadn't said that. Just because I've taken absolutely no interest in my appearance for so long, doesn't mean I can't improve. Maybe if I'd had a mother, I might be more in touch with my feminine side. But I was raised by nuns, and their definition of femininity had nothing to do with fashion. Girly stuff was not their strength. But raising a smart, confident woman was. So I'll go with that.

"You know, I'm sorry. I'm enjoying dressing up. I'm just not used to it, and I didn't think I was very good at it. But I'm trying."

"Dress however you like. You always look great to me."

I smile and put my arms around his waist, landing a kiss on his cheek.

We stroll around town, through a farmers' market where a flock of nuns peruse the wares. I look for familiar faces, but the habits they wear are different from the Sisters of Mercy. I think of Sister Dolores and look forward to seeing her again.

A photographer is at work in the adjacent park, his subjects a mime and a lovely red-haired model in a frothy pink pinafore over a white bodysuit. The poses are playful, mock kisses and lots of hugs as the model is careful not to smear her outfit with her cohort's white grease paint, black eye makeup, and crimson lipstick.

The photographer motions to the woman, easing her sideways. As she turns, she sights Drew and freezes. The photographer urges her sideways again, then turns to see what is distracting her. "Foster," he says.

"Hey, Seth, how are you?"

"Good."

"Rea, this is Seth Friedman. He photographed me for a big ad campaign a while back."

"Nice to meet you," Seth says, extending his hand. I take it. "Likewise."

Seth slings his camera strap over his shoulder. "That was quite a few moons ago. See you've hit the big time. Seen all your films. Great work."

"Thanks," Drew says.

"I heard you were in town doing *American in Paris.* It's all over the trade pubs, lots of Oscar buzz."

"Oh, I don't know. But the script is great, and Sandy Marshall is a pro. It's a great set. Great cast. Lucky to be on board."

The model steps closer along with the mime. "Hi," she says. "I'm a huge fan."

"Thanks," Drew says. "Nice to meet you."

The mime moves in, putting both hands up as if against a wall. Drew smiles and mirrors the pose. They make matching faces—sad, happy, surprised, then happy again. Moving along the imaginary wall, they come to the end and hang their elbows on some pretend shelf. They tilt their heads sideways. It's hilarious. Playful, and something I could never do.

They both break into laughter and shake hands. "Pleasure to meet you," the guy says. "Big fan too."

"Thanks," Drew says. "Appreciate your kind words."

****

We have lunch at a quaint outdoor bistro where we order French onion soup garnished with melted Gruyère and a giant crunchy crouton. A crisp pinot grigio complements the savory potage. Apple crisp tops off the meal, and we continue our stroll down the main street. Drew garners stares and the occasional request for an autograph. I marvel. Even in Paris he's a major celeb.

The day ends as we exit the Louvre, images of famous masterpieces linger in my mind—sculptures, *objets d'art*, paintings, drawings, and archaeological finds. The *Mona Lisa,* and *Venus de Milo*, believed to depict Aphrodite, the Greek goddess of love. Found in pieces, made of Parian marble, it's missing both arms and stands over six feet tall. The architecture of the building alone is breathtaking as it was originally the Louvre Palace, built in the late twelfth century under Philip II. The stone statues, marble staircases, and carved banisters, the tiled floors, all incredible. To think of the time and amount of craftsmanship, not to mention the mere hard work, boggles the mind. Drew takes my hand as we walk along the banks of the Seine on our way back to the hotel.

"I'll admit I enjoyed that way more than I expected. It's been a wonderful day. No, a perfect day."

He smiles his movie-star smile, and my insides turn to goo.

Chapter Thirty

Drew heads off to set after three false starts, each time returning for "one more kiss." I promise not to have too much fun without him. John is at my beck and call, and he's picking me up at noon for my planned outing.

Windows down, the warm breeze flutters my hair, which I let fall loose around my shoulders. At work it's always up or back, out of my way. The sun is bright, the sky a cloudless cerulean blue. "Lovely day," I say.

"Beautiful," John says.

The carved wooden convent doors loom large, my feet planted firmly on the top tier of the three half-moon steps. Nearly nine years have passed since I walked these hallowed halls. I tap the brass door knocker several times and wait. I realize I'm holding my breath and force out an exhale. The door opens, and I am greeted by Sister Mary Katherine's ever-angelic countenance. She frowns, then her eyes open wide, her chin drops. "*Ma chère coucou!*" Her hand covers her mouth, and she makes the sign of the cross on her chest. "Andrea? I can't believe it's you. What are you doing here?"

"*Bonjour*, Sister, how are you?"

She slaps her chest. "I am well, thank you… But I am being rude, please, please come in." She turns sideways and sweeps her hand in a welcoming gesture.

I step onto the black-and-white mosaic floor, my eyes traveling over the familiar wood-paneled foyer. The giant grandfather clock beside the oval stained-glass window of a cross chimes one. The aroma of something baking fills my head. The sisters had a sweet tooth, and there were always fresh-baked sundries to satisfy nighttime cravings. I still can't eat a chocolate brownie without my mind visiting their old-world kitchen with its wood-burning stove and oak countertops. Of course, they had a gas stove also, but oh…the things they could make over a wood fire.

"I've unexpectedly returned to Paris for the summer, and I immediately needed to pay you a visit."

"Come in, come in," she says. I follow her into the sitting room, and we sit facing each other on the navy and white floral couch. "I am so glad you did. Dolores has shared all your letters, and I know she saves them and reads them often. You've completed medical school, no? And you are officially a physician?"

"I am."

"We are so proud of you, Andrea. Look at you, all grown up and a doctor."

I smile at the sister's praise. They were always generous with it, and I now understand how vital it was to my survival. "How is Sister Dolores? Is she here?"

Mary Katherine's eyes drop, and she sighs, her hands folded in her lap. "I'm sorry, but no, she's in hospital."

My pulse quickens. "What's wrong?"

"She was diagnosed with breast cancer a few days ago. She is receiving treatment."

I have a million *doctor* questions, but I hold my tongue and start slowly. I have to go to the hospital immediately. "Can you share any details?"

"I saw her yesterday. It is stage zero which is the

best you could hope for. They are removing some tissue, and she will have to undergo radiation, but the prognosis is good."

"You're correct; that is about the best diagnosis you can get." The tension in my muscles lessens. "I assume she's at St. Mary's?" This hospital is only a few miles away, and the place where I had my appendix out as well as receiving five stitches in my foot after stepping on a conch shell on the beach at the tender age of seven.

"Yes. Will you visit? She would be most happy to see you."

"Absolutely. I'll head right over."

The good sister rises. "Excellent. I will let you go, but promise you will visit again. I want to hear all about your life. Every tiny detail. Promise?"

"Of course. As I said, I will be here most of the summer."

"Good." She comes close and kisses one cheek, then the other. Her hands take mine, and her gaze fixes on me. "It is so good to see you, Andrea. Give Dolores my best, and tell her I will be along later. I baked brownies for her."

"I will."

John is at the curb, and I instruct him to take me to St. Mary's, giving him a short explanation of my need to visit the hospital.

"I'm so sorry. This is a friend?"

"I attended school here, and the nuns took me under their wing since my father rarely visited. I consider them my real family."

John nods, he peers back at me in the rearview mirror. "Understood. Would you care to stop and pick up something? Flowers, perhaps?"

"An excellent idea. Thank you, John."

I select a large bouquet of pink roses and green hydrangeas from an outdoor stand and settle into the backseat, arriving at St. Mary's a few minutes later. "You can take a lunch break, and I'll call you when I'm ready to leave. I should be here for at least an hour or two."

"Thank you, Dr. Tasson. I'll be close by."

"Please, John, call me Rea. We have a whole summer together."

John smiles in the rearview mirror. "I'll try…hard to break *force de l'habitude.*"

I stand at the reception desk, posies in hand, and am directed to Sister Dolores's room. I wonder if Mary Katherine called to advise her of my visit. Apparently not, as she gasps at my presence. Her hands slap her cheeks. "*Oh, mon Dieu,* Andrea!" She's not wearing her nunnery attire, her short gray hair on display.

"*Bonjour*, Sister. How are you feeling?"

"Right now, my heart is pounding, but it has nothing to do with my state of health."

I glance at the monitor, her heart rate slightly elevated.

She pats the bed. "Come sit. Let me have a look at you."

I hand over the flowers, and she cradles them like a babe in arms. "*Belles fleurs. Merci.*" She places them on the side table. I sit near her feet, but she pulls me close and hugs me, then kisses each cheek.

"So, pray tell, what are you doing in Paris?"

"I'll be here for most of the summer. With my boyfriend. He's an actor and is filming here for the next few months."

She frowns.

I realize I haven't written to her since Greg died. I'm not sure I want to go through the entire saga with her. Keep it short and sweet. Well, not so sweet.

"I thought you would be married by now, to that doctor, Greg?"

"Unfortunately, he died. I'll admit I was in a bad way for several months, but then this amazing man literally crashed into my life, and, well, he's wonderful."

Dolores taps her bottom lip with her index finger. "Well, I am so sorry for your loss, but happy you have recovered. But you say he's an actor? How does your father feel about that?"

The good sister listened to me rant and rave about my father on too many occasions to count. She always listened patiently, nodding her head, and rarely offered an opinion. As I got older, she was all about forgiveness and eventually wore me down to the point where I let him back into my life. "Well, it's complicated. Since they are both in the business, it's not like they can ignore each other. But Drew has stepped up big time. Called him and took him out for coffee, laid his cards on the table, and, well, I think he scored some points. Remains to be seen from here."

"Good. This Drew sounds like a standup man. I am happy for you."

"I think I might love him."

"Well, then, *magnifique*."

"Enough about me. I want to know how you are doing. Sister Mary Katherine gave me the major details, but I want to speak to your doctor."

As if the walls had ears, he marches into the room. If you looked up handsome and debonair in the French dictionary, his picture would be there. His pale green eyes land on me. "*Et qui avons-nous ici?*" he says.

Chapter Thirty-One

"This is my doctor," Sister Dolores announces. "Doctor, this is Dr. Andrea Tasson from America. She is a friend and a former student at our school. We have kept in touch all these years, and she came to visit and found me here."

He extends his hand. "Jean Paul Lavigne," he says, "at your service."

I stand and accept his greeting. "Pleased to meet you," I say.

"*De même*. Are you a medical doctor?"

"I've just completed a first-year residency as a trauma surgeon." I decide to skip the change in specialty.

"Excellent." He turns to Sister Dolores. "And how is my favorite patient today?"

Sister Dolores beams. "I bet you say that to all your patients."

He clutches her chart to his chest. *"Mon Dieu,* I do not." His impish smile makes him appear younger than his probable forty-something years.

"I've reviewed your scans and test results, and I'd like to go over your treatment plan."

Sister Dolores inhales and lets it out slowly. "Please, I'm anxious to get started."

He looks at me. "Are you comfortable discussing this in front of your friend?"

"Absolutely. She's like a daughter to me."

Her declaration warms my heart, and I sit down on her bed and take her hand. "I will be here every step of the way. I won't leave until I know you are in a good place." I refocus on the handsome physician. "Go ahead, Doctor."

"It is stage zero, a ductal carcinoma, which means there are atypical cells in the lining of your milk ducts. But those cells have not spread beyond the wall of the duct to reach surrounding tissue, your bloodstream, or lymph nodes. Of course, if not treated, it has the potential to become invasive."

Sister Dolores nods but doesn't respond, but I say. "So, your diagnosis is DCIS, ductal carcinoma in situ?"

"Yes. We will remove the area of DCIS plus a small margin around it, but we will be able to preserve most of the breast. I doubt you will need reconstructive surgery as the area is quite small. After the surgery, we will follow up with radiation and hormone therapy."

"Tamoxifen?" I say.

"Exactly." He refocuses on Sister Dolores. "Radiation treatment utilizes high energy beams to destroy any atypical cells left behind after surgery. Treatments are given five days a week for several weeks. It is done as an outpatient."

"Then I should be able to perform my duties at school by the beginning of the term?" Sister Dolores asks.

"You should. The side effects of the treatment are minimal, burns—like a red rash—and fatigue, but that should be the worst of it."

"How soon is the surgery?" she asks.

"I have you on the schedule for tomorrow morning. Excluding any complications, you should be able to return home later that day. Dr. Tasson, do you have any questions for me?"

"I think you've covered it expertly. I'm good."

Dr. Lavigne nods his head. "Then I'll leave you to your visit. I'll check on you later in the event any questions or concerns have arisen."

"Thank you, Doctor," Sister Dolores says, and he makes his exit. "He's quite handsome, isn't he?"

"Sister!"

"I don't mean for me; I mean for you. If you didn't have a new boyfriend, I'd try to set you up."

"He's wearing a wedding ring."

"Oh? I hadn't noticed."

I close my eyes and shake my head.

We spend another hour catching up. She tells me tales of how incredibly impolite students are these days. "Especially the American ones," she whispers.

We laugh and commiserate and eventually hug goodbye. "I'll be here tomorrow for your surgery and stay with you until you are released. I can take you home and get you settled."

On my way out, I hear my name. I turn to find Dr. Lavigne behind me. "Dr. Tasson, I wanted to follow up with you to see if you have any additional questions. Would you care to see the scans and lab results?"

"I don't think that's necessary. Sounds like you have everything under control."

"Perhaps I could buy you a *café?*"

We sit at a table for two under a red-striped awning in a nearby cafe. Brilliant red potted geraniums adorn the window boxes under the open leaded-glass windows. The day couldn't be more perfect—the sun warms my back, and the light breeze wafts the aroma of coffee around us.

"*Bonjour, Docteur*," the waitress says. "*Qu'est-ce que je peux vous offrir ?*

"*Un cappuccino, s'il vous plaît,*" Dr. Lavigne says.

"Same for me, thanks."

The waitress departs.

"Thank you for taking such good care of Sister Dolores, Doctor."

"Of course. And please, call me Jean Paul. So, you were her student?"

I don't plan on relating the whole sordid story of being dumped on the good sister's doorstep at the age of five, but I find myself saying more than I planned.

"My mother died when I was a baby, and my dad wasn't around much. He shipped me off to school here and rarely visited. Sister Dolores would bring me to the convent, so I wouldn't be alone in the dorm during the holidays and even for summer vacations. I had my own room near the kitchen. Even though she could be fun, her idea of Christmas was devoted to prayer and meditation. And singing, lots of singing in church. I read nonstop, and she became a mentor in that regard, giving me access to the convent library. I'm confident I read every book they had."

Our orders arrive, the cream artistically presented in the shape of a heart, along with two warm croissants and a side of butter.

Jean Paul sighs. "I operated on her mother last year, and now she always gives me a complimentary pastry with my coffee." He spreads butter on his croissant.

"You realize there are twenty-seven layers of butter in a croissant," I chide.

Jean Paul purses his lips. "My wife tells me the same

thing, but I'm irredeemable."

The words continue to pour out of me. "The sisters had a profound effect on my development. They ministered to the poor, and I often accompanied them as they tended to the less fortunate, spending many hours in soup kitchens, hospitals, and as I got older, the nearby prison. I don't think they realized how vital this part of my education was. There were two places where I know the good sisters changed my life forever—taking biology and tending to the destitute. I do believe my interest in medicine began there."

"Hmm," he says, then sips his coffee. "I might take issue with that. The medical profession is filled with people who've suffered a tragic death of a loved one at an early age."

"I have heard that. The inability to save someone you love sparks the need to save others. But I was too young to know any better."

"It can still manifest later in life when you fully grasp your loss. Of course, your exposure to helping the less fortunate also likely contributed to your desire to become a physician."

The delightful coffee tantalizes my taste buds, and I almost purr. I didn't realize how much I missed Paris. Especially the coffee and croissants.

"So, you wish to be a trauma surgeon?"

Oh, dear, now he's opened a can of worms. I sigh. "Well, I completed my first year of residency as a trauma surgeon in emergency medicine, but I've had a change of heart and switched to psychiatry."

"A drastic change, and you've forfeited a year, no?"

"I know, but…" I have no intention of detailing a life of abandonment, having experienced two painful deaths, and…well… I imbibe more coffee. "I've experienced a good deal of trauma in my life, the emotional kind, and seen results of undiagnosed and untreated mental illness in the ER, and I think my time would be better spent ameliorating that type of trauma. I believe mental illness is a neglected field."

"I commend you. I agree completely." He leans back in his chair and crosses his arms over his chest. "Your father is the famous Hollywood director, James Tasson, no?"

"How do you know that?"

"My wife saw it on some celebrity news show. There was a picture of you and your boyfriend. My wife is a fan." He laughs.

I'll never get used to the relentless need for celebrity gossip, hopeful that someday it will end, and I can be a regular, boring person again.

"His biker films were well received here. I wound up buying a motorcycle myself. Much to my mother's chagrin." He laughs again. "My wife insisted I get rid of it before she would marry me."

"Probably a good idea. I've seen enough victims of motorcycle accidents to agree with her."

"Me too. It was a phase. I thought it made me cool. I was not that cool in *lycée.*"

"I don't think any of us were that cool in high school." I smile. "How long have you been married?" I sip more of the scrumptious brew, savoring the delightful aroma.

"Fifteen years this August."

"Children?"

"Two girls, eleven and thirteen."

"How delightful. What are their names?"

"Monique and Sophia."

"How lovely."

Dr. Lavigne's pager goes off and he glances at it. "I'm afraid I must head back to hospital." He drains his cup and returns it to the saucer. "I will see you tomorrow. Before the procedure?"

"Yes, I'll be there before she heads to surgery."

He places money on the table.

"I can get this," I say.

"*Absurdité*." He stands. "Perhaps you can come for dinner one evening. My wife and daughters are fascinated by all things American and would love to meet you."

"Thank you. I'd love to meet them."

"Good. *Au revoir*."

I linger a few minutes longer, finishing my coffee, reveling in the dreamy atmosphere, and wishing Drew were here. I call John, and he tells me he'll be at the entrance to the hospital in fifteen minutes. A ringing noise emanates from my purse, and I retrieve the cell phone and flip it open. "Hey," I say.

"How's your day?" Drew says.

"Good, I have lots to tell you."

"Everything okay?"

"It is. How is your day going?"

"Great, everyone is incredibly welcoming and I'm feeling very Jerry Mulligan."

I laugh. "It's hard to picture Gene Kelly without his dancing shoes."

"I know. This portrayal is a little darker, but I'm embracing it. You know, the brooding artist who's down on his luck."

"Go, you," I say. A woman's voice calls his name.

"Be right there," he says. "Gotta run, luv."

"Okay. Call before you go to sleep."

"We have a night shoot, but I'll find time to call. Love you," he says and hangs up.

I stare at the screen. "Love you too," I whisper.

Chapter Thirty-Two

John picks me up promptly at seven the next morning, and we are soon en route to St. Mary's Hospital. The silence uncomfortable, I decide to get to know my driver. "So, you were born in Paris?"

"I grew up in Sèvres."

"Oh, aren't they famous for their porcelain?"

"Yes, both of my parents worked at the factory."

"But you decided to try something else?"

"They didn't make much money, and my brother and I decided we didn't want to live on the verge of poverty for the rest of our lives. He works in a bank and is nearly finished with his finance degree."

"And you?"

"I was lucky to receive a scholarship to The *Cours Florent,* here in Paris. I graduated two years ago."

"Is that for acting?"

"Yes."

"So why are you a driver?" Oh, I think, perhaps that was rude.

"I am a driver for a studio, which gets me in the front door, and I hear about auditions through the grapevine there. I've done some local theater and a few commercials, but I'm still waiting for my big break." He holds up one hand, fingers crossed.

"Does Drew know all this?"

"*Oh, mon Dieu,* I would never take advantage like

that. It would be inappropriate."

We arrive at St. Mary's hospital, and John jumps out to open my door.

"Thank you, I'm not sure when I'll be leaving. I'll call when I need you."

"No problem. I'll be nearby."

I enter the cheery hospital room—my flowers found a vase—to find Sister Dolores in the bedside chair.

"I'm famished," she exclaims.

I smile. "You can eat after your surgery. Don't be difficult."

With that, Dr. Lavigne arrives in his scrubs, a petite, auburn-haired woman at his side. He claps his hands together and says, "Is my favorite patient ready?"

"As ready as I'll ever be," Sister Dolores says.

"This is easier than going to the dentist," I say. "You'll take a short nap, and it will be over before you know it."

Nurses bustle about, helping her onto a gurney and adorning her head with the required, and unattractive, surgical cap.

"Would you like to scrub in?" Dr. Lavigne asks.

"I don't have privileges here."

"I've taken care of everything. You're welcome in my OR."

Sister Dolores grabs my hand. "Oh, yes, please."

"Of course," I say. "I would be happy to be at your side."

"Wonderful." He turns to the woman in pink scrubs beside him. "This is Dr. Monet. She will prepare you."

"Please, Elizabeth," Dr. Monet says. "A pleasure to meet you, follow me."

I kiss Sister Dolores on both cheeks. "See you in the

operating room." I squeeze her hand, then follow Elizabeth to the doctor's locker room. She opens a closet to reveal the cache of scrubs, and I select my size.

"You can use my locker for your things." She rotates the combination lock and stands aside, then takes a seat on the metal bench.

I hang my blue sundress on the hook inside the locker, retrieve a clip from my purse and secure my hair in a messy bun, then add my purse, and slip into the required uniform.

"Dr. Lavigne says you've recently changed your residency specialty from trauma surgery to psychiatry. That's quite a switch."

"So says everyone."

She doesn't comment further, then stands and shuts her locker.

"Follow me," she says again.

We enter the surgical prep room, and I am introduced to nurse Elyna who hands me a cap, which I don. I scrub my hands using the requisite two-minute procedure alongside Dr. Monet, while the nurse ties a mask around my face. My hands held high, she slips on the latex gloves and a gown.

We enter the chilly chamber as Sister Dolores is wheeled in. Dr. Lavigne is already inside, speaking with the anesthesiologist. I stand at the good sister's side. "How are you doing?"

"A little nervous, but I've prayed and am confident the Good Lord will look after me."

"Good. I'm sure He will." I smile, knowing she will see it in my eyes.

The anesthesiologist explains what comes next, and she counts backward, only reaching ninety-six.

****

Returned to her room, a groggy Sister Dolores opens her eyes. I rise from the chair and take her hand. "You're awake. How do you feel?" Her lips are stuck together, so I grab the nearby pitcher and pour some water into the glass and add the straw. I press it to her lips, and she takes a long sip. "Better?"

"Much. Thank you." She rests her head against the pillow and inhales slowly. "How did it go?"

"We should probably wait for Dr. Lavigne to speak with you, but from what I saw, it went splendidly. They were able to remove all the affected tissue, and the scar is minimal. You should recover quickly."

"Thank God, or rather, thank the world of medicine for their effective treatment."

I smile. "I'm so happy this went smoothly and your prognosis for a long life is strong."

Dr. Lavigne enters and affirms my assessment, saying the good sister can return to the convent later that afternoon.

"I can take her. I have a car."

"Excellent," Dr. Lavigne says. "The nurse will give you an appointment at my office in two weeks. And an appointment for your first radiation treatment here at the hospital. If you have any questions or feel poorly in any way, don't hesitate to call my service."

He turns to me. "A pleasure meeting you, Andrea, and I'm still hoping you will come for dinner one evening. I will be in touch soon. And if you're inclined to bring your boyfriend, I know my daughters and my wife, would be most excited."

I laugh. "Of course, hopefully, he can get away."

The discharge papers arrive, followed shortly by

lunch, and we can leave after that. I run to the cafeteria and grab a chicken sandwich and iced coffee and return to eat alongside my patient/friend.

I call John, and he arrives promptly at one-thirty, helping the sister out of her wheelchair and into the back seat alongside me.

"He's quite handsome," Sister Dolores whispers.

My eyebrows arch. "What's with you and handsome men?" I ask. "Aren't you married to Jesus?"

"Well, that's kind of metaphorical, and besides, it's not a sin to look."

"But it is a sin if you're thinking inappropriate thoughts." I giggle. I can't believe I'm having this conversation.

"Well, I'll go to confession."

I laugh louder, attracting John's stare in the rearview mirror. I cover my mouth to stifle my near hysterics and give Sister Dolores a sideways glance. "You're awful," I say. "Stop talking."

Chapter Thirty-Three

We arrive at the convent, and Sister Mary Katherine stands in the open doorway, her arms stretched wide. "Welcome home," she shouts as she dashes down the steps. John has the car door open and holds Sister Dolores's arm as she exits.

"Thank you so much, young man. You're quite the gentleman." She squeezes his arm and lingers a few seconds.

"My pleasure, Sister. I hope you make a quick recovery. I will say a prayer for you."

"You're very kind, thank you."

I tell John to return in an hour, after I get Sister Dolores settled and ensure she's okay.

Sister Mary Katherine has her best friend in hand, and we enter the familiar vestibule, and I shut the door behind us.

"How is she doing?" Sister Mary Katherine asks me.

"Physically, fine, but she's incorrigible when she talks about my handsome driver. Not to mention her handsome doctor." I smile, and Sister Mary Katherine mirrors my face, then places her hand over her mouth.

I glance back and forth. "Both of you? Seriously? You're acting like two teenagers."

"Well, we're nuns. We're not dead. Besides, we both had boyfriends before entering the order," Sister Mary

Katherine says.

I never, ever thought of this.

"In Sister Dolores's case, probably too many boyfriends."

My chin drops. Do I want to hear this? Yes, I decide, I most certainly do.

Sister Mary Katherine walks to the sitting room, and we follow. She has set the round wooden table with biscotti and coffee. "I have sustenance. I'm sure the hospital fare was wretched."

We sit, and Sister Mary Katherine hands me a cup with one sugar and cream. They both know my coffee order. Hell, they taught it to me.

"So, how many boyfriends are we talking?"

Sister Dolores takes a bite of cookie, then sips her coffee. She closes her eyes and moans. "Heavenly. Nobody can hold a candle to you in the bakery department, Mary Katherine."

Sister Mary Katherine smiles.

"So?" I prompt.

"Well, first there was Pierre. I met him when I was fourteen and thought he was the most beautiful boy I'd ever seen. Blond hair and big green eyes, tall, nearly six feet. And he was an amazing artist. I still have the sketches he drew of me. And he was a great kisser. My first."

Okay, now I'm worried about TMI. I've opened Pandora's box, and I have no idea what will fly out. I don't say anything, and she continues.

"Then there came Claude. He was a new student, and everyone was after him. He was a footballer and helped our team win the championship that year. We were together until he got recruited by a semi-professional team, and eventually we grew apart. He became a professional footballer but retired some years back. He was my first true love, and I thought we would be together forever. I lost my virginity to him." She takes another bite of cookie and drinks her coffee.

Definitely TMI, way too much. I figured all nuns were virgins. How does Jesus feel about marrying a fallen woman? Okay, how archaic am I? But these were beliefs of a young girl, and I guess they're still buried deep in my subconscious somewhere.

"Well," I finally say, "I had no idea you were an experienced woman."

"That's not all of it," Sister Mary Katherine adds. "Tell her about Philippe."

Oh, no.

"I met Philippe in college. He was a year ahead of me. He was studying architecture, and we spent many days and nights exploring the most unusual and archaic structures in the city, places I never would have known existed. He was magical, he also could draw, and I have those sketches too. When he graduated, I hoped he would propose, but he wound up getting a job with a prestigious firm in the States and off he went. We agreed I would follow once I graduated but alas, he found a new love in America. They married and have three children. They live in Boston, I think. I was heartbroken, and, well, I decided I was done with men and joined the convent."

"Sounds a little spiteful. Not what I would say is a calling to the church," I say.

"I know. I was running away, and this seemed like the safest place. But I've grown to love my life, and I have found great joy in serving others."

"Well, I'm glad you are happy."

"Your turn," Sister Dolores says to Mary Katherine.

"Oh, no, I think we've sufficiently shattered Andrea's image of us, and I don't want to add to the damage."

I laugh. "You two are hysterical. I had no idea."

We switch to talk of the school and how students these days are so undisciplined and distracted by the outside world. When I was a student, we were very insular, the sisters were our only contact with the outside world, and we didn't experience much folly. It was all about academics as well as the arts and service to God.

"It's a struggle these days," Sister Mary Katherine says, "and the parents don't offer much support. Not that they ever did. Many of them were happy to send their daughters to boarding school and let us do the parenting while they had ample means to travel the world and indulge in extortionate adult festivities."

Sounds familiar. And I thought it was just my father. Apparently not.

Sister Dolores sighs. "I'm suddenly tired. I think I'll lie down for a bit."

"Of course," I say, "anesthesia has a lingering effect like a hangover, and a nap will help you rejuvenate." Hmm, a hangover probably isn't the best analogy to use with two nuns. Although…

"I'll take her up and get her settled," Sister Mary Katherine says.

"Are you sure? I can stay and help."

"We're fine," Sister Dolores says. "You've been an angel. Go now and spend time with that hot boyfriend of yours and let me rest." They both smile.

"Incorrigible," I say again. "Both of you."

A flock of nuns suddenly swarms us. I recognize

Sister Genevieve, and Sisters Lucy Anne, Margaret Mary, and Agnes Stephen, who coached athletics, her signature red high-tops with her nunnery attire a sight to be seen. Several others are strangers and must have arrived after I graduated.

"Sister!" they collectively exclaim.

"Thank the Lord you are okay," Sister Genevieve says." She turns to me. "Andrea, is that you?"

"Yes, Sister, it's good to see you again. I'll be back to check on you in a few days," I tell Sister Dolores. "Get some rest."

Chapter Thirty-Four

It's nearly ten, and Drew is slumbering beside me. The brilliant sunshine warms the covers, and I slide my hand across his firm chest. He smiles, eyes still closed. "Mmm," he mumbles. "Sleeping in with you is becoming a habit." He turns on his side and presses his erection against my belly. "Good morning, luv."

"Morning."

"Three whole days off."

"I know. What are we going to do?"

"More of this," he says, sliding a hand between my legs.

The sex is luxurious, slow, and easy, then forceful, passionate, my climax an uninhibited release of control, of self-consciousness, of everything. Like a tangled bunch of twinkly lights inside you that blows a fuse. Drew's mantra is the woman always comes first, and he never fails to deliver, his climax never far behind. The antithesis of making love to Greg. Half the time I don't even think he knew I hadn't climaxed. I close my eyes and try to forget. All of it... *Stay in the moment, this moment, with a man who loves you deeply and always, always, puts you first.*

He lies atop me, his lips near my ear. "Am I crushing you?" he whispers.

"No, I like to feel your weight on me, it anchors me to Earth."

His head pops up and he kisses me. The dessert to our lovemaking.

"I'm thinking we could visit my parents today. Stay over and come back tomorrow. We'd still have time to do some touristy things. What do you think?"

"Sounds great."

"Good, it's a little under three hours by train. There's one leaving at two this afternoon. We can be there in time for dinner."

"Train? Sounds romantic. I love traveling by train."

"Then I'll call my mother and let her know."

I head to the bathroom to shower and hear Drew on the phone.

"Hi, Mum. Yeah, we should be there around five, for dinner. And don't make a big deal and invite the entire family. I don't want to overwhelm her." A pause, then, "Great, I'll call when we get off the train."

We dress and pack a few things, then sit on the deck and indulge in the perfect continental breakfast. I could get used to this.

"My dad will pick us up at the train station. It's only a twenty-minute drive to the house."

****

John deposits us at the train depot at one-thirty. We buy our tickets and board the well-appointed car. A far cry from the trains in L.A. and New York.

I scan the vista of farms and country cottages, cows milling around, goats trying to play with them, but they munch grass and ignore them. My eyes grow heavy, and I lean my head on Drew's shoulder.

"Hey, luv, wake up, we're here."

I open my eyes as the station comes into view. I stretch my arms above my head and yawn. "Sorry, I guess I dozed off."

"From what you told me about your work schedule, I think it might take the entire summer for you to catch up on some much-needed sleep."

"You might be right."

Drew grabs the bags from the overhead compartment, and I follow him down the three steps to the platform.

Drew must have called from the train, because a man, an older version of Drew, rushes toward us. He has a full head of salt-and-pepper hair, a wide smile with perfect white teeth, and the same deep blue eyes.

"Andrew!" he says, and surrounds him in a giant hug, patting his back affectionately. He pulls back, still holding Drew by his arms. "So good to see you, son."

"Hi, Dad. It's been too long."

He turns to me. "Dad, this is Rea Tasson. Rea, this is my dad, Tom."

I extend my hand. "So nice to meet you." But he wraps me in his arms and hugs me tight, then releases me.

"Wonderful to meet you. We're so glad you guys could visit." He takes the duffels from Drew's hands, turns, and we follow.

The red Saab travels the winding country road, I in the backseat and Drew alongside his dad. They talk about this aunt or that uncle, this cousin and that, and I realize Drew has a large extended family, something I've only witnessed in movies, books, or TV. I'm suddenly wary. I've never considered myself to be nervous around a crowd, but this is different. People will be measuring me, wondering if I'm worthy of being with Drew.

We turn into a long driveway lined with silver

birches. Off in the distance sits a beautiful three-storied stone structure with two brick chimneys and a wide front porch. To the left and right are rows and rows of grapevines, staked and netted to ward off predators.

"Geez, Dad," Drew says, "I told you not to invite the whole goddamned family."

I peer out the windshield where ten to fifteen people crowd the space between two white pillars. Oh, God.

"Well, all your grandparents live on the property, so there was no getting out of that. And three of your aunts live down the street. No way to avoid them either. And you are famous, in case you forgot. We had all to do to keep the entire town from showing up."

Drew looks over his shoulder. "Sorry, luv, I hoped to keep this small and intimate."

"No worries," I lie. "It's fine."

Tom parks the car and everyone waves, but only one person steps off the porch. A petite woman with curly, cinnamon-colored hair tied up in a yellow grosgrain ribbon, clad in a flowered peasant dress and black ballerina flats walks toward us. Drew opens the door and I step out.

"Andrew! I missed you terribly."

He wraps his arms around her small frame and kisses the top of her head. "Missed you too, Mum, it's been too long."

She gazes adoringly at him, placing her hand on the side of his face. "You look good. Happy. It does a mother good to see you like this."

Before he can introduce me, she turns. "Rea, I can't tell you how happy I am to meet you." She hugs and releases me, her smile warm and welcoming, her skin smooth and creamy white, a touch of pink frosting her cheeks.

"Hello, Mrs. Foster. Nice to meet you."

"Please, Eleanor. Come."

She takes my hand and leads me toward the house, and the onslaught ensues. I've memorized tomes of scientific names, but there's no chance I will remember this litany of monikers. His mother makes the introductions while Drew is swamped by the swarm of adoring cousins, mostly female, and obviously fans of his work. I hoped I'd meet his two sisters, but they're both away at college. We sip homemade lemonade and make small talk until finally the crowd disperses. Only Drew's grandparents and parents remain.

"Come on," Drew says, "I'll show you our room. We can freshen up."

"We can sleep in the same room?"

"Of course. It's 1998, and my parents are very evolved."

He secures my hand in his as we trod the banister-lined staircase to the second floor. I stop midway, focused on the family picture gallery on the wall. In one photo, a young Drew has his arms around two smaller girls in matching white dresses. "Are your sisters twins?"

"Yup. They're five years younger."

"Identical or fraternal?"

"Fraternal, but they loved to dress the same."

I scan the collection of photographs, a life on display. Happy faces, silly faces, the faces of joy. A family.

"Come on," he says, tugging me forward.

The room's décor is reminiscent of an old English manor, pale green and cream striped wallpaper, a four-poster bed with canopy and tufted cushions on a white eyelet comforter. A love seat sits at the foot of the bed, upholstered in a dusty green floral print adorned with pink accent pillows. A cream-colored coffee table atop a floral print rug, and two green plaid armchairs complete the sitting area, and watercolor prints of country wildflowers line the walls.

"This is lovely," I say. "So homey."

Drew smiles. "Well, you wouldn't want to stay in my old room. The sports paraphernalia alone would overwhelm you."

"Oh, you're an athlete?"

"I played football, what you guys call soccer, and I'm decent with a tennis racquet. I actually had a scholarship to university for football, but I decided to attend the London Academy for the Dramatic Arts. I did some local theater, then just before graduation, I got booked in America for a clothing campaign, then landed *New Horizons* off that."

By clothing, he meant an underwear billboard. "I remember that ad. It was everywhere."

"Okay, you got me. I was mortified, truly."

I smile. The girls in my dorm were drooling over him in that commercial. If they only knew I was here with him now. "You never told me much about your career, and I guess I never asked. Sorry about that."

"Well, I never asked you about yours either." He drops down on the bed, kicks off his shoes, lies back, and cradles his head in his hands.

I sit beside him on the edge of the bed. "Funny that you ask. I just had this conversation with Sister Dolores's doctor. We had coffee."

"Oh?" Drew says. "You had coffee with what I assume is some handsome French doctor? Do I need to worry?"

Chapter Thirty-Five

I smile and slap his chest. "He's married and no, you're stuck with me."

"Good. Stuck works. So, what was this conversation?"

"Well, I always thought I pursued medicine because the sisters took me on their pilgrimages to soup kitchens, homeless shelters, and even a prison, to minister to those in need. But he disagreed. Jean Paul said statistically most people pursue medicine because someone close to them died. Thus, the subconscious need to save others. I hadn't thought about that, but it could certainly be true for me. Sister Mary Katherine, my biology teacher, was the one who made me understand people die from pathogens or accidents, and it has nothing to do with God, which I thought an odd revelation levied by a nun. People always told me my mother was too sick, and God took her to take care of her. It always infuriated me. Why couldn't the people who loved her on Earth take care of her?"

Drew takes my hand. "I think both could be true. Or you got the double whammy."

"It seems like that always happens to me. I don't get one kick in the teeth; I get two or three."

"Yeah, but it proves you're a survivor. And honestly, I don't think many people could have gone through what you have and come out on the other side as a functional human being."

I slide my sandals off and snuggle next to him on the soft duvet. I lay my head on his shoulder. "Did you always want to be an actor?"

"I wanted to play professional football for Chelsea, our home team. But I got injured a couple times and decided maybe something tamer would be more to my liking. I'm not exactly a huge guy, so taking a hit hurts."

Drew was a sizable man in my opinion, but I guess in the field of professional sports, that might not be the case.

"My sisters and I always put on little plays for the family, and we got rave reviews. Once we made a pact to talk in an American accent for the entire summer. We got really good at it, but it annoyed the hell out of the family."

"I could see that."

"I got cast in the lead for the school play my second year in high school, and I shamelessly admit I loved the applause. I was a reasonably popular kid as a footballer, but the acting made the girls chase after me. It was heady, and my ego loved it."

"What about your sisters? Do they have the acting bug?"

"Not a chance. They have more admirable pursuits. Mary is a journalism major, and Lizzy is studying environmental biology. Both want to change the world for the better."

"You're lucky. You have the perfect family, a perfect life."

"I've had my bumps."

"Oh? Do tell." I sit up and face him.

Drew sighs, gazing at the ceiling. "When I was

seventeen, my girlfriend, Addie, drowned."

"Oh, God, no, how awful."

"She was on vacation in the Caribbean with her parents. She was an only child. She went out for a swim early one morning and never came back. She was an expert swimmer, so no one can understand what happened. Her body washed up on the shore about ten miles down the beach. They ruled it as natural causes, but not knowing what happened is still torturous to think about."

I take his hand and kiss it. "I'm so sorry."

"I haven't had a serious girlfriend since." He smiles at me. "Until you." He squeezes my hand. "In some ways, I think it's subconscious. When you get hurt like that, your brain makes you avoid getting you in a situation where you can get hurt again."

Huh, I think. Pretty much my M.O. Even with Greg, I didn't allow vulnerability into the relationship. "I agree. Vulnerability isn't my strength, but I understand now, if you don't reveal your emotions and weakness, you can't have a healthy relationship. It allows for deeper understanding and evokes empathy you need for a relationship to go the distance."

"Well, listen to how much you've evolved, Dr. Tasson," Drew says.

"Yeah, I'm scaring myself." I change the subject. "It must have been great having siblings. I wish I'd been so lucky."

"Well, in the early days, it was annoying. I desperately wanted a brother, and they loved to make me the king in our childhood role-playing games. They would dress me up in a cape and a crown made from foil." He laughs. "Maybe that's where the acting bug

208

started."

Drew turns on his side and faces me, his arm draped over my hip. "You wished you had siblings, does that translate into having kids of your own?"

Oh, God. No. I bite my lip so as not to say it out loud. I'm sure Drew wants kids. Most people do.

"It's okay. You can tell me the truth." He pushes an errant strand of hair off my forehead and caresses my cheek.

"I don't think so. I have no idea how to be a mother. I'm sure I would be terrible at it."

"I disagree. Your job is literally taking care of people. I think you've got the skill set."

"I'm not sure I have the emotional skill set."

"Well, then we'll just have to work on that." He drags his thumb over my lips, parting them, then leans in for a kiss. My insides flame, like they always do when he touches me. I don't think I could ever get enough of this man.

****

His mom makes balti curry for dinner, chicken with spices—mustard, garam masala, cumin, garlic cloves, and turmeric, served over rice. It's traditionally made with goat or lamb, but she's adapted it to a wider audience. She explains the difference from a traditional curry. The last ten minutes you cook it at high heat in a flat-bottomed wok, or balti dish, thus its name. It's aromatic and delicious.

We sit outside in the lush garden, under a flowered trellis with twinkly lights, around a table which easily seats twelve. All four of Drew's grandparents have joined us, and his grandfather, Albert, pours a cabernet from the family vineyard.

"I've made my famous blackberry cobbler for dessert," announces Grandmother Foster.

I study the four elders, smile lines creasing their faces, and I try to imagine the years of joy in belonging to such an amazing family. The conversation is lively and sometimes downright hysterical. The British sense of humor vacillating between sardonic and witty, to raucous disregard for convention. Simultaneously sarcastic, scatological, and intellectual.

I'm seated across from Eleanor. She's rubbing her temples, her eyes closed. "Everything okay?" I ask her.

Her eyes open and she stares at me. "This awful headache came out of nowhere. I'm not much for headaches."

I notice one eye is a little bloodshot, and my diagnostic skills kick in. "Are you feeling any numbness, dizziness, or confusion?"

"No, I'm sure I'm just tired. I've been working in the garden nonstop. I tend to forget I'm an old woman." She smiles and rises. "Let's get these dishes cleared, so we can have Grandma Foster's famous blackberry cobbler."

Drew and his father insist on helping his mom in the kitchen, and the threesome cart the dishes into the house. Drew returns with two bottles of champagne as Grandma Foster rises. "I'll get the dessert." She turns to her husband. "You brought the whipped cream, right?"

He frowns. "Of course, dear."

The sound of breaking dishes startles us. Drew flees inside as we hold our collective breath. "Rea," he shouts. "Come quick!"

I run inside to see his mother lying on the terracotta tiled floor. His father kneels on one side, Drew on the other. His father is slapping her cheek. "Wake up, Ellie, wake up!"

"What happened?" I ask.

"I don't know," Tom says, "she was standing at the sink when she suddenly leaned to one side. She gripped the counter to right herself, and I ran to grab her, but she collapsed before I could get to her."

I kneel beside Drew and place two fingers on her carotid artery, her pulse strong. She's not unconscious, and she's breathing, but her face is contorted, one side of her mouth droopy, one eye half closed. She tries to speak, but it's garbled. "She's having a stroke." I grab her hand. "It's okay, Eleanor, I've got you. We're going to get you help."

"Oh, God," Drew exclaims.

"We need to get her to a hospital right away. How far is it?"

"Only about ten minutes," his father says.

"Good, because there's a new drug that is effective at reversing the effects of a stroke if administered in the first hour."

"My sister is a nurse and the head of the emergency room there. I could call her. Maybe she's on shift," Tom says.

"Excellent, and we should alert the EMTs. They can give advance notice to the ER."

Drew calls 999, their version of our 911, and explains the emergency to the operator.

Tom is on the phone with his sister. "It's Ellie. She's had a stroke, and we've called emergency services. Drew's girlfriend is here, and she's a doctor and tells us there's a drug that if administered in the first hour can reverse the symptoms." A pause. "Okay, great, we'll be there soon."

The flashing lights and sirens tell us help has arrived.

"Maggie is on shift, and they have the drug. I think she said it's called tPA."

"That's it. Good."

The EMTs secure Eleanor on the gurney as I give them my report. "Do you want to ride with us?" the female says.

I look at Drew and his father. "Would either of you rather—"

Drew cuts me off. "No, you go. We'll be right behind you."

"Okay, then, let's go," I tell the EMT.

I hold Eleanor's hand, reassuring her that she's going to be okay. A tear escapes, and I wipe it away. She tries to speak, but I shush her. "Try to stay calm. Deep breaths, in and out." I breathe along with her, and her pulse slows.

We arrive at the hospital in nine minutes. I give the attending doctor my assessment, and he orders imaging to determine if it's an ischemic or hemorrhagic stroke. The majority of strokes are ischemic, caused by a blocked blood vessel in the brain that cuts off oxygen supply, resulting in a neurological deficit. The tPA dissolves the clot, and if not too many brain cells have been killed, the patient can return to normal.

Dr. Simpson invites me to the imaging center, and we wait for the scan to post. We both sigh. Thankfully, it's an ischemic event. "We'll administer tPA immediately," he says.

I return to the waiting room, and Drew and his father rush toward me. "Good news. It was an ischemic stroke, essentially a blood clot in the brain. The tPA will dissolve it and she should be fine."

His father surrounds me in a tight hug. "Thank God you were here," he says.

He pulls back, his eyes brimming with tears.

"Glad to help," I say.

Drew puts his arm around me and kisses the side of my face. "You're an angel."

I'm pretty sure I blushed.

Chapter Thirty-Six

We leave about two hours later, assured Eleanor is nearly recovered and finally asleep. Tom decides to spend the night, and Drew and I head back to his house.

We assure his grandparents that Eleanor will recover, and I'm subjected to an onslaught of hugs and a flood of tears and praise. He'd called his sisters from the hospital and alerted them to his mom's condition and updated them after getting the good news.

"They both have major papers due on Monday but offered to come home immediately," Drew says, "but I told them we were here and she would be fine and they could come next weekend."

Exhausted, Drew and I fall into bed.

"Explain to me how someone gets a stroke."

I snuggle into his side. "The most common factors are high blood pressure, high cholesterol, smoking, obesity, and diabetes. Does your mother have any of those? She's not overweight and I doubt she smokes."

"I honestly don't know. It's not like I'm up to date on her health."

"Well, she's lucky it was ischemic because a blood clot can be treated without surgery. Two million brain cells die for every minute of stroke, so every sixty seconds increases a patient's chance of suffering permanent damage."

"That's why we had to get her the drug so fast."

"Exactly. There's also a hemorrhagic stroke, where a blood vessel ruptures. It's more difficult to treat, usually it requires surgery, but it has to be done quickly to avoid permanent damage."

"Is that the same as an aneurysm?"

"Not exactly, but a burst aneurysm can cause a hemorrhagic stroke."

"Jesus. Now *my* head hurts."

I sit up and place my fingers on his temples and trace tiny soothing circles. "There, there, sweetie."

But he's not done. "Are strokes hereditary? Because if they are, I want you always carrying that drug around with you."

I smile. "Not necessarily, it's more a history of disease, like high blood pressure and cholesterol. Those tend to run in families."

"Well, honestly, now I'm scared shitless. How do you do this kind of stuff all day? The stress alone would give me a stroke."

I drop my hands into my lap. "Thus, my switch to psychiatry. You're right, the schedule for a trauma surgeon is highly unpredictable, demanding, and stressful, which can make maintaining a healthy work-life balance difficult. I hadn't thought about it much because I had no life anyway. And Greg and I were in it together and didn't give much attention to our life outside of the hospital. But I did my research before deciding to switch my residency. Being a trauma surgeon is both physically and emotionally exhausting, and many patients arrive in your trauma bay that you can't save. They have the highest burnout rates and are at risk for developing psychological trauma and PTSD during their career."

"Jesus. I'm glad you decided to give that up."

"Me too."

Drew falls asleep, but I'm still awake. The near death of his mother haunts me. I couldn't bear to watch him go through such a tragedy. He's asleep on his side, facing me, puffs of air crossing his lips. He turns onto his back, and I sling my arm across his chest. "I love you," I whisper. But it falls on deaf ears.

Eventually, I drift into dreamland.

I'm in my dorm room at school, the summer after graduation, about to return to the States. It's a sultry August night, and I decide to skip the planned evening at the homeless shelter in lieu of packing for my upcoming departure.

A shiver runs down my spine. A chill on such a warm night?

"I'm sorry I left you."

I turn to face a beautiful woman, dark auburn hair and large brown eyes with long black lashes. My eyes. Her petite frame is clad in a flowing white gossamer gown. She stands in front of the full-length mirror, and I search for wings, but strangely, no reflection is evident at all.

"I shouldn't have left you alone with your father. I was selfish, angry, and I never considered how horrible it would be for you. My beautiful daughter."

"Mom?"

"I loved you very much. I need you to know that. I was so overcome with sadness, I couldn't see a way out, and I made a terrible choice. I don't expect you to forgive me. I can't forgive myself, but I need you to move on. To let all this anger and sadness go. Open your heart. You deserve to be loved, and it's right in front of you.

I'm sorry your father didn't do right by you. He is a good man, but he can't find his way out of his grief. Try to forgive him."

My heart is racing, my pulse throbbing. The urge to run seizes me, but my feet are frozen in place. Tears erupt, and sobs rack my chest. My mother grabs me and shakes me...

"Hey," he says, "you were dreaming." He turns on the bedside lamp. "You're crying? What's wrong?"

I slowly sit up, resting my head against the tufted headboard. "I dreamt about my mother. She was here and spoke to me."

Drew remains silent as he wipes the tears off my cheeks with his thumbs.

"Well, not here, I was back in my dorm room, at boarding school."

"Okay. What did she say to you?"

"It's a dream. It doesn't mean anything."

"Humor me. What did she say?"

"She asked me to forgive her and to leave behind the sadness and anger I've been carrying around. That I deserve to be loved and I should open my heart and let someone in."

"Good advice."

"It's a dream!"

"It's said people from the other side can talk to you in your dreams."

"You believe in ghosts?"

"I don't *not* believe in ghosts."

"You're kidding?"

"Or it could be your subconscious giving you good advice."

"So now you're a dream therapist?" I throw back the

covers and run to the bathroom and slam the door. The gloomy woman in the mirror is familiar. I must be losing my mind. Again. Ghosts? He seriously went there.

A soft rap on the door. "Luv, let me in."

"I need a minute."

Chapter Thirty-Seven

The handle turns and Drew is standing behind me. His arms encircle me in a warm embrace. His chin rests on my shoulder.

"I think I understand," he says.

"Understand what?"

He turns me to face him, his hands around my waist. "Nearly losing my mother is the worst thing that ever happened to me, other than losing Addie. I can't imagine my world without her, so for the first time I felt a little of what you must have gone through."

"I don't know…losing someone you've loved, someone who's loved you, isn't the same as losing someone you never met. Kind of like abortion."

His eyes narrow. "I don't get what you mean."

"I've often thought a child born into poverty, abuse, a terrible life, is way worse than never being born at all."

"Noteworthy analogy. Maybe you're right."

I extricate myself from his embrace and sit on the closed commode, my head in my hands. "Why can't I get past all this? It's all in the past. The dream is right. I need to let it all go."

Drew squats in front of me and takes my hands in his. "I think life can only be *understood* backwards, but it must be *lived* forward. You understand what happened. Your mom suffered from postpartum depression and couldn't find a way out. Your father has enormous guilt over not seeing how much pain she was in and not being able to save her. He never meant to hurt you by sending you away."

"You're right. I need to stop letting my past determine my future."

"In my experience, the things we worry about are almost never the things that actually go wrong, and the things that do go wrong, you couldn't have dreamt up." He pulls me to my feet and hugs me, then plants a chaste kiss on my lips. "Come on, let's get a shower. We've got things to do, and then we need to head back to Paris. I need to be on set tomorrow."

Drew's expertise at shower sex never ceases to amaze, and I exit the steamy cubicle anxiety-free, rejuvenated, and ready to face the day.

****

We arrive at the hospital an hour later. His mom looks great, his dad, not so much. We hand over fresh clothing and wait outside while she changes. The doctor appears and gives us our marching orders. "I've signed the discharge papers, and from what we can tell so far, it seems your stroke was cryptogenic, which means without a known cause. I'll see you in two weeks at my office and we'll do some follow-up testing."

"What are the chances of it happening again?" Eleanor asks.

"Statistically, one in four patients has another event. But we're going to keep a close eye on things until we figure it out."

Tom takes his wife's hand and gives a squeeze. "It's going to be okay. We dodged a bullet, and we'll be prepared in the future."

"My office number is on your discharge papers. Call

and make an appointment for two weeks from now."

We pile into the car and arrive home to waiting grandparents. Hugs and kisses abound, along with lots of "Thank God Rea was here." Glasses of lemonade are passed around, and eventually the mood calms.

"Rea," Eleanor says. "I need to speak with you." She comes toward me, and I stand. "Alone."

She takes my hand and tows me through the sitting room and up the stairs. We enter a room with pastel blue striped wallpaper and another four-poster bed with a navy-blue duvet. She lifts the cover of the wooden jewelry box on the double-wide dresser and plucks a silver trinket from the velvet tray.

"I want to give this to you. As a thank you for saving my life." She steps closer and opens the fastener. The filigreed heart dangles in front of my neck.

"Eleanor, this isn't necessary. And I didn't save your life; the drug did."

"Not in my book. We would never have acted so quickly if you hadn't been here."

"But I'm sure this is a family heirloom, and, well, I'm not family."

"You are to me. I love you and regardless of what happens with you and my son, you will always be family to me."

I find these words incredulous. How could this woman love me? She's only known me a day.

She ignores my words and secures the chain around my neck, then turns me toward the mirror. "It was a gift from my mother."

I want to protest. She has two daughters. Shouldn't it go to them? But then again, they're twins, so choosing would be impossible. "Thank you. It's beautiful."

"I know you have to leave, but promise you'll come back soon. With or without Drew."

"I will," I promise.

Drew and I depart on the two p.m. train, and I settle into my seat, dropping my head on his shoulder. "I see my mum gave you her locket," he says.

"I tried to say no, but she wouldn't have it." I sit up and face him. "She said she loved me."

Drew smiles. "Of course, who wouldn't love you? You're amazing, and beautiful, I might add. Not to mention generous. Jillian told me you paid for her tuition her last year in medical school. After her mother spent her tuition money."

Damn Jillian. I swore her to secrecy. Why would she tell Drew? "She wasn't supposed to tell anyone."

Heat rises in my cheeks. This is all too much. I'm not looking for attention, or…? I don't know what. All these years I told myself my mother never loved me, and my father never loved me. No one loved me, and now this almost-stranger says she does. I'm suddenly exhausted. The train departs the station, and the clickety-clack of the wheels on the rails lulls me to sleep.

Back at the resort, we unpack and order room service and sit on the back deck to await our sustenance.

"When do you have to be back on set?"

"Tomorrow, noon."

"At least we can sleep in."

"About that, I wondered if you'd like to come back with me. You could meet everyone and crash in my trailer for the night, then return to the hotel the next day."

"Seriously?"

"Yeah, I think it would be cool for you to see what I'm up to."

"I'd like that."

The waiter arrives, setting out *salade Niçoise*, shrimp skewers, and a warm baguette. He pours two glasses of cabernet, then vanishes quietly.

"I'm going to miss this bread," Drew says.

Chapter Thirty-Eight

We arrive on set a little before noon to Drew's waiting assistant. "Anything happen while I was gone?" Drew asks.

"A few minor rewrites and we need to reshoot the scene in the café, but otherwise we're still on schedule, and Sandy is very happy," Lisa says. "Hey, Rea, good to see you again."

"Hi, Lisa. Thanks. You too."

"How's your mom?" Lisa says to Drew. "We heard what happened."

"How?"

"It was on the local news. Someone at the hospital saw you and squawked."

Drew shakes his head and sighs but refrains from comment. I'm beginning to understand his life. He can't go anywhere without somebody reporting on his whereabouts and offering an opinion most of the time too—how he's dressed, what he's eating or drinking. It must be exhausting.

"She's fine thanks to Rea. Saved her life."

"I guess having an M.D. for a girlfriend doesn't suck," Lisa says.

I'm tired of receiving all the credit, but I decide to let it go, realizing the futility of continued excuses.

We follow Lisa onto the sound stage, and Drew introduces me to some of the crew. He settles me onto a director's chair with his name printed on the back, and Lisa offers me iced tea. "Do you want something to eat?" she asks.

"No, thanks. We had a big breakfast."

I'm face to face with Gwen Davis. "Hey," she says. "You must be Rea. Drew talks about you all the time."

I'm caught off guard by her dazzling beauty. The same blue eyes as Drew, her petite, trim frame clad in a tight white cami and slim-fit faded jeans. Her long blonde hair cascades over her shoulders nearly to her waist, her perky and vivacious persona overwhelming. My mind flashes to Drew being in bed with this stunning woman, and my stomach knots. Stop it, I admonish myself. Get your mind out of the gutter.

"So nice to meet you," I mumble. "Are you guys having fun on set?" Okay, where did that come from, and why would I say something so stupid? Yeah, must be my subconscious talking, and it better shut up.

"This project is a blast, and we're in Paris, so what's not to like?" she says.

A crew member barks out some lighting instructions, and another calls Gwen's name. "Gotta run," she says. "See you later. We should all have a drink."

Drew settles into the chair beside me and peruses some pages he pulls from his back pocket.

"Rea," I hear again and look up to see Oscar-winning megastar Megan Street. She extends her hand. "I'm so excited to finally meet you."

Finally meet me? Why would she say that?

"Drew misses you terribly. So glad he brought you to set for a visit."

"It's a thrill to meet you. I love your work."

"Thank you, so kind of you to say that."

She talks with Drew about an upcoming scene until Drew is called away. "Be back in a few," he says. "Megan, make sure she stays out of trouble." He winks.

Megan takes Drew's seat. "You know, I knew your mother," she blurts.

All the breath whooshes out of me. What? In all these years I never met anyone who knew my mother. Anything I heard was secondhand, gossip, sensational tabloid stories.

"She and I met doing summer stock on Long Island. A quaint little theater called the Gateway Playhouse. We had a blast. We roomed together that summer."

I should say something, but nothing meaningful comes to mind.

She continues. "We got some bit parts in a few off-Broadway productions, but then we decided to move to L.A. together for pilot season. We lived in a crappy little apartment in the Park Wilshire. We went on a ton of auditions together, often for the same part. She usually beat me out. She finally booked a pilot, but it never made it to network."

"Megan, I've never met anyone who knew my mother, nor anyone who could tell me what she was like. This means the world to me."

"Well, she was the life of the party. When she entered a room, all heads would turn. She'd gotten cast as the lead in a new Scorsese movie, and her career was about to take off. She met your father at a party at his house."

And then it hits me, like a sledgehammer to the head. "Did my mother ever make that movie?"

"No, why?"

"Was she pregnant with me?"

Megan frowns and looks away, as if trying to remember. "Ah, no, I think there were some studio issues and the movie never got made. Happens all the time."

And there it is. I'm sure she's lying, although she's probably trying to spare my feelings. I always knew I'd caused my mother's death but could never back it up with fact. My mother got pregnant, and losing that role sent her over the edge. It was my fault.

There's no reason to take this out on Megan, so, like always, I bury the anger and move on. "My father was already directing by then?"

"Yes, he'd had his first blockbuster, and everyone wanted to work with him. Winning an Oscar attracts actors like flies to sugar."

"Did they ever work together?"

"No way. They agreed that would be a bad idea." She pauses. "Your mom was kind and caring, a bighearted soul."

"That's so nice to hear. Most of what I know is second or third hand. Tabloid stuff. And my father never talks about her, even to this day."

Her gaze focuses on the floor. "When your mom died, I was filming in Italy. I didn't make it back for the funeral. I've always regretted it." She looks up and takes my hand. "I was devastated. Although we hadn't seen each other in recent months, I still felt a tremendous amount of guilt that I wasn't there for her."

"I appreciate that. I think she really needed a friend, and it seems my dad was too busy working to see she was in trouble."

"I know. I did meet up with him when I got back from Italy. He was a total mess. I told him these kinds of things often go unnoticed by those closest to someone, but he said he could never forgive himself." She smiles. "I did meet you that day. You were the most beautiful baby."

My stomach churns at the revelation of these recollections.

"I know your father had difficulty giving you the attention you needed, but the nanny adored you, so I hoped you were happy. When I heard he planned on shipping you off to boarding school, I called him. I told him he'd regret it, but he was dead set on it. Said you were smart as a whip and needed proper schooling. He didn't think schooling in L.A. would meet your needs. Plus, he was convinced he couldn't give you what you needed because his projects took him away for extended periods of time. He said you'd be better off without him."

Drew returns, script still in hand. "Megan knew my mother," I say.

His eyebrows arch. "I had no idea."

"I've never met anyone who knew her up close and personal. Megan has been wonderful, telling me they were close friends and giving me insight into who she was."

"That's amazing," he says.

"It truly is," I say.

Someone calls Megan's name, and off she goes, promising we'll catch up later.

I watch Drew do a scene with Megan, Sandy directing from behind the camera lens. They're in her fancy apartment, where she offers to sponsor him in an upcoming art show. As I know this film by heart, I realize this is the scene after the lonely heiress notices him displaying his work on the streets of Montmartre, where she buys two paintings and brings him back to her swank apartment to pay him. While there, Drew's character accepts her invitation to a fancy dinner party.

There's a scene change, and Drew's wardrobe is now a tuxedo. They continue in the apartment where he returns dressed to the nines and realizes he's the only guest at the dinner party. Offended, he tells her he's not interested in being a paid escort, but she insists her only intention is to support his career. It's fun watching Drew act his part, and I realize he's good at this. Really good. His indignation at thinking he's being used as an escort by the lovely heiress is convincing and at the same time hysterical. I cover my mouth so as not to disrupt the scene with my giggles.

The crew and actors break for dinner, and I find myself around a table with Gwen, Megan, Lisa, Sandy, and Drew. I can see how actors on a film set become fast friends, almost family, and I guess, sometimes a lot more. Thankfully, I don't have to watch any intimate scenes between Drew and Gwen. Not sure I would have found those quite as entertaining.

"Hey!" someone shouts. "We need a doctor!"

Everyone looks my way. "Don't you have someone on set?" I ask.

"Somewhere," Megan says. "But you're right here."

Drew grabs my hand and pulls me upright. We come upon a man prone on the floor of Milo's swanky apartment. A man is on his knees beside him. "What happened?" I inquire.

"I don't know. We were moving some lights when I heard a groan. He clutched his chest and keeled over."

I kneel beside him and place two fingers on his carotid. No pulse. His lips are blue. "What's his name?"

I ask.

"Hank," a voice above me says.

"Hank," I yell. "Can you hear me?" I dig two knuckles into his chest and vigorously slide them back and forth. No response. "He's having a heart attack," I announce. "Someone call an ambulance. Do you have an AED?"

Chapter Thirty-Nine

"Yeah," a male voice says. "I'll get it."

I start compressions, counting to the beat of "Staying Alive," like they taught us in medical school.

The machine arrives and I stop compressions, instructing Drew to take over, making him hum the well-known ditty. I turn the device on by pressing the green button, peel off the sticky pads, pull up his shirt, and attach the leads to each side of his chest. "Clear," I say, and Drew stops compressions and everyone moves back. I hit the red button and check for a pulse. Nothing. "Again," I say, and hit the button a second time.

Come on, buddy. Don't die on me.

My fingers press against his carotid. I hold my breath. A pulse. Thank God. "We have a heartbeat," I announce. People applaud. I smile. We don't get this adulation in the ER.

Hank moans but doesn't open his eyes. I rest my hand on his chest, counting the beats. Sirens sound in the background.

He's loaded onto the gurney, stable for now. Sandy takes my hand in both of hers. "Thank you so much. I'm so glad you were here."

A pall hangs over the cast and crew, people whisper in small groups, then start to wander off.

"We've got an early call time," Gwen says. "I think I'll turn in. Night, Rea. I'm so glad we met. And nice work, by the way."

"Thanks," I say.

Megan is next. "Hope to see you again soon. Don't be a stranger."

"I can't tell you how much I will treasure your stories about my mom. It means a lot to me."

"Of course. We'll catch up again soon. I promise." She embraces me in a warm hug, what I imagine a motherly hug would feel like, then excuses herself for the night.

"Shall we head back to my trailer?" Drew says.

I place a hand on his chest. "I think I need to go home. I mean back to the resort. I'm…I don't know, feeling a little overwhelmed."

"Well, you did save two lives in twenty-four hours. Two for two, two days in a row. Pretty impressive, if you ask me."

I frown, placing my other hand alongside the first and lean in. "Hmm…maybe it's you. Bodies keep dropping around you."

Drew feigns shock, his chin drops, his eyes widen. "I beg your pardon."

I laugh. "Honestly, that's a normal Monday morning at work, so that's not overwhelming. First, your mom gives me the locket and says she loves me, then meeting Megan and hearing all about my mom…I'm feeling…emotionally overwhelmed."

He wraps his hands around my waist. "I think that's a good thing. I would sit with those feelings for a while."

"I agree. And I'm thinking of sitting with them in a tub of bubbles."

"Now I've created a monster. A bubble monster." He smiles.

"Sounds like a children's book."

"It does. Maybe when I'm old and gray and my career is in the toilet, I'll write that book."

I smile. "You do that." I sigh. "But seriously, I'm trying so hard to understand my father, and Megan gave me some good insights." I break from his embrace and sink into a chair, and Drew sits beside me. "I never got to be a kid. I lived in a grown-up world until I got shipped off to boarding school. But I didn't make friends well. I was too introverted, shy. And I didn't speak the language, which was a huge barrier for a long time. Plus, I didn't know how to be a kid, to be silly, to break the rules, get into mischief. I played it safe, wouldn't even consider taking a risk."

"Well, I made enough mistakes for both of us." Drew takes both my hands and rubs his thumbs over the backs. "And I'm a firm believer in doing things that scare you. It's how you grow."

"Well, then I'm seriously stunted in my development."

"We'll have to work on that. Do you want to go skydiving?"

"What? Are you crazy? Is that something on your bucket list?"

Drew roars, throwing his head back in raucous laughter. "No way. I have absolutely no desire to jump out of a plane at fifty thousand feet."

I wipe my forehead, mocking relief. "Phew. You had me worried there for a minute."

"Besides, I think you already do pretty daring stuff. Your whole career is life and death, which is downright terrifying in my book. Besides, who we are as children doesn't necessarily define us as adults."

I drape my arms over his shoulders and lean in again. "I swear, you are the wisest man I've ever met. Are you sure you're only twenty-five and not sixty?"

"If so, I look pretty damn good for sixty." He winks.

I kiss him, long and hard. Maybe I should stay.

"Are you sure you want to go home and leave me here all alone in my under-sized bed?"

"That seals the deal. No way will I get any sleep under those circumstances."

"I planned on no sleep for an entirely different reason." He wags his eyebrows.

I slap his chest. "I better go. When will you make it back to the hotel again?"

"Hopefully, this weekend. It's Sandy's kid's birthday Saturday, and she's giving the crew the day off, so she can spend it with her family."

"Great. I want to spend some time with the sisters this week anyway."

"Come on, I'll walk you to the car. John is on call." He pulls his phone from his pocket and presses a button. John must be on speed dial. "Hey, where are you? Rea is heading back tonight. Okay, we'll head there now. Thanks." He returns the phone to his pocket. "He's out front."

Drew takes my hand, and we exit the studio lot. "Oh, by the way, did you know John's an aspiring actor?"

"I didn't. I thought he just worked livery for the studio."

"He mentioned he's been auditioning. He attended The Cours Florent here in Paris and graduated a few years back. He said he's done some local stuff, he has an agent, but is trying to break into the American scene."

"That's a great program. I'm impressed. I'll keep

him in mind. Maybe I can hook him up with someone."

"Great, but don't tell him I said anything. I wouldn't want him to think I was interfering."

"Luv, this whole business is based on who you know and who can make a connection for you. I'd be glad to help him any way I can. But don't worry. Mum's the word."

****

I arrive at the hotel near midnight and scan the bathroom for bubble bath. A classic wine bottle silhouette sits on the glass shelf above the bidet; its white and the gold label reads, LOLLIA *le bain moussan*. It could easily be mistaken for an expensive rosé. I read the description: *Tiny, luxurious bubbles chatter in this moisture-rich blend of Avocado & Olive Fruit Oils infused with notes of Lavender, Honey Blossom, White Orchids, and warm Indian Amber & Tahitian Vanilla. "Relax" – it's virtually impossible not to with this alluring fragrance.*

Sold. I run the water hot in the round soaking tub built for two, wishing Drew were here. Maybe I shouldn't have left. The bubbles extend several inches above the rim, and I turn off the water, dip a toe in, and sink into the luxurious, perfumed foam. In the corner sits a terry cloth pillow, and I arrange it behind my head. My second bubble bath and it's even more decadent than the first.

Wrapped in a towel, I take my cell phone from my backpack and grab the charger. The screen announces a missed call and voicemail...from Drew. I play the message. "Hey, luv, just checking to make sure you got home safely. I guess you're in the tub. I can't sleep. Call me back."

Naked, I slip into the silky sheets and hit one on the keypad. Even if he hadn't assigned that number for his speed dial, I would have. He's definitely my number one.

"Hey, luv," he says.

"Hey."

"How was your soak?"

"Delicious and decadent. You've spoiled me for life."

"That is my life's goal."

I laugh. "So why can't you sleep?"

"Why do you think? I'm missing my girl."

"Well, I won't lie, I'm having second thoughts about leaving. I wish you were here beside me."

"What are you wearing?"

I laugh again. "My birthday suit."

"Good, then you're ready."

"Ready for what?"

"Have you ever had phone sex?"

"What? No!"

"And another first for the sexy Dr. Tasson, who fulfills all my fantasies."

"I'm not sure I…"

"My voice commands will guide you and let your imagination run wild. Turn off the lights and slide down on the covers. Fancy that I'm there beside you. Close your eyes, open your mind and…your legs."

Oh, my. I obey.

Chapter Forty

I sleep like a baby. It's after nine and I call the desk and order breakfast. Wrapped in the pink silk robe Drew gifted me, I smile. I'm loath to admit I'm enjoying all the things money can buy way too much. Expensive lingerie, a magnificent hotel, private jets, and yet…I feel guilty. I've never been one to indulge in such luxury. I have enough money to buy anything I want, but I never do. I guess it's okay to enjoy a little extravagance now and again. As long as it doesn't go to my head. I *am* on vacation, but soon I'll be back to wearing scrubs with my hair slicked into a ponytail, sans makeup, lucky to get a shower every day. I suddenly wonder…does Drew want me to doll myself up more? Maybe I'm too plain for him, and he's trying to jazz me up. Costuming me? A makeover? Yikes. Is he trying to mold me into some sexy-actress persona?

Breakfast arrives, and I tell the waiter to set it up on the bedroom deck. He pours the coffee and removes the cover on scrambled eggs and bacon. "Thank you," I say.

"Avec plaisir, madame." And he leaves.

I call the convent to arrange my visit, then call John to confirm my itinerary.

I munch a ripe red strawberry and splash some cream in my coffee along with a spoonful of sugar and stir, then sip the aromatic brew. Coffee in Paris cannot be equaled. Drew will miss the bread, but I will miss the coffee.

My cell phone rings.

"Hey, luv. I slept great after our virtual liaison, how about you?"

I place the porcelain cup painted with blue irises on the saucer. "Same here. That was hot. Let's do more of it."

"You're on," he says.

"How's your workday today?" I pop a blueberry into my mouth.

"We're shooting the scene in the club where I first meet Gwen's character and she tries to blow me off."

"Cool."

"Oh, and guess what? I got John into the production. The actor playing the bartender in the club bailed, and I got him in. He's stoked."

"Wow, that was quick. That's wonderful."

"We're doing some reshoots now, and we don't film the club scene until tonight, so he's still available to drive you around today."

"I'm going to visit the sisters at the convent, so it will work out fine. Plus, I can always get a cab if necessary. I don't mind in the slightest."

"Great. Well, I gotta run, luv. Call you later."

"Bye."

"Bye, luv."

I finish breakfast, go for a brisk swim in the ocean, then head to the shower.

Dressed in an apricot-hued sundress and black patent leather sandals, I find John at the curb outside the lobby. He exits at the sight of me and holds the back door open. "Morning."

"Morning. Thank you," I say, sliding into the back

seat. He shuts my door and sits behind the wheel.

"Beautiful morning," he says.

"It is. The weather has been great, not a single rainy day yet."

"This is the high season in Paris, peak tourism because of the long days and sunny weather. And the humidity is moderate. It is the opposite of America. Here the humidity is highest in December and lowest in July."

"Are you doubling as a weatherman?" I ask. "An actor, a driver, and now a weatherman? You're quite the multi-talented man."

John laughs, his playful eyes meet mine in the mirror. "I have some news. I got a small role in a new film."

"That's amazing. Congratulations."

"I'm sure you had nothing to do with it," he says, then winks.

I smile. "Me?"

"I know you did."

"How could you know that?"

"Because you are a kind soul, and I'm convinced your mission in life is to help people."

"Well, I'm not confessing to anything. You wouldn't have been offered the part if you didn't deserve it."

"You're very kind, and I am thanking you nonetheless."

We arrive at the convent around noon, and I rap the door knocker three times.

Sister Mary Stephen greets me. "Andrea, so nice to see you again. I've heard all about your travails. You're a guilty pleasure around here." She opens the door wide. "Please come in."

"Guilty pleasure?" I say, a crease between my eyes.

"Well, you're dating a handsome, famous gentleman, and you're a physician. Smart and lucky in love, a very glamorous existence I would say. The stuff of dreams."

I frown. These nuns are freaking me out. I never imagined this kind of stuff crossed their minds. I figured they were all about their vows—poverty, obedience, and what's the other one? Oh yeah, *chastity*... Hmm...

"How is Sister Dolores feeling?"

"Well, we keep insisting she rest, but you know how she is. Spending too much time in the garden."

Sister Mary Katherine joins us. "Andrea, how are you?" She kisses my cheeks.

"Good, thank you. How is our patient?"

"Recalcitrant. As always."

I smile.

"Come. She's in the sunroom having tea."

I follow her into the morning room where the sun beams through the venetian blinds, casting stripes across the oriental rug. Sister Dolores is in her white cap, sans veil, wearing a simple gray caftan. "Andrea! So good to see you."

She pats the couch cushion beside her, and I sit. "I've brought you some reading material." I hand her a crime novel and a fantasy best seller. I know she loves a good thriller and she's a fan of magic. "Have you read these?"

"Not yet. I've been wanting to read this book. Our students are wild for it."

"I've been too busy to read much for leisure, but I'd like to read this too. I picked up a copy for myself."

"Good, we can do a book club," Sister Dolores says.

"So, how are you feeling?"

"Quite well. A little tired, and I start my radiation treatment tomorrow. Not looking forward to it, but I'm sure the Lord will shepherd me through it."

"I'm sure. It won't be too terrible. Mostly it causes swelling of the breast, some pain, and the skin will redden and can blister. It will feel tender and even itchy, and dry peel, or flake, as treatment continues. You can also get a sore throat and of course, extreme tiredness. I'm sure Dr. Lavigne will explain all of this. Call me if you have any questions or concerns or if you need anything at all." I place a hand on her knee, and she covers it with her own.

"You're a dear and a comfort to show up in my time of need."

"It's the least I can do."

"Tea?" Sister Mary Katherine says, teapot in hand.

"Yes, thank you."

We spend a few hours reminiscing and generally assessing the state of the world and the need for more compassion and understanding among its inhabitants.

I return a few more times, content on Sister Dolores's progress. She seems a tad wearier than when I arrived, but that's to be expected. And as the summer draws to a close, I know I'm going to miss her. Miss her like a mother.

Chapter Forty-One

"Are you sure you don't mind?" I ask.

"Not at all."

"He's got two daughters who I know are fans. He even hinted his wife might be a bit of a groupie."

"It's okay. If it wasn't for the fan public, I wouldn't have a career. I'm good."

The summer is ending, and I leave for home on Friday. Drew must remain for two more weeks, and I try to convince myself it's a good thing. I'll get a chance to start my new residency focused, able to commit to whatever work schedule is required before Drew returns.

I promised Jean Paul we would come for dinner and am barely getting it in under the wire.

We arrive at a brick, two story residence with large arched windows, peaked in a steep roof. A silver Peugeot is parked in front of the two-car garage. There's a courtyard entrance with a magnificent garden, precisely trimmed hedges and shrubs form symmetrical lines dotted with plants of simple color palettes—pink, yellow, with the occasional pop of purple. The abundance of lavender perfumes the air.

The door opens and Jean Paul steps out, his two daughters beside him. "*Bienvenue,* " he says, arms outstretched. "Welcome." He kisses both my cheeks.

"Drew, this is Jean Paul Lavigne."

"So nice to meet you," Jean Paul says. "These are

my daughters, Monique and Sophia."

Their smiles couldn't be any bigger. "Hello," they both say.

"So nice to meet you," Drew says.

He ushers us inside, and it feels like a breath of fresh air. The décor is modern, yet simple, beiges and browns, with the occasional gold or auburn accent. Monet-style artwork dots the walls, and the French doors leading to a rear garden are open.

A tall thin woman with black hair pulled into a tight bun enters from the left. "*Bienvenue,*" she says. "Welcome to our home."

"This is my wife, Julia," Jean Paul says.

After the predictable double kiss adorns our cheeks, she steps back and says, "We've been excited to meet you both."

Well, not really, I think. This is mostly about Drew. But I can't blame them. I'm kind of a fan girl myself.

We sit in the garden around a cream-colored metal table set with white china, crystal glasses and black and white gingham placemats and napkins. A vase of fresh flowers from their garden centers the table. Dinner is grilled salmon with roasted potatoes and green beans. Cheese and a baguette served after the main course and *crème brûlée* for dessert.

I learn Julia is a human rights attorney, and it's obvious Jean Paul is extremely proud of her work, citing numerous international cases that had great impact on the world. Sophia and Monique are animated and articulate, unafraid to interject their opinions on grownup topics.

We depart after Drew signs some memorabilia the girls have accumulated from his fan club and slip into the back of the car, John at the helm.

"I enjoyed that," Drew says. "I'm having a great time in Paris. And I have you to thank."

He kisses my cheek, his fingers laced through mine.

I ruminate on the lovely evening. This is what it's like to be part of a loving family like Drew's. To have a family meal with great food, great conversation, and great people. I sigh. I want that.

****

Drew isn't due home for another week when the film is scheduled to wrap.

Returned to work, on the first day of my new residency, I stand at the nurse's station reviewing notes on a recent admit to the ER. I've been called in for a psych evaluation.

"British heartthrob, Andrew Foster, who's filming the much-anticipated remake of *An American in Paris,* was recently sighted at Tiffany & Co on the Champs-Élysées in the company of his costar, Gwen Davis," a reporter on Hollywood Tonight announces. My gaze darts to the TV screen along with all seven of my coworkers. By now, *everyone* knows I'm dating Drew.

Jillian enters the space and I glance her way. She frowns as all eyes fix on the screen. "What's going on?" she says. "A fifty-car pile-up on Highway One again?" She stares at the TV.

Drew stands at the counter alongside Gwen as they peer into the case. He points to something under the glass. "Looks like a budding romance between the two," the reporter says. "Word is they've been very chummy on set and Ms. Davis recently announced her split with longtime boyfriend, Luke Jenson. Neither are strangers to on-set romance as both have had flings with costars."

It's like my heart is outside my body.

"Isn't Foster dating somebody here in the States?" the host asks.

"Yes. Andrea Tasson had been in Paris for most of the summer but recently returned home, and odds didn't have them lasting very long. They come from totally different worlds. While the cat's away…" He winks.

"But her father is Oscar-winning director James Tasson, so that's not completely accurate."

"Yes, but he sent her off to a French boarding school to keep her away from the Hollywood scene. And it's obvious he's not on board with her dating an actor. I wouldn't be surprised if he's happy to learn Mr. Foster is moving on."

"Thanks for your report, Mario. Keep us posted."

"Will do."

All eyes swivel from the screen to me. "Asshole," Jillian says. "He has no idea what he's talking about."

I know Jillian's right; however, my pulse is racing. I take a deep breath and exhale slowly. Or maybe she isn't. The odds are likely right. The chance of us going the distance isn't something anyone would bet on. We *are* from completely different worlds. And I can't compete with some gorgeous actress Drew is spending an inordinate amount of time with. Probably *in bed* with. Even if it's make-believe, as he so often assured me, it could easily turn into the real deal.

"Reporters live for this stuff," I say. "I just have to keep ignoring it. I'm used to it." But I'm not. And I don't think I ever will be. Besides, I expected this. Everyone I care about leaves in one way or another. It's only a matter of time.

Jillian grabs my upper arm and pulls me into the hallway. "You're not convincing me."

"You didn't really think this would last, did you?"

She hesitates before saying, "I didn't at first, but seeing you two together, I believe he really loves you. And he's a good guy. You know he is. Don't believe all that Hollywood bullshit. You know better."

"Yeah, well my father…"

She cuts me off. "Don't you dare quote your father. He's the last person you should listen to." She digs a finger into my chest and keeps poking, punctuating her words. "I saw you with Greg, and he wasn't half the man Drew is. I don't mean to speak ill of the dead, but I dated him, remember? And he wasn't that affectionate or supportive. He wasn't the guy for me, and I wasn't sure he was the guy for you either."

The more I'm around Drew the more I can see the truth about Greg. I thought we were the perfect match, neither of us overly emotional, nor affectionate, but now I see it as not particularly loving either. Something I didn't think I was capable of.

"You're a completely different person around Drew. I've never seen you so happy. And relaxed. You're not a human tornado that has to get everything done immediately. You always take care of everyone else, and he's the first person who's ever taken care of you. I know he loves you. Trust me."

"I don't want to think about this anymore."

"Call him, I'm sure he can explain."

"I will." But I don't.

Chapter Forty-Two

I end my shift at nine and head out, stopping for takeout Chinese food on my way home. I should call Drew, but it's late and he's probably working. I envision him wrapped around his beautiful costar, pretending to have sex, or perhaps, having sex for real. Stop it, I chastise myself. He's never given you any reason to think he'd cheat. He's a stand-up guy. He loves you. And you love him. Yeah? Then how come you haven't declared it yet? He's been patiently waiting. Maybe he's done waiting.

Another day goes by, and I'm in bed reading about depressive disorders, trying to keep my own miserable thoughts at bay. Drew has called six times, but I've been loath to pick up the call. I'm not sure why. Postponing the inevitable, I guess.

The keypad downstairs beeps five times. Someone has put in the code. I sit up straight, clutching the large tome to my chest. Footsteps on the stairs. I hold my breath.

"You haven't answered my calls." Drew fills the door frame, dropping his duffle on the floor.

"What? I...uh...I've been busy, working double shifts."

"Bullshit. You saw that piece on the news about me and Gwen in the jewelry store."

"So?"

"So, you believe what they're spinning. I called to explain, but you've been ignoring me."

"Look, Drew, this relationship was a long shot. It's been great. You're great. But I can't compete with all the incredibly gorgeous, sexy, actresses you're around every day. It will be a never-ending parade. I wouldn't expect you to resist."

"I thought we already settled the competition argument. This isn't a competition."

"I don't blame you. I honestly can't give you what you want, what you need."

"I'll be the one to decide that." He approaches the foot of the bed and crawls onto it, like a lion stalking his prey. He straddles my hips with his knees and sits on my thighs. "Do you want to know why I was in that jewelry store?"

"You don't have to tell me."

"Well, I *am* going to tell you." He reaches into the pocket of his three-quarter zip sweatshirt. "Gwen was helping me pick this out, after I called Jillian to coach us." I stare at the famous aquamarine box, trying to breathe. "I planned on something more elaborate and romantic for this moment, but since we appear to be in crisis mode, it turned into more of an emergency triage."

"No, Drew, you can't be serious." I cover my mouth with both hands.

"Serious as a heart attack. I think that's language you can comprehend."

My hands fall, landing on his thighs. "But…"

He places three fingers against my lips, like he often does when I'm about to say something stupid. "Marry me. Let's spend the rest of our lives together. I want to grow old with you, always having you by my side. I can't imagine my life without you in it." He drops his hand.

"Drew…"

"I'm not done. I love the butterflies I get when I see you smile. I want that smile for the rest of my life. And I love you just the way you are. So say yes." He opens the box to reveal a smaller turquoise box and flips it open.

"I love you," I finally say.

"I know."

"I'm sorry it took me so long to say it out loud. I say it to myself all the time. And when you can't hear me. I should have said it out loud."

"Well, it's a good thing because I'd look like a total asshole with this ring. Besides, I heard you the night you thought I was asleep. At my parents' house."

"What? Why didn't you say anything?"

"Because if you wanted to say it to me when I was awake, you would have. Baby steps, I figured. You were trying it on for size."

"Where did you learn so much patience?"

"Good question. Maybe from my sisters. Navigating their world required endless patience. The drama, the hysterics, I could never understand why they got so upset at the most inane things. Luckily, they've outgrown it. I don't know two women who have their feet more solidly on the ground." He pauses. "Except you."

I smile. "I love you, and I will love you forever." I kiss him, long and luxuriously. God, I missed him. And here I thought it was over. What an ass. Old habits, I concede. Just because everyone in your life so far has abandoned you, doesn't mean it has to happen again.

"Open it," he urges.

Nestled in the black velvet is an oval cut diamond surrounded by a diamond encrusted rope band of white gold. It's stunning. I laugh. Gwen and Jillian have excellent taste, but I'm sure it was totally Drew's call.

"What's so funny?"

"Nothing," I say. I gaze into his deep blue eyes. "You want to marry me? I'm a mess. I'm not sure I'll ever be anything else."

"Well, you're my mess, and I will cherish you always."

He frees the ring from its nest and slips it on my finger. My heart swells with my love for this amazing man. I've never been this happy…and terrified, at the same time.

****

Drew didn't return to Paris, the edits required only voice-overs which he completed remotely. We're lounging on the deck, swimming, reading, sipping Margaritas on this perfect Sunday afternoon. The wireless phone beside me rings. Unknown caller. "Hello," I say.

"Rea, it's Megan Street, how are you?"

"Megan, hi. Drew and I are slumming it in the backyard, enjoying a rare day off."

"Wonderful. Congratulations on your engagement."

"Thanks, how did you know?" Well, that's a stupid question, it's been broadcasted on virtually every news source available to humans.

"Well, I knew beforehand. After Drew and Gwen went shopping at Tiffany's and the press tried to turn it into something scandalous."

"Yeah, I'll never get used to it. How do you stand it?"

"Oh, I'm boring. Married to the same guy for thirty years, two kids, none of whom are in the business. They leave me alone."

"Well done," I say.

"Besides offering my congratulations, I wonder if we could meet this week. I assume you're probably working, but I can come to the hospital."

"Oh? Sure, I'm on shift all week. I usually aim for a lunch break around noon."

"Great, I have something I want to give you. How about tomorrow? Noon in the hospital cafeteria?"

"I'll see you there."

"Thanks. Say hi to Drew."

"I will."

The call ends and Drew says, "Megan Street?"

"Yeah, she wants to meet me with me. She has something to give me."

"Hmm, I'm intrigued," Drew says.

Me too.

****

I sit at a table in the cafeteria sipping iced tea when Megan enters wearing jeans, a tailored white blouse, and oversized tortoise shell sunglasses, her hair in a sleek ponytail. I wave, and she beelines toward me. Nobody seems to notice a mega-movie star entering our unexciting cafeteria.

"Hi," she says, enclosing me in a motherly hug, which I enjoy way too much.

"Do you want something to eat?"

"Just coffee. I can't stay long. I have a production meeting at two, and you know how the traffic can be."

"How do you take it?"

"One sugar and regular milk."

I return with the steaming paper cup and place it in front of her, then take a seat opposite.

She sips, then smiles. "Not bad." She folds her hands in front of her. "I have a story to tell you."

Chapter Forty-Three

Megan inhales and exhales slowly. "I already told you I was in Italy on a film set when your mother died, and I couldn't get away. We hadn't seen each other in several years. We'd call each other on our birthdays, but that was about it. I was on the East Coast, and she was here, and our paths never crossed. When I got home a month later and visited your dad, he was a mess. I tried to comfort him and just listen, but he was angry. He blamed himself for not seeing your mom was in trouble. I think he still does. Anyway, I offered a shoulder to cry on and asked if I could do anything." She smiles. "When I saw you, I was enchanted. You looked so much like your mother. And since I had two boys, the visage of a baby girl beguiled me. I held you for a few minutes before your nanny—I think her name was Ava— whisked you off for your nap."

"Funny coincidence," I say, "Ava is now Drew's agent."

"No kidding? That is bizarre." She sips her coffee. "Anyway, your father said he was on his way to Morocco for his next film, and he begged me to dispose of your mother's belongings. I asked if there was anything he wanted to keep. Her wedding ring, perhaps. He said he already had it, and lifted it out of his shirt, hanging on a gold chain. But everything else he wanted gone by the time he returned, and he didn't want a stranger to do it."

I don't remember ever seeing my father wearing that ring. Maybe he stopped when he married Jade.

"It took me the entire weekend, but I was glad, and sad, to be charged with the untenable task. Ava helped, and you were there in your baby seat watching with curious eyes.

"The reason I'm telling you this is that I saved two things." She reaches into her purse and pulls out a gold bracelet with a charm, half a heart with the words *best friend* on it. She holds up her wrist to display a matching one. "Your mom and I got these the year we were in New York. I thought you might like to have it."

She opens the clasp. I offer my wrist and she secures the fastener. My throat tightens, but I manage to utter, "Thank you, Megan, this means a lot to me." I twirl the delicate bracelet around and grasp the charm. I've never had anything of my mother's and never thought to ask why.

"There's something else. I took her wedding dress. I preserved it in case you might want it someday." She reaches into her purse again. "Here." She hands me a photograph of my mom and dad on their wedding day. "I can send it to you if you want."

I can't contain my emotions any longer, and the tears well. "Yes, thank you. I want the dress," I whisper.

Megan squeezes my hand. "Oh sweetheart, I didn't mean to upset you."

"They're happy tears, Megan. And honestly, Drew has helped me accept my feelings, good and bad. I didn't know how shut down I was until I met him."

"He's a remarkable man. And I know you make him very happy. He talked about you nonstop, and we all could see how much he loves you. He said he'd been so lonely, but the minute he saw you, he knew he would never walk away from you, ever."

"I never could have imagined someone like him in my life, but I'm thankful he is."

"Love is all that matters in this world. I know your mother would be happy to know you've found it. And she'd be thrilled to see you in her dress."

"This means more to me than you could ever know." I can't take my eyes off the photo. My parents beam at the photographer, my father's arm around my mom's waist.

"You look so much like your mother," Megan says. "I think the dress will fit, maybe some minor alterations."

I study the face of the woman in the photograph. Same big brown eyes. Same auburn hair.

"Are you sure you're all right? I don't want to leave if you are upset."

"I'm good. Thank you so much for all of this."

"Good. I'll send the dress tomorrow. Well, I better go. I promise to keep in touch. You too. Call me anytime."

We rise and embrace, and Megan departs, no one the wiser that the famous Megan Street has just graced our campus.

Home late from my shift, I find Drew in bed reading a script.

"Hey, luv," he says, laying the paper on the duvet and sitting up. "Long day."

"Yeah, but it's nothing compared to the days of trauma surgeries. Not as many life and death situations." I strip out of my scrubs and toss them into the hamper and slip on a cami, brush my teeth, and slide under the covers. "You don't have to wait up."

"I don't mind, plus I've been thinking about the wedding. We haven't set a date or decided what kind of wedding we want."

"Can't we elope? I don't think I'm up for anything too pretentious. I have simple tastes."

Drew chuckles. "I've noticed. I was thinking about getting married in Paris. I took the liberty of calling Sister Dolores, and she said we could have the ceremony at the convent chapel. We can invite my parents, grandparents, and sisters. They could bring dates if they want. Then, I figure there's Ava, Megan and her husband, and Bobby and his wife and of course your dad and Jade. That's barely twenty people. What do you think?"

I lay back on the pillow, my head cradled in my hands. "You called Sister Dolores? That's a bold move."

"You're not pissed, are you?"

"I guess not. Sounds like you've thought this through."

"I talked it over with my mother, and she suggested the vineyard, which would be nice, but that would include my whole damn family and well, I want something more intimate."

I smile, taking his hand. "It's perfect."

He beams. "Sister Dolores said they would do a candlelight dinner in the garden. I told her my mum would help with anything she needed and I'll write the checks."

"My father can pay for it."

"I don't think money is an issue for any of us."

"The garden is beautiful."

"Now we just have to set a date. How's early

October?"

"That's only a month away."

"I know, but I can't wait to marry you."

I cuddle up to his side and kiss his cheek. "Me too."

"I assume Jillian will be your maid of honor?"

"Yeah, I already asked her. Who's standing up for you?"

"Honestly, it's a bit of a dilemma. I'm not close to any of my mates from home anymore. And I haven't got any friends here. I thought about John. We've gotten close, and I'm thinking of starring him in my film." He holds up pages. "I've written a script. It's a coming-of-age story about a teenage misfit in the 1920s who comes to America from England to find his fortune. He's befriended by a Black family with a son the same age, who've recently migrated to New York from Kentucky."

"It sounds great. Can I read it?"

"You want to?"

"Sure, I'd love to."

He smiles. "I'd be thrilled if you read it."

"Done," I say, taking the screenplay from his hand and sitting up. I flip to the first page.

"Anyway, I decided to ask my father to be my best man."

I drop the script on my lap. "Wow, that's cool. Very cool. Was he thrilled?"

"Beyond thrilled."

Chapter Forty-Four

I open the brown paper to reveal a white box reinforced with metal grommets. I remove the cover and part the pink layers of tissue paper. All the breath is trapped in my chest as I grasp the gown by the shoulders and pull it from its nest. Sleeveless, with a beaded, deep V-neckline, and lace bodice. An A-line skirt with a court train enhanced with seed pearls and sequins adds a touch of sparkle over the delicate lace.

Tears. Again. I don't cry for my entire life, and now it's become my daily routine. Almost.

I drape it over my arms like a treasured child and march up the stairs. I open the closet door in the spare bedroom, about to hang it, when an image stops me...the last dress hanging there. Suddenly I'm superstitious. A jinx? What happened the last time I hung a wedding dress here? My jaw locks, I can't breathe. I recoil as if bitten by a viper. No way. It has to go somewhere else and somewhere Drew can't find it.

I run into our bedroom and lay the dress on the bed. I'm like a woman possessed. I grab the phone and hit speed dial two.

"Hey," she says.

"Jillian, thank God you're home. Can I come over?"

"Sure, what's wrong?"

"I'll explain when I get there." I hang up.

The dress repacked and tucked safely in the backseat

of my car, I arrive in Jillian's driveway. She flings open the screen door.

"What's wrong?" she says.

"Nothing, sort of…" I retrieve the treasured box, and she lets me pass. I march into her bedroom and place the box on the bed. "Is Brian home?"

"No, he's at the restaurant. You're scaring me. What's going on?"

I take a few deep breaths and begin. "I met with Megan Street the other day, and she told me she had my mother's wedding dress and she'd send it to me if I wanted it. Of course, I said yes, and it just arrived."

"Oh, my God. You're kidding? That's amazing."

"I know. So, I opened the box and was about to hang it in the closet in the spare bedroom, when…"

"Shit, the room Greg used? Where you had your other dress?"

"Exactly and suddenly I felt—"

"—it would be bad luck if you hung it—"

"—in the same place as the other dress."

"Well, apparently we're on the same page," Jillian says. "Okay, let's calm down. Let me see it." She approaches the bed, hands on her hips.

I unpack it and hug it to my body.

"Wow. It's incredible. And in great shape."

"Megan said she had it preserved."

"Have you tried it on?"

"Not yet."

"Well, let's go, girl. I want to see it on you right now."

I strip out of my jeans and T-shirt while Jillian unzips the back and holds it open for me to step into. She pulls the zipper up and fastens the tiny buttons covering it, then walks around to face me. Her hands fly to her mouth, smothering her gasp. I have known Jillian for almost ten years and never seen her cry. Not even when her mother stole her tuition money intended for her last year of med school.

"God, Rea, it's beautiful. You're beautiful." She takes my hand and tugs me toward the full-length mirror on her closet door.

I study the reflection in the mirror. A woman I do not know, and yet she's familiar. It's as if my mother is in this room. In this dress, with me.

"It fits perfectly," Jillian says. "You just need some heels."

My hands slide across my breasts, around my waist, over my hips. For someone who never dresses up and who doesn't enjoy dressing up, I feel wonderful, like I'm in a chrysalis, protected, shielded from the cruelty of my childhood. And once I marry Drew, I will be free, a butterfly taking flight, happy and able to face whatever life brings. With Drew at my side, I can do anything, be anything. I always thought a person should be fearless and confident on their own, but having a partner by your side, fortifying you, being a safe place to fall…is the best of both worlds.

Coming to my senses, I say, "Can I leave it here?"

"Of course. I'll keep it safe until the big day."

****

The toaster pops and my phone rings…again. This is the third call.

"Someone you're avoiding?" Drew asks.

"What? No." I grasp the hot English muffin from the toaster and plop it on the white plate alongside the offending telephone.

"That's the third call you've silenced in the last five minutes."

It rings again and this time Drew glances at the screen.

"Your dad?"

I roll my eyes. "Nosey."

"Why don't you want to talk to your father?"

I sigh, too loudly. "You know we don't have the best relationship."

"You said you've forgiven him for his past transgressions."

"I have, mostly."

"How come I'm not convinced?"

"That's your problem." I rub my face with both hands and come close. "I'm sorry, I shouldn't snap at you."

He places his hands on my shoulders. "Forget it, it's none of my business anyway."

"I know why he's calling."

"I'll bite."

"He's called twice already this week. His new movie premieres next weekend, and he wants me to attend. I told him I wasn't sure I could make it. I'm on shift that night, and I'd have to get someone to switch with me." I nibble a finger. "He's insistent I be there. He's hinting it's something special, and he's anxious to see what I think. Although it's a little late for my review since it's already in the can."

"If it's important to him, then you should make the effort."

"Have you heard anything about it?"

Drew is putting too much peanut butter on his muffin. I take the knife from his hand. "What are you doing? Trying to overdose on peanut butter?"

"I…I was distracted." He picks up the knife and scrapes some off, returning it to the jar. He takes a long draught of his coffee then moves to the kitchen table.

"Well," I repeat, "have you heard anything about this project?"

"Not much, just that it's something out of his wheelhouse. It's all been very hush-hush. NDAs and all. The press release isn't even scheduled until after the premiere."

"Isn't that unusual?"

"Kind of, but sometimes, when a project is anticipated to be a mega-blockbuster with a famous director and stellar cast, they try to hype it up by keeping it hush-hush."

"You'll come with me?" I ask.

"Of course. And I'd love to see you all dolled up again."

"Seriously?"

"Yeah, you in heels and an evening gown is hot."

I sit beside him at the table and give him a sideways glance. "You're such a guy."

"Hey, don't denigrate me, I have my weaknesses."

I smile. "Okay, I'll tell him we'll attend."

Chapter Forty-Five

The next day at work, I complain to Jillian. "I have to attend another premiere tomorrow."

"Oh, woe is you. Most people would kill for your life."

I sigh. "I know, I should be grateful, but I never thought my life would take this turn."

"You're engaged to the hottest guy on the planet. And the nicest, I might add. Don't make it sound like it's a burden."

"You're right. Sometimes I'm just an ass."

"What are you wearing?"

"Oh, I hadn't thought about that. I have the blue number Drew bought me for his premiere."

"Are you out of your mind? You can't show up in a repeat dress. Even someone with your fashion illiteracy would know that."

I sigh, again. "I don't have time, and Drew won't care…" But then I think, maybe he will. He outright said he couldn't wait to see me in an evening gown and heels. Damn.

"We both get off at four, and we're going right down to Celeb Wear. Bethany will hook you up."

****

We enter the trendy boutique and thankfully Bethany is working. She rushes over. "Hey, I saw on *Hollywood Tonight* that you're engaged.

Congratulations. Well done."

I'll never get used to this. The paparazzi have been lurking everywhere. Shouting at me to give a comment, but I've successfully ignored them to date.

"Thanks, Bethany."

"Hey, Jillian, how are you?"

"Good. Rea is going to her father's premiere tomorrow, and she intended to wear the same thing she wore to Drew's."

Bethany's eyes widen. "Heavens, no…"

"Not if I have anything to say about it," Jillian says. "So I dragged her down here as soon as she told me."

"Thank goodness."

I roll my eyes, even though I know their assessment is spot on.

"Let's get to work. Something full length?"

"I think so. And I'll need shoes and probably a clutch."

"Done," Bethany says.

I'm in a dress, then out of a dress, in another, then out… It takes about forty minutes until both Jillian and Bethany gasp. It's a black strapless gown with a tulip hem, a small pink rhinestone rosebud perched at the center of my cleavage. "I guess this is it," I say.

"Absolutely," Jillian says.

"One hundred percent," Bethany offers. "You're a knockout in that."

We add a sparkly pink clutch and black patent pumps, and Bethany insists on earrings similar to the rosebud on the dress. "Wear your hair up," she insists.

And the look is complete. Never in my wildest imagination did I think I'd be living this life. Even for a moment. And I'm glad it is just a moment. I couldn't keep this going, nor would I want to. It's entirely too much, and I can't imagine what it's like to be Gwen or Megan and have to keep up appearances like this. But I'm glad to do it on occasion and especially for those I love.

We return to my house, and I open a bottle of chardonnay. Jillian and I kick off our shoes and settle on the back deck. The ocean is calm tonight, but there's a prediction for stormy weather tomorrow. The red carpet might be a disaster.

The back door opens to reveal Drew dressed in khaki cargo shorts, a pink golf shirt, and his Tevas. "Hey, I thought I heard you come in. I thought you were off at four. I expected you before this."

He sits at the end of my lounger and props my bare feet on his knees. His thumbs dig into my arches, and I struggle not to purr.

"Your girlfriend here was planning on wearing the same dress she wore to your premiere," Jillian says. "A fashion intervention was required, so I marched right down to Bethany for emergency triage."

"Good work. Even I know that would have been a huge faux pas."

I frown and give them both the finger.

****

He walks into the bedroom, and I'm naked, face down, on the bed. A tornado ravages my thoughts. A sense of foreboding about the premiere tonight is swirling in my gut. How did I wind up in another Hollywood Moment?

"Tempting as this view is, we're going to be late if you don't get a move on."

"I know. I'm going."

He comes over and smacks my butt. "Get in the shower."

I obey.

****

Drew is fastening a cufflink as I walk out of the closet in my new dress. "I need help with this friggin' thing," he says. His eyes land on me. "Wowie zowie, you look beautiful. I don't think I've ever seen a more beautiful woman."

He comes close and kisses me gently, and suddenly I don't want to go, well, not suddenly. I haven't wanted to go for the entire week. I want to stay here, in the arms of this loving man. Order a pizza, listen to tunes, or watch a classic movie. Anything but traipsing to another movie premiere.

"Thanks," I say. "Glad you approve."

"I approve all right, and there's not a woman in Hollywood who can hold a candle to you. You're a knockout."

"You're sweet, but I'd much rather be home with you, just hanging out."

He smiles. "You'll be okay. It'll be fun. You'll get to see Ava, Megan, and Gwen."

"Megan and Gwen are going?"

"Yup."

He thrusts his wrist at me, and I thread the cufflink through the holes in his sleeve and center it. "There, and you're looking pretty sharp yourself, Mr. Hollywood Heartthrob."

"Enough of the mutual admiration society. The car is here. Let's jet."

We arrive and take our place in the queue of limos until our turn comes. "I'll pull up when I see you come out," the driver says. "I'll wait in the side lot. If I'm not here, I'm assigned the fourth space on the right."

The red carpet is the usual shitshow, and I brave the bright lights, screaming fans, and annoying reporters shouting inane questions. "Drew, when's the wedding? Rea, where's the wedding? Where's the honeymoon?" God, get me out of here.

My dad is looking dapper in his usual Tom Ford tuxedo, shaking hands and kissing the horde of fawning women swarming him while Jade lingers in his shadow. His full head of silver hair and pearly white smile have earned him the Hollywood title of Silver Fox. I swear, how has he done this his entire life? It's exhausting just watching him.

Suddenly, Ava is at my side, dressed in a full-length red gown, rhinestone epaulets adorning her shoulders.

"Rea, congratulations. I'm so happy for you both." She hugs me. "I already congratulated Drew." She winks at him.

"Thanks, Ava. You'll be coming to the wedding?"

"I wouldn't miss it for anything. Have you set a date?"

"We're working on it," I say.

"If you need help with anything, just ask," she says.

Megan is next, and she introduces me to her husband, Eddie, a criminal attorney. He's tall and dressed in the required black tuxedo. He extends his hand. "So nice to meet you, Rea. I've heard so much about you."

"Thanks. Pleasure meeting you."

He leans in and whispers, "I bet you love these things about as much as I do." He pulls back, and we share a seditious smile.

"You have no idea," I say.

Gwen is next. Her pink chiffon gown swirls around her like a cloud of cotton candy, her blonde hair cascading over her shoulders, one side pinned up with a rhinestone—probably an actual diamond—barrette. "Congratulations." We air kiss, touching cheeks, so as not to smear lipstick on each other.

"Thanks," I say again.

A tall blond man is at her side. "This is my boyfriend, Jax," she says. "Jax, this is Rea, Drew's fiancée."

"Nice to meet you, Rea."

The lights flash on and off, the signal to enter the theater.

"Sis," I hear, and Bobby barrels toward me, his wife, Sally, in tow.

"Hey," I say as he engulfs me in his usual bear hug, the pink rhinestone adornment at my cleavage digging into me. Sally and I embrace, and she kisses my cheek. She's a hair stylist and, as always, her coiffure is impeccable and elaborate, an iteration on a French braid, something I could never manage, although I can execute a flawless appendectomy.

As we enter, my father is waiting by the door. "Rea," he whispers, taking my hand and pulling me to the side. "You being here means the world." I study my father's face. His usual confident, calm persona is nowhere in sight. He looks…nervous, a slight sheen on his forehead and upper lip.

"Of course, Dad. I'm happy to be here. I know I don't always say so, but I am." Okay, so a bit of a lie.

"This is something special to me, and I don't care what the critics or anyone else says; only your opinion matters."

I find this odd, and unsettling. Why would he care about my opinion?

Chapter Forty-Six

"Dad, is everything all right? You're not acting like your usual self."

"It will be after tonight. I'm sure of it."

"Okaaay," I say as the house lights flash again.

"We better get our seats," he says. "I have to make my remarks, and we can talk after."

He walks away with Jade, and Drew takes my hand, leading me down the aisle. We sit in the front row, a little to the right. Bobby is next to me. "Does Dad seem weird to you?" I ask Bobby.

"Yeah, he's definitely off. I have no idea why."

I pose the same question to Drew.

"He's a little tense. We're all like that on premiere night."

I'm not convinced.

My father makes the requisite introductions, the producers and cast, the screenwriter, et al.

When he introduces Gwen, my eyes widen. I turn to Drew. "Gwen is starring?"

"Yes," is all he says.

"Wait a minute, this means she'd already filmed it when you worked together in Paris."

"Yes," he says again.

"And she didn't tell you anything about it?"

"She signed an NDA, so she couldn't." Drew squeezes my hand too tightly.

"Something's up," I say. "I don't like it."

"It'll be fine. Just hold on to me."

Hold onto him. Why?

And then my father says, "This movie was a labor of love. At times a very painful one, but one the world needed to see. I hope you enjoy it, and maybe you'll learn something too." He descends the stage, and the lights go out.

A personal one? Dread invades my soul. Oh, God.

The title flashes in giant, bold, red letters—*REGRETS*. The opening scene depicts a young woman on stage in a small theater. I wouldn't have known this if Megan hadn't shared… Oh, my God. It's my mother, and Gwen is playing the part. She dyed her blonde hair brown. They move to the city and do some off-Broadway work, some stints in the dancing entourage. There's even them in a gift shop buying the friendship bracelets. Then they take the road trip to L.A. for pilot season. It's all there—my parents' whirlwind romance, my birth, her death, me going to boarding school in Paris, names changed to protect the innocent. Yeah, not so much. I don't recognize the actor playing my father, and he's not in many scenes, focusing on the other characters, nor the little girl who's…*me*. Even Sister Dolores is portrayed. It ends with me starting my residency and Greg's death. At the conclusion, there's my father, sitting in his director's chair, dressed all in black, giving a PSA about postpartum depression and drug overdoses, the warnings, and numbers for help.

If a human doesn't breathe for two and a half hours, they're dead. How am I still alive?

The blood flow in my hand is non-existent, having clutched Drew's the entire time. Before the lights come on, I extricate my hand and flee. Up the side aisle, through the lobby, out the front door. I speed toward the limo parked in the assigned spot as promised. I drop into the back seat, exhaling what little breath I have left. I close my eyes. "Take me home," I order.

"What about Mr. Foster?"

"He's staying for a while. Just take me home."

"Yes, ma'am."

"Quickly." I look over my shoulder and see Drew descending the theater steps.

"Yes. Ma'am."

We enter my driveway, he already has the code. I extricate myself before the car has fully come to a stop and barrel toward the front door, fumbling with my keys, dropping them twice. A feral scream escapes me.

"Are you okay?" the driver says.

I ignore him, finally turning the key in the lock and slamming the door behind me.

I kick off my pumps and flee out the back door, down the three steps to the beach and run toward the crashing surf. A flash of lightning splits the night sky, a crack of thunder follows, rattling my bones.

But the moon is out, giant, hanging over the horizon, ready to splash into the endless abyss of the pitch-black water. The ocean is furious, but not as furious as I am. I halt, the foaming seawater pummeling my ankles. The next wave strikes higher, soaking the bottom of my perfect onyx gown in icy saltwater. I struggle to stay upright. Time stands still as wave after wave strikes me, each blow a sharp lash, a punishment for trusting—my father, Drew, Megan, Gwen—everyone in my goddamned, fucked-up life. The coldness numbs me, a sweet escape, no more feeling, no more pain, no more anything. I can't even cry. Back to the old me. The one who feels *nothing.*

Hands seize my upper arms, and I'm yanked backward. He turns me around, and I stare into Drew's moonlit face. He doesn't say anything. His hair nearly covers his eyes. Lightning strikes again followed by a sharp clap of thunder. The sky opens, and we are deluged with sheets of stinging rain.

"How could you do this to me?" I say, too calmly.

"I didn't."

"You knew," I shriek. "You knew and didn't warn me."

"I didn't know much. Gwen gave me a thumbnail sketch, but since she'd signed an NDA, she wasn't allowed to even tell me that much, and I was sworn to secrecy."

"I don't give a crap about an NDA. You should have told me."

"Gwen gave me the heads-up because she wanted me to be prepared in case things didn't go so well."

"Well, shit, Drew, they didn't, did they?" I try to wrench free, but his grasp is tight, preventing me from escaping into the churning sea.

"Think about it for a minute. This was your father's way of offering a public apology. His attempt to make things right with you."

"You've got to be kidding. How could making this public make me feel any better? Dredging up all that pain, the abandonment?"

"If you'll get out of your own head for one goddamned second, you'd realize what your father experienced was a hundred times worse than what you did. And how is what happened with you and Greg any different from what happened between your father and mother? He missed, or ignored, the signs like you did. You both suffered tremendous guilt about the death of someone you loved."

This truth hits me hard. I have no right to judge my father because I am guilty of the same sin. And yet I've punished him repeatedly.

"Your father was in no condition to take care of you. Giving you over to the Sisters of Mercy was the best thing he could have done. Yeah, you didn't have a mother, but you had something almost as good. Those nuns were your mothers, and they raised an extraordinary woman. The best woman I know."

This realization hits twice as hard. Lots of people have terrible mothers, and fathers, ones they do not choose and can't do anything about.

A shadowy figure stands on my back deck, his hands in his pockets, his head hung low. Something cleaves in my chest, and a dark cloud leaches out. I look at Drew.

"Give him a chance. He's flagellated himself in front of the whole world for the sole purpose of gaining your forgiveness. I think the PSA at the end could save lives. Hell, even if it's one life, that's a good thing."

I extricate myself from Drew's hold and make my way to the deck. My father descends the three steps onto the sand. I face him, rain pummeling us. "You should have warned me."

"I feared you wouldn't come."

"Or you could have shown it to me privately."

"I hoped you'd consider it an homage to your mother and how proud I am of you. And you might truly forgive me. And it would serve as a public service announcement for people to learn about postpartum depression and drug use. Maybe even save a life."

My hands fist at my sides. "How could you abandon your own child? To send me away and never see me, never get to know me?"

He sighs, dragging his hands down his face. "Because…she's all I saw when I looked at you."

For the first time I *see* his pain. Even in the near darkness. I *feel* his pain, and it's greater than my own.

He grabs my upper arms. "But now I only see you. My beautiful, brilliant daughter. I'm so sorry you didn't get the father you deserved. I was afraid. It was my fault your mother killed herself. I was more worried about my career than her. I was selfish and ignorant, arrogant and immature. I knew nothing about postpartum depression. And I needed to acknowledge my mistakes in front of the world, my regrets. To take responsibility for abandonment of my only daughter. Who I am so proud of. Who I love with all my heart."

"I always felt it was my fault, and Megan confirmed it when she said Mom lost the part in that Scorsese movie, and even though Megan said it wasn't, I knew it was because she was pregnant with me."

My father doesn't say anything which confirms my suspicion.

"But it wasn't anybody's fault," he says, "and we both have to let it go. Stuff happens and you only have so much control."

I sigh. "I don't know…but I do know we have to stop punishing ourselves."

A glint of reflected moonlight strikes my eye. Around his neck, something shiny, gold. My mother's ring. I grasp it between two fingers. "Megan told me you had this, but I've never seen you wear it."

"I put it away when I married Jade. But I needed it near my heart tonight."

I smile, letting the paragon of their love go. Suddenly I feel lighter, as if I could float away on a thundercloud. "I'm sorry I made a spectacle."

"Don't say that. You have nothing to be sorry for. It's on me, all of it."

I wrap my arms around his waist, and he secures me in a warm hug, his chin resting on my head. Our breathing aligns, and our heartbeats sync. "Okay," I whisper. "It's done. The past be gone and only the future exists from this moment on."

He pulls back, and his smile is like a warm breeze on a chilly day.

Two hands grasp my shoulders and I turn.

"Safe to approach?" Drew says.

"Yes," I say. "It's done. It's over."

"Thank God," he says.

We ascend the three steps together, Drew's hand in one and my dad's in the other.

The kitchen screen door slams behind us. "I need a drink," I say.

"Me too," they both say.

"And a towel," Drew adds.

Drew pours two fingers of scotch in three glasses. "I love you," I say, "both of you," as we raise our glasses. "To Mom."

"To Mom," they say.

I can only describe the next week as paparazzi on steroids. The entertainment media lost its collective mind, and reports of my histrionics were everywhere. One reporter claimed he had it on good authority that the whole event was a publicity stunt to boost box office revenue. It wasn't, but it did.

Drew and I fielded phone calls—Ava, Lisa, Megan, Jillian, but no Gwen. Bobby called Dad a complete and utter asshole. I finally relented, and Dad and I made a statement to the press that all fared well in Tassonland. And, thankfully, it's been quiet these last few weeks.

Chapter Forty-Seven

We board the private plane at nine p.m. along with Ava, Bobby, and Sally, Jillian and Brian, my dad, and Jade. Megan and Gwen, along with their significant others, are arriving separately. Drew's family will be traveling by train and should get there before us.

Champagne flows freely, along with an assortment of food to sustain us on the eleven-hour trip—breakfast options, more substantial fare, plus delectable finger food and bite-sized sweet treats. Chairs transform into beds. This is *sooo* less stressful than flying commercial. I tell myself it's the last time I'm indulging in such decadence. It's bad for the environment.

We arrive at our hotel around eleven a.m., check in, unpack, my dress secluded in Jillian's room, and enter the lobby to a flurry of guests. Kissing, hugging, lots of animated conversation. I meet Drew's sisters and their boyfriends. The family resemblance unmistakable.

I sight Gwen, and she beelines toward me. She takes my hand. "Rea, I wanted to call you, but figured I'd rather tell you how sorry I am in person. It was awful seeing you on set, knowing about *Regrets* and that I had played your mother. I begged James not to spring it on you, but you know your father. He said if you knew, you'd never see it. Maybe he was right, but I still felt terrible deceiving you. Can you forgive me?"

"I understand, and in the end it all worked out. He

was right, and I know you were prevented from saying anything. There's nothing to forgive."

She hugs me and whispers near my ear. "Thank you."

I am released, and we share a smile. "All good."

We munch some lunch in the hotel restaurant. Drew's parents are hosting a rehearsal dinner at the hotel, sans rehearsal. The ceremony will be simple, and we're confident we can pull it off spur of the moment.

"Let's head back to the room," Drew whispers. "I need a nap."

Sure, I think. *A nap* is often Drew's euphemism for sex. "I'm saving myself for marriage," I say.

Drew laughs. "Too late, luv."

****

The hotel hosts a magnificent dinner, no doubt coached by my future mother-in-law and professional chef, Eleanor Foster, and the wine is top shelf, from their vineyard. I'm seated between my dad and Drew, his parents beside him. His grandparents sit across the table, and I marvel at their affection for each other. Should I be so lucky to live a long happy life with my picture-perfect husband.

It's ten p.m., and I take Drew's hand. "Let's turn in."

"Sorry, luv, but I think your gal pals have other plans. You're sleeping with Jillian. They already came for your stuff."

"What?"

"Something about a bridal shower."

"No. Oh please, tell me…"

"Looks like Brian is bunking with me. Good thing we have two queen-size beds. And the guys are having a cigar-smoking, brandy sniffing evening. Hopefully, no strippers." He glances sideways and frowns. "Hmm, maybe I'd like strippers."

"Oh, God." I pinch the bridge of my nose.

Jillian is standing beside me. She takes my hand. "Okay, girl, you're mine until the wedding."

"Jillian, this isn't necessary. I'd rather stay with Drew. We don't have to adhere to any traditions…"

"Not an option. Let's go."

She tugs me toward the elevator. I glance over my shoulder, looking forlornly at Drew. He makes a tiny wave, then blows me a kiss. Arriving on the twelfth floor, we walk to Jillian's room, 1215. The door opens, and *all* the female persuasion is there. Drew's sisters, grandmothers, and Jean Paul's wife, Julia, Megan, Gwen, Sally, Jade, Ava, and Eleanor.

"Surprise!"

Oh. My. God. Eleanor comes over and anchors a short bridal veil to my head. They seat me in a chair and Jillian ties my wrists to the arms with white lace.

"So, you don't make a run for it," she whispers.

"Seriously? This is too much, and I can't believe you're doing this to Brian. You're in the City of Light, the most romantic place in the world, and you're making him sleep with Drew?"

"He's a big boy. He'll get over it. And besides, we're here for you guys."

I shake my head. "We have to be the two most unromantic women on the planet."

"Tell me…"

We play Never Have You Ever, and a few too many secrets are revealed. Who knew the grandmothers led such thrilling lives? Grandmother Foster, who grew up in France, danced the cancan in a famous cabaret club, and Eleanor and Tom eloped, and their parents were not happy. I'm kinda wishing I'd done the same because I'm not so great at this kind of stuff. Never do I ever…enjoy being the center of attention. The wedding will be bad enough. But alas, I should say, "Good enough. Get over yourself, woman."

There is more champagne and presents to open—lingerie, massage oils complete with massager, and even a sex toy—from the grandmothers. "In the hands of a man, this can be quite stimulating," Grandmother Foster says, an unmistakable twinkle in her eye. Oh. My. God.

We laugh and cry, the good kind of crying, and I'm incredibly moved to be a part of this circle of women. The joy, the camaraderie, the bond of womanhood, something I've never experienced. The love.

****

The sunlight pierces the side openings in the blinds, and I groan. A little too much champagne. I should have brought IV bags with me. They do wonders for a hangover. The clock announces 11:20. Damn. I never sleep this late.

"Wake up, sleepyhead."

Jillian already had breakfast delivered, and she pours coffee. "Oh, thank God. I need caffeine."

The phone rings, and I pick it up. "Hey," Drew says. "How was your night?"

"You wouldn't believe me if I told you. Your grandmothers are wild women."

"Tell me. Honestly, I think there are some things I wish I didn't know."

"How was yours?"

"I'm still a little queasy from the cigars. Hopefully, I'll rebound quickly."

I laugh. "Thought we'd escape unscathed from the tawdry wedding rituals, but I guess not."

"Well, it was all done with love, and we survived."

Barely, I think.

The convent chapel is filled with flowers. Bouquets of aromatic lavender, green hydrangeas, and pink alstroemeria adorn each pew, with two giant arrangements on either side of the altar. Sister Dolores greets me at the entrance, her beatific smile relaxes me, and she hands me a matching bouquet and a smaller one to Jillian. Sister Mary Katherine stands behind her, along with Sister Genevieve and others I don't know. Their hands are clasped, their heads lowered, as if in reverence.

"*Ma chérie*, you look angelic. So beautiful," Sister Dolores says. She kisses both cheeks and holds me at arm's length. "Such a journey you've made, and seeing you so happy makes my heart full."

"Thank you, Sister. You've been a major part of that journey, and I can never repay you for everything you've given me."

"Nonsense. My love for you has no bounds, and I will love you forever."

A tear erupts. Oh, no, I promised myself I wouldn't cry. Again, an entire life of not crying and now…Jesus. And now I've taken the Lord's name in vain….*in his house.*

Megan and Eleanor are fussing over my train as Jillian assists. Butterflies flutter my stomach. A tightness twists my chest. I finger the silver heart around my neck, the one Eleanor gave me. I wish my mother was here.

"Are you all right?" Megan says.

"Yeah, I miss my mother."

She grasps the bracelet surrounding my wrist, the one she gave me, and holds up the charm engraved with Best Friend. "She's right here." She places a hand on my chest, her touch warm. "And here."

I swallow back the tears and smile. "Thanks. And meeting you has brought me so much closer to her. Thank you."

"Of course. Now walk down the aisle to that magnificent man, and live happily ever after. You deserve it, and so much more." She kisses me, then walks to her seat.

My gaze wanders down the aisle where a priest waits at the altar, donned in traditional church vestments. Drew and I are both technically Catholic, but we wouldn't consider ourselves practicing Catholics. In my case, science is my religion. But for the sake of our families, we are willing to partake in a traditional church ceremony. No mass, however. That might be a little too sacrilegious.

My dad takes my arm as the organ plays "Canon in D" by Pachelbel. "I love you," he says. "I've always loved you. I wish I'd been able to show you sooner."

"I know. Me too."

He kisses my cheek. "Let's do this," he says, his smile wide.

I focus on Drew standing at the end of the aisle, his father at his side. I want to run to him.

The ceremony is simple, and saying those magic words, *I do*, sinks deep into my soul.

And then, it happens. I should have seen this coming, but it catches me off guard. Sister Genevieve sings her signature ballad, "Climb every mountain, ford every stream, follow every rainbow, till you find your dream." And there isn't a dry eye in the church. Even the priest has his handkerchief out, dabbing his eyes. The refrain ends, and I mouth, "Thank you," to Sister Genevieve, and she smiles.

"I now pronounce you man and wife. You may kiss the bride." And Drew does. A real kiss, the kind that makes me weak in the knees. We turn to face the congregation, and applause, whoops, and hollers fill the air.

White flower petals rain on us as we march down the aisle. Outside, on a perfect day of warm sunshine and a cool breeze, we make our way to the backyard garden where the sisters have prepared a wedding feast fit for French royalty. The novices and postulates act as servers, and we sit at a grand table under twinkly lights laced through a trellis adorned with trumpet vines, bougainvillea, and morning glories.

Toasts are offered—my dad, Jillian, and Tom. And I suffer through jokes and praise, terrible dad puns, and things I'd forgotten. All infused with unconditional love. A life of abandonment has metamorphosed into a life filled with more love than I ever could have imagined.

****

In February my father wins best-picture and best-director Oscars for the movie of my life. Gwen wins best actress, and the girl who plays me wins best supporting actress. A year later, Drew wins the Oscar for lead actor for his role in *An American in Paris.* But my prize bests them all by a mile. My water breaks right there in the lobby of the Dorothy Chandler Pavilion.

At midnight, I deliver twins.

We miss all the after-parties.

Chapter Forty-Eight

"Is this really the exact spot where the car crashed?" Jessie asks, eyes wide.

We walked a long way down the beach while my story unfolded before making our way back. It'd been ages since I thought about such things. So much of it made me smile as I related the strange circumstances of meeting my husband of forty years. Drew became a famous director and producer in his own right after eventually leaving acting behind, except for the occasional part just for the fun of it.

"Yes," I say as I flash back to seeing Drew trapped inside the black Porsche that night. "It was right here, right where we are standing."

"Gosh, Grandma. What a crazy story. It's like destiny or fate or something. Don't you think?"

My smile is wide as I take Jessie's hand to walk back to the house. My daughter walks alongside us. I should get back to show my face among the Hollywood elite here for the express purpose of being seen at this iconic funeral soiree.

"Oh, I don't know, Jessie. Sometimes I do think so. But who knows? Life takes some strange turns every now and again. And you never know where you'll wind up."

We find ourselves at the steps leading to the back deck. I'm not quite ready to go in, as I perch myself on the bottom step for a minute, facing the crashing surf. I envision Drew walking along the sand with me. I miss him so much.

The three of us sit in silence, when I hear the back door open. I don't turn around, assuming it's someone I don't want to talk to. Or maybe it's Mark, telling me there is some problem with the food, or perhaps we are out of alcohol already. This crowd certainly can knock back the booze.

Hands are on my shoulders. Knees hug my waist as he perches on the step behind me. "Miss me?" he whispers in my ear, giving me a sweet kiss on the neck, sending tiny shivers down my spine.

I can't smile wide enough.

"Grandpa," Jessie yells. "You're back."

"Hi, Dad," my daughter says.

I turn to face him. "God, I missed you. I'm so glad you're home."

"I'm so sorry, luv, I couldn't get a flight out fast enough. Remind me never to go to Japan again. It's way too far away from you. We had to finish the last day of shooting, and if we didn't, it would have been hell trying to get everyone back again. Not to mention expensive. This movie is already too far over budget for my liking. And believe me, there were plenty of people pissed at not being able to make it back in time for your dad's funeral. But no one could say anything since if I wasn't going to get there in time, they certainly couldn't whine about it."

Drew gives me another sweet kiss. "Do you forgive me? I'm so sorry I wasn't here for you during this. Was it awful?" His arms surround my neck, and I lean against his chest. I breathe in his scent. It rejuvenates my spirit. I hate it when he goes on location so far away. I always get the feeling he's never coming back. Even after all this time, the sense of him leaving me sometimes gets the better of me.

"Of course, I forgive you. And yes, it was awful. I fully expect you to make it up to me. And in a big way," I tease.

"I've already got it covered. Just you wait and see."

I glance up. His face is mysterious. His impish smile taunts me.

"What have you got up your sleeve?"

"It will have to wait until later, as soon as everyone is out of here."

"Grandma told us the story of how you met," Jessie blurts.

"Oh, really?" Drew says. "You mean the day I crashed into her life?"

"Yeah, that's what Grandma said. She showed me the exact spot where your car crashed. Right over there," she says pointing to the fateful location.

My daughter stands. "Come on Jess, let's go back inside and see how your father and Jay are holding up. We need to get going soon. It's getting close to Jay's bedtime."

Drew takes my hand and leads me into the kitchen. "I guess I should make the rounds before everyone is gone. Otherwise, I'll have to hear about it later."

"You're right. I haven't exactly been playing the perfect hostess myself."

****

The last of the guests finally leave, and Mark is finishing up with the caterers. I can't wait for this to be over. To be alone with Drew. I haven't seen him in a month, and I miss him terribly. Darkness has blanketed the ocean as I look out the back window at the crashing surf. I have lived in this house for forty-four years. Forty of them with Drew. The house my father gave me to alleviate his guilt from shipping me off to France and out of his life. Oh, Dad, I think, your life has come to an end. I know you had some tough years after Mom died, and I know how looking at me every day caused you more pain than you could bear. I understand that is why you sent me away. We mended our fences and even though the early years were truly awful, the later years were better. It never should have happened to either of us. We should have had a better life together.

"Penny for your thoughts?" Drew whispers in my ear as he comes up behind me, encasing me in his strong arms.

"Just thinking about Dad, and what a terrible life we had in the beginning."

"Yeah, you did have a rough time there for a while."

"Excuse me, Dr. Foster, we're done cleaning up and we will be out of your hair in a minute," the caterer announces. "It was a pleasure serving you, and again, please accept my condolences on the loss of your father."

"Oh, thank you, Maria. Everything was wonderful. Thanks so much."

"My pleasure. Good night then, good night, Mr. Foster."

"Good night," we both say.

Finally, we're alone. Drew pours us both a glass of wine, and he tows me out to the back deck. It's a beautiful spring night. The stars are bright, and the full moon is almost too brilliant. Jessie has stirred up my memories, and I see us as a young couple again, swimming in the ocean and the pool, having dinner together that night, and making love right here on the chaise lounge built for two.

We take a seat on the steps leading off the deck, our favorite perch to sip wine and listen to the sounds of the ocean. "I see *The Bubble Monster* hit the New York Times bestseller list," I say.

Drew smiles. "I heard." He laces his fingers through mine, his thumb stroking the back of my hand. "Not sure how I ever got around to writing it. Mostly at night when I was missing you with nothing else to do. It always makes me smile when I think of you taking your first bubble bath."

My cell phone rings, and I dig it out of my pocket. "Huh," I say, "it's Jean Paul. Hello?"

"Rea, I'm so sorry to inform you that Sister Dolores has passed. Last night, in her sleep, at the retreat where she retired."

"Oh, no. How sad."

"I know how fond you two were of each other, but be at peace. She led a long and wonderful life and died peacefully."

"You're right. And I am. Thanks for letting me know. Will there be services?"

"Yes, but it isn't necessary for you to make the trip. She knows how much you loved her."

"I would consider it, but I have a big event I must attend, so it would be impossible."

"Of course. Take care."

"Thanks for the call, Jean Paul. Take care."

"Bad news?" Drew says.

"Sister Dolores died. Peacefully, in her sleep."

Drew places his hand on my knee. "I'm so sorry."

"Thanks. She meant the world to me, and I miss her

every day."

"I know. But you can't attend the services because you're getting your award Saturday night."

The APA is giving me a lifetime achievement award largely based on my work with the use of supervised hallucinogens in the treatment of depression, but also for my middle school initiative where I've toured the state with the governor to speak to young teens and their parents about mental health. Not a fan of self-aggrandizement, I'm uncomfortable accepting such praise, but Drew related his experiences with winning four Oscars, two for acting and two for directing. He said if people want to offer their praises it's best to accept and just be humble.

"So, it's been a tough week. How are you holding up?" my loving husband asks.

"I'm okay. Luckily, he didn't suffer much. Quick and painless, that's the best way. And the same for Sister Dolores." Although I eventually became a psychiatrist, I witnessed more pain and suffering than I cared to remember in the early days of my training.

"It seems Jessie was quite enamored in her enthusiasm for our love story," Drew says with a chuckle. "You know, it would make a great movie."

My eyes widen, I hold my breath. No…

Chapter Forty-Nine

"Oh God, no, Drew. My father did, and it nearly killed me. I'd die if I ever saw it on the big screen. Promise me you'll never do that to me."

"I promise. But it would make a great movie. You must admit that."

"No, never, I'll never admit it."

We are both quiet for a few minutes as I ponder the preposterous notion of my life as a film. Again. My thoughts are interrupted by the ominous sound of his voice.

"Rea, there is something that's bothered me for a long time, but I've never had the nerve to ask you."

I'm startled by his words. We tell each other everything. I have no secrets from Drew. Well, there was the time I blamed the broken headlight on the grocery cart in some phantom parking lot, and then the time I told him I couldn't get his tuxedo from the tailor in time for his premiere because of some fabricated traffic jam, and the time...well, those don't count. I always told him the truth about the important things. But now I'm off center, worried. What could I have kept secret from him all these years?

I don't say anything at first, afraid of what might be coming. I turn and look at him, my brow inching towards a frown. His face is serious in the moonlight as my pulse spikes.

"What is it?" I say, not really wanting to know.

"That night, the night after I crashed the car on the beach, would you have really killed yourself if I hadn't been here?"

My heart stops. Get the paddles. Somebody restart it. I close my eyes in sheer horror. I have asked myself this question a million times. I've repeatedly self-analyzed my psyche that night. I have discussed it with colleagues. I have made lame excuses. Yet, each time, I come up with the same answer. Yes. Yes, I would have. I had the intent, the plan, the means. Yes, I would have done it. I have never said it out loud before, to anyone. Not even to myself. But maybe the time has come to admit it. I don't think I could lie to him. Not now, probably not ever, not about something like this. I'm terrified of saying the words.

I look lovingly into his face before my mouth opens. "Yes." I cannot say anything more.

He looks at me with an unnerving intensity. What is he thinking? Does he suddenly see me as weak? Mentally ill? Unstable? I find myself sinking into an old familiar hole. I'm twenty-five again.

"Rea, I have a confession to make."

The tables turn. First, I feel like the accused. Now I'm not so sure. What is he saying, what untruth could he be withholding from me? And, after all these years?

I can't decide who looks more terrified. I don't know what to say.

Drew is on his feet, my hand trapped in his. We leave the wine glasses behind. He leads me down the steps, my feet hitting the sand hard. We walk around the corner of the steps to stand close to the foundation of the house. The shovel I used to plant the beach roses to replace the one that died sits against the side of the house. I've always been terrible at cleaning up after myself as I admit the garden tool has been sitting here for over a week and I'd totally forgotten about it.

Drew lets go of my hand and grabs the shovel. He digs into the sand near the base of the house. He heaves it down again after depositing the mound of sand on the ground. Again and again until there is a hole about a foot deep. The shovel drops to the ground. Drew kneels on all fours, rummaging in the newly dug hole. Standing, he hands me a square-shaped object covered in wet sand and what appears to be an old flip phone.

"Here," he says, placing the ominous portent in my hand. "Open it."

It doesn't want to open. Like it's glued shut. I take my fingernail and pry open the two flaps. Drew's twenty-five-year-old face stares back at me. It's his driver's license. There are three credit cards as well. I open the billfold and find four hundred and sixty-five dollars in there. I gaze into my husband's face with a bewildered expression.

"I bought two beers that night for seven-fifty each and tipped the bartender twenty bucks. I started out with five hundred dollars."

He continues to peer at me. I'm confused. He said he lost his wallet. He'd searched down by the water, and it wasn't there.

"I don't understand," I say.

"I didn't lose my wallet. I buried it here in the sand. Along with my mobile phone."

"You mean it's been buried here this whole time?"

"Yes, and I never called anybody either. Not my agent, not my publicist, no one. Not until two days later."

"I don't understand," I say, again. "What do you mean? You told me you couldn't remember anyone's number, you left messages for your agent and your publicist, you tried to leave, but your knees hurt too much, and no one was around to give you a ride…and so you came back."

"I lied. I had my wallet. I knew everyone's number. I never left to find a ride."

"But…but…why?"

"I don't know. The moment I saw you, I didn't want to leave. It was like I was drawn to you for some reason, and then after you left for work, I went to take a shower with the intention of leaving and maybe calling you the next day for a date. But then, I found all those vials of pills in the medicine chest and stuff from some guy, and the wedding dress, and I got a creepy feeling. I meant what I said that night, I wasn't going to leave until I got it all out of you."

"Oh, Drew, I don't know what to say. I can't believe we're reliving this night all over again, after all this time."

"I didn't bring this whole thing up to make you feel bad. I did it because I have a surprise for you."

How could this be taking a U-turn, again? Where is he going with this?

"Drew, you're freaking me out, why are you doing this?"

"Come on, come with me." He pulls me toward the back door. We walk up the steps, across the deck and enter the kitchen. Drew leads me to the front door where he stops me.

"Happy birthday, Rea." He kisses me.

I'm confused, my birthday? Oh my God. I'd

forgotten, having been consumed with the wake and funeral for my father. Tomorrow is my birthday.

"I forgot it was my birthday," I say to the love of my life.

Drew kisses me again. I swoon. Sometimes I can't believe he still has this effect on me after all these years. I am molten chocolate in his arms.

"Rea, I love you. I love you more than anything in this world. I have loved you from the first moment I saw you on the beach that night. I don't mean to upset you; I only want to tell you how much I love you. Come on, don't you want to see your birthday present?"

His embrace makes me feel warm and safe, just like it always does. I don't want to leave it. "We never buy each other birthday presents any more. What have you done?"

"Well, this is a big birthday, but more importantly it's something I want to give you regardless of the occasion. Come on."

I follow him out the front door, my hand in his. The bright moonlight flashes across the inky black paint. I peer into the night to see the outline of a car. Getting closer, I can make out the form of the black Porsche. I turn and look at him. "Oh, my God, don't tell me you found it? The Porsche you were driving that night?"

"No, I've kept it all these years."

"What? You're kidding. Where was it?"

"Well, Bobby kept it for a while. I bought it from the rental company. It wasn't worth much because it was pretty much totaled. Bobby kept asking me what I wanted to do with it, and I couldn't give him an answer. Eventually I stored it and forgot about it. About a year ago I decided to restore it and thought it would make a great birthday present. So here it is. What do you think?"

"Oh Drew, it's wonderful. I mean, it's a beautiful car in its own right, but it means so much more."

"Let's take it for a ride," he says, like a kid with a new toy.

"All right, but I'll drive. You're still a terrible driver."

We slide into the red leather seats. It smells like a new car, but it holds ancient memories. I push in the clutch and turn the key in the ignition. The car purrs to life. I ease off the clutch, giving it some gas as we make our way down the driveway, past the gates with the security code I long ago changed to Drew's birthday. The three of us speed down the coastal highway as the thoughts of our life together dance in my memory. Drew reaches over and takes my hand as I keep the other firmly grasped on the steering wheel.

"Happy birthday," he says.

"Thanks," I answer, "And thanks for saving my life."

"You're welcome," he says with that adorable movie star smile of his.

I take a deep breath as I think about it, *the crash*, the crash that saved my life.

THE END

A word about the author...

Caryn McGill is the author of seven novels, spanning several genres, some under the pen name Kendra Greenwood.

Born on New York's Long Island, Caryn McGill resides on its bucolic East End. When not writing you can find her whipping up something scrumptious in the kitchen or fusing glass into decorative pieces.

Find Caryn McGill online: FB at caryn.mcgillwrites, Twitter @carynmcgill, and www.writeonsisters.com where she formally blogged.

Thank you for purchasing
this publication of The Wild Rose Press, Inc.

For questions or more information
contact us at
info@thewildrosepress.com.

The Wild Rose Press, Inc.
www.thewildrosepress.com